# BECOMING YOU

## By the Author

Getting Lost

Keep Hold

The Fifth Gospel

Becoming You

Girls With Guns
(novella collection with Carsen Taite and Ali Vali)

Visit us at www.boldstrokesbooks.com

# BECOMING YOU

*by*
## Michelle Grubb

2017

ISBN 13: 978-1-62639-811-5


This Trade Paperback Original Is Published By
Bold Strokes Books, Inc.
P.O. Box 249
Valley Falls, NY 12185

First Edition: February 2017

CREDITS
Editor: Cindy Cresap
Production Design: Stacia Seaman
Cover Design by Sheri (graphicartist2020@hotmail.com)

# Acknowledgments

A heartfelt thank you to everyone who has read one (or more) of my books. It truly is a privilege to tell stories that are enjoyed the world over.

As always, thank you to everyone at Bold Strokes Books, especially Radclyffe, Sandy, and Cindy.

For Kerry. For always.

# CHAPTER ONE

"What I don't understand is why you'd want to go out with someone who looked like a man?" Hannah was absorbed in a magazine article about sexuality.

Airlie shrugged, feigning disinterest, and continued reading the travel pages. If she had a chance, when Hannah wasn't looking, she'd check it out later. Not that she needed to hide reading the piece, Hannah was practically reading it aloud in the terminal.

"I just don't get it. Surely lesbians fancy hot looking chicks," Hannah said.

"Like you?"

"Yes, exactly like me." Airlie rolled her eyes. "But seriously, all lesbians don't have to look like men, do they?"

Airlie glanced over the top of her reading glasses. "I don't know, Hannah. How would I know?" She felt heat redden her neck. Her reaction to the topic of homosexuality, and the subsequent effort to quell the thought, was becoming exhausting.

Hannah continued. "Logically, if you *were* attracted to women, and not men, surely you'd want to be with someone who looked like a woman, not a man. Am I right?"

"Maybe." Airlie sipped her coffee. "Can't you just be attracted to a *person*?"

Hannah unfolded her lanky legs. "Wouldn't that make us all bisexual?"

"I don't *know*, Hannah. We're not attracted to women, so how would we know?"

Just as Hannah was poised to impart additional wisdom, the waiter appeared, as if on cue, to deliver lunch. It was a welcome distraction, anything to steer the subject elsewhere.

It was an emotional day. Traveling to Europe together was a dream they shared and had promised to fulfill before turning thirty. Now both twenty-eight, after two long years of planning, they were at the airport, bags checked in, and booked on the five p.m. flight to Dublin. Twenty-six hours of flight time ahead of them.

Airlie despised flying. It was a long way to fall if *all* the engines failed. Regardless of the length of flight, her pale skin inevitably became dehydrated, and her ankles would swell to the size of footballs. She remembered the last time she had been at the airport preparing to take an international flight. It was four years ago and she'd been traveling to Thailand with her then fiancé, Sam. It had now been three and a half years since she last saw him.

Airlie strode purposefully from the trendy, overpriced airport café, thankful the focus had shifted from sexuality to the all-important duty-free shopping. Laden with perfume, electronic gadgets, and the maximum limit of vodka, they waited patiently at gate three for boarding. Airlie slouched in the poo-green modular chairs. Typically energized, Hannah wandered through shops searching for a hat.

"What about this one?"

Airlie shook her head.

"This one?"

It was worse than the first. She frowned and shrugged, wondering if she had to suffer this until boarding.

Airlie shoved her hands into the pockets of her favorite faded jeans and watched as Hannah left the store empty-handed before wandering into a bookshop.

Her mind again wandered back to her time with Sam. In her early twenties, and completely naive, Airlie had convinced herself that life was okay. Hers appeared to be no more or less exciting than anyone else's was. She had great friends—not too many—an easy job at the hotel, a boyfriend who was nice enough, and if someone had asked her if she was happy, the answer would have been a resounding yes. But in the back of Airlie's mind was the niggling notion there had to be more. In her misguided wisdom, she determined that more love would dissolve her sense of incompleteness. Barely registering that she was possibly only a quarter of the way through her life, she agreed to accept Sam's proposal of marriage.

Sam was a catch, or so her friends used to say. Even her mum thought he was a lovely young man, a sure sign you've got it wrong. Above all, he truly loved Airlie, and no matter how appallingly she began to behave, he appeared determined to ignore her insolence.

Little confrontations soon took over from civil conversation, and they fought incessantly. Airlie had commenced a journey of self-destruction, but she needed to destroy their relationship first. Pushing Sam away to concentrate on her own demise was a priority. A priority she couldn't explain, but nevertheless, one she would fulfill with relentless determination.

Predictably, the hostility became unbearable, and one day Airlie snapped. "What the fuck is your problem?" She'd never spoken to Sam so harshly. The tone and the words were foreign to her.

They were in the middle of yet another heated discussion. This time, the topic was saving for the wedding, honeymoon, and a deposit for a house. Sam had moved back home to save, but Airlie refused to stop renting with Hannah. It was an unexpected revelation, but suddenly Airlie's life seemed mapped out. Marriage, house, kids, and then death.

The atmosphere at dinner had been strained. It was one of the few occasions Airlie had given in to his rather reasonable demands to come over. She'd tried not to show her increasing agitation with him in front of his parents, but now, in the isolation of his bedroom, Airlie was a different person.

"What is *my* problem? You're asking me what *my* problem is. Are you blind?" His face portrayed confusion, but he remained calm. "We never have any time alone, and we're supposed to be getting married next year, although God only knows when."

Airlie walked to the window, peering through the blinds at cars passing by. Each of those cars carried at least one person who had their own problems. She wanted to be one of those people, lucky enough to be driving past the storm gathering momentum in Sam's room.

"Look," Sam said. "This is madness. I just want to be with you. We're never close anymore."

Airlie stared at him. She knew what was coming.

"We hardly have sex anymore."

She inhaled deeply. "So that's what this is all about?" Of course it wasn't. Sam had never demanded sex, and it was the truth, she couldn't remember the last time they were intimate. Still, something in her refused to let it go. Sex with Sam was a chore. She loathed the routine foreplay, the sweaty thrusting, groaning, and the faked orgasm that would thankfully end it. There was no spark, no passion, nothing.

She was treading on dangerous ground. From deep inside, something began to stir. It was an unexplainable feeling, a rising of frustration and rage, and it was poised to explode. While she wasn't exactly angry with him, he was to be her source of relief. She was intent on pushing this argument until something broke, until he broke, and her torture finally ended.

"That's not what this is about and you know it."

"You might want to rethink, because this is as good as it gets."

Sam was hurt. "So you mean this nonexistent sex life is as good as our sex life will get?"

She shrugged.

"Well, you can just forget it. I'm not signing up for that. I *didn't* sign up for that."

"I beg your pardon?"

"Jesus, Air-Bear, I can't talk to you anymore. I'm beginning to wonder if I ever could. When was the last time we made love?"

"Fuck off, Sam." She hated that pet name, and she hated the fact that she couldn't recall one time she made love to Sam. Sex, yes. Making love, never.

"When did you become so selfish? I don't know why I'm even bothering. By the way, while we're on the subject, we haven't had sex in eleven weeks. Don't you think that's just a little too long between drinks?"

"Do you want to know *why* we haven't had sex in eleven weeks, since you're counting?" Her eyes narrowed. "You're a lousy shag, Sam, that's why!"

Airlie could feel her temples pulse, and her entire body trembled. "You say you don't know why you're even bothering? Then don't. Let's not fucking bother? Clearly, you'd be happier if we didn't."

"Fucking bother, huh? I should be so lucky." His vicious tone suggested he might pick her up and throw her across the room like an old rag doll. He wouldn't, though; he was a good man. He turned toward the window, his grimacing face in his hands. "For God's sake, Air-Bear, calling it quits isn't what I want."

It was what she wanted, and it became glaringly apparent Sam wasn't going to be the one to end this. Nevertheless, ending it was all Airlie could think of. It consumed her.

She stepped back and stared long and hard at the back of his head. She thought he might be crying. "I don't want this anymore, Sam."

The words sparked a wave of relief that tingled through her entire being. This nightmare would end here, tonight, now. Her calmness was frightening, and the enormous relief intoxicating.

"I think it would be a huge mistake for us to get married." His sobbing grew as she began collecting her things.

"Airlie, c'mon." Sam spun around, his eyes willing her to stay. "This is stupid. We can work this out."

Airlie grabbed her keys and ran from the bedroom, down the dark hall, out the front door, taking the steps two at a time, before jumping in her car. She slammed and locked the door. Not once did she look at Sam as he hammered the windows begging her to stop. Airlie sped off, bravely chancing a glance in her rearview mirror at the sobbing heap of Sam's body on the side of the road. Cars drove past him, probably with at least one person in each thanking their lucky stars their problems weren't as bad as that poor young man's.

When she arrived home, Airlie thought she could stop running.

Her running had just begun.

# CHAPTER TWO

Despite how little one actually accomplished during an international flight, it was surprising to discover how exhausting that journey could be. With a spare seat between them, Hannah and Airlie graciously took turns attempting sleep with their head in the other's lap.

The flight was long, extremely long.

"Shoulder?"

"No," said Hannah.

"Shoe?"

"Nope."

"Socks?"

"Nope."

"Sex?" Airlie was desperate and on the verge of quitting.

"No. What? *Where?*"

"Nowhere, I was just checking." She sighed heavily to evoke sympathy. "Can I have a hint?"

"It's inside the plane."

I spy wasn't all it was cracked up to be. "I know. Sandwiches?"

"No." Hannah smiled. "But good one."

"Shit?"

"Can you see shit? I don't think so."

"I can't see it." Airlie pulled a face. "But I can sure smell it. That's rotten."

Hannah recoiled. "Who would do that on a plane?"

They tucked their noses down their tops. When Airlie eventually surfaced for air, the smell lingered.

"Let's see how far we can get past the flight attendant into first class," said Hannah.

It was nearly midnight, Australian time, and they had been flying for a little under six hours. So far, sleep had eluded them. They wandered about the cabin, passing other bored passengers. A commotion at the toilet to the rear was gaining attention. Attendants darted in and out, clad to the armpits with latex, managing the source of the stench that was slowly seeping through the cabin. Strangers shot accusing glances at other passengers and promptly either stood up or adjusted themselves in their seat to turn away from the possible culprit.

As they approached the front of the plane, everything certainly appeared more impressive; the food smelled better, there wasn't a hint of poo in the air, and the ambient light gave the impression of an expensive hotel. More impressive than the cramped, gloomy old hostel in the rear.

Hannah straightened, and in her best posh Australian accent said, "Eton's first on the list. I'll have to choose a school sooner rather than later."

Eton, the posh, boys-only, private school near Windsor Castle, was sure to impress, except that was the sum total of Airlie's knowledge. Prince William or Harry or someone royal had attended. She improvised. "You'd be an asset. They'd be lucky to have you. Latin teachers are difficult to come by, I'm sure."

Hannah lowered her head. "Latin? How fucking boring."

Airlie grinned, and they advanced deeper toward first class territory.

They progressed past one checkpoint and were nearly five rows in when a lovely young flight attendant, with a voice higher in octaves than a soprano, spoke from behind. "Perhaps, ladies, you could discuss your appointment at Eton on the way back to your seats in economy."

"Damn," muttered Hannah.

"So close," whispered Airlie.

"It was the Latin, wasn't it?" asked Hannah. "Too much?"

The flight attendant smiled. He passed them two bottles of gin from the galley. "In future, you might appear more convincing if you remember to re-button your jeans and replace your shoes."

They looked each other up and down. Defeated, they turned and smiled curtly before making their way back to the stinky, crowded rear end of the plane.

All that remained was a thorough investigation of the in-flight entertainment. Airlie eventually declared there was nothing to watch. They squirmed until a nice lady from the row in front took pity on them, feeding them licorice allsorts while they moaned all the way to Hong Kong.

❖

Hong Kong airport was vast. Airlie had an urge to remove her shoes and slide along the gleaming polished floor. There were shops, restaurants, boutiques, cafés, and bars everywhere. It was possible to spend a fortune in Hong Kong airport *if* anything had been open.

"McDonald's is open," said Airlie.

"Macca's is *always* open."

"It's not special, is it?"

"No, it's very normal."

Airlie knew all this sitting around was a struggle for Hannah. "If I go and steal some napkins and salt and pepper and straws and stuff, will that cheer you up?"

"We're not twelve."

"No, but will it cheer you up?"

"It might if you get in trouble," said Hannah.

"Okay, here goes."

As she turned to give Hannah a cheeky wink just beyond the threshold of McDonald's, the lady from the row in front strolled down the gleaming terminal and stopped next to Hannah. Airlie waved at them. She knew Hannah would be explaining her mission but was too tired to feel embarrassed; she'd never see any of these people again.

At the counter, a rather short man lunged from behind the ice cream machine to greet her with a bag of food and a beaming, toothy smile. Without giving him a second thought, she continued to gather salt and pepper, until the little man thrust the bag at her chest.

"Okay, sorry, thank you. All there. Sorry 'bout wait. You go now, okay, thank you."

"I think you've made a mistake," Airlie said.

"No, no. No mistake now." The tiny man's eyes lit up. "But extra fries for long wait. Okay? Bye."

Airlie looked left then right, but no one was interested in claiming the food. Perhaps someone had ordered but couldn't wait any longer before rushing off to catch their flight. She shrugged and triumphantly swaggered out to rowdy applause. Hannah and the other lady were in stitches. On the off chance that Ronald McDonald himself might come chasing after them, they darted down the nearest escalator and out of sight.

Airlie peered into the bag. "We have nuggets, chips, and cheeseburgers. Who wants what?"

Delighting in their misappropriated goods, they ate enthusiastically. The lady from the row in front introduced herself as Olivia. She was smartly dressed, traveling on her own, and probably only a few years older than Airlie. Besides her warm, wide smile and perfectly straight teeth, her expensive jeans and olive green blazer were impressive. Although her dark hair was short, simple, and stylish, Airlie guessed she probably paid a couple hundred dollars for the privilege.

"So are you traveling onward from London, or is that your final stop?" asked Olivia.

"No, we're heading on to Ireland." Airlie dumped the empty McDonald's bag into a bin on the way back to the departure lounge.

"Really? I live in Ireland—on the west. I've just been home visiting for a month."

"Have you lived there long then?" asked Airlie.

"Sixteen years this July. So yes, long enough. How long are you planning to stay?"

"We have working visas, so a year at the least," said Hannah.

"That is," Airlie crossed her fingers and winked at Hannah, "if all goes to plan."

"If it all goes belly up, hopefully we'll at least have a good time before we have to pull the plug," Hannah added optimistically.

As they waited to board the plane, Airlie marveled at the spectacular lightning show and the crashes of thunder rolling in the distance while sheets of rain lashed against the mass of glass that separated them from the wild weather. Tropical storms in Hong Kong weren't unusual.

The bulky plane soared into the dark night sky, skipping along on the tail of the storm. They ate dinner yet again, and Airlie was convinced sleep couldn't be far away. She was exhausted. The cabin lights were eventually switched off, almost every seat reclined, and for the rather large gentleman about three rows back, sleep obviously came easily, if his snoring and snorting was any indication. Having been a light sleeper all her life, Airlie was prepared for just that kind of disruption and produced earplugs for them both. Within minutes, they were snuggled down, blankets beneath their chins, plugs in, eye masks on, and settled for a most deserved slumber.

After thirty minutes, Airlie was agitated. Within another five, Hannah was too.

"It's impossible to get comfortable in these bloody seats." Hannah's long legs were no asset on a plane. "I bet they're all comfortably horizontal in first class."

"Want me to get some more pillows? Might help?"

"Nah, maybe we should try the TV again."

They quickly concluded that the television wasn't the answer.

"Let's have a drink." Airlie had spotted a tasty Shiraz on the wine list.

"Why not? Can't hurt."

"Press your buzzer then," said Airlie.

"You press yours. You suggested it."

"Go on, press it."

"You're on the aisle. Best if you press yours." Hannah released the latch on the tray table in preparation.

"You do realize that regardless of who presses the button in this row, the same light illuminates? They don't have a map of every seat to tell them who needs assistance." Airlie hadn't flown much, but she at least knew that.

"Of course I knew that."

Olivia turned around, beaming an entertained smile. "I'll press my buzzer and get us all a drink, eh?"

Upon arrival of the second drink, the flight attendant suggested that for the comfort of other passengers, perhaps Olivia should move if they were going to continue drinking and chatting. As if attending a child's slumber party, Airlie shuffled into the middle and Olivia, with pillow and blanket in hand, settled into the aisle seat.

Within half an hour, they learned that Olivia was married to

Gavin, he was Australian, and they had moved to Ireland before they were married. Back then, Olivia's profession as a town planner was sought after due to the booming Irish economy and a high demand for infrastructure. Airlie had been way out; Olivia was forty-one and had no children.

To pass the time, they played word games, story games, battleship, number games, connect four, and now they were tackling the jumbo crossword in one of the newspapers.

By this stage, Hannah had turned to rest her pillow on the closed window shutter. Apparently, trying to think of intelligent answers had made her tired. "I'm gonna try to get some sleep, kids. Night night."

"Night, Han." Airlie gave her knee a gentle squeeze.

"Sleep well, Hannah," whispered Olivia.

Fifteen minutes later, Airlie and Olivia were quietly jubilant as they completed the crossword. Hannah was sound asleep. Airlie was ready for lights out, but not quite ready for sleep. Olivia intrigued her. It occurred to her that she'd not met many truly interesting people in her short life. She knew many people who *wanted* to be interesting, people who *thought* they were interesting, but they were mostly just wannabes. Olivia didn't just talk of the things she wanted to do, she talked of the things she *had* done. The dim cabin felt cozy, and the heating was turned up to induce slumber. Hardly anyone was walking the aisles, there was no line for the toilet, and not a flight attendant was in sight.

"Do you miss Australia?" asked Airlie. "I mean, it must be hard to come home and leave again, emotionally, I mean." She shrugged. "I reckon that must be hard."

"Have you ever lived away from home?"

"No. Not in another country. The farthest I've lived away from my parents is four hours by car, and to be honest, sometimes that didn't seem far enough."

"Not many people understand what it's like to live away from home. You make a new home, return to your old home, leave your old home, and go back to your new home, which is essentially now just home, and then do it all over again, almost annually."

"I guess you're always saying good-bye to someone you care about. That's got to be difficult."

Olivia let out a small but kind laugh. "You've been in this world before, Airlie; you have wisdom beyond your years."

Airlie enjoyed the compliment. "What's it like where you live?"

"Cold. But beautiful. We live near a beach called Roaring Bay. It sounds so cliché, but Gav and I bought our little cottage for next to nothing, and over the years we've made it our own."

"Can you see the beach from your house?"

"You can indeed. It's a lovely view from the garden."

Airlie thought how charming it would be to relax on a warm summer's day, sipping a pint, watching the waves crash on the shore.

As if reading her mind, Olivia said, "It's a great beach, but it's not like an Australian one. The best nights are when a storm is rolling in." She sighed. "But enough about me. What about you? What do you do for a living?"

"I'm in hospitality—hotels. Quite boring really. I'm not convinced I like people enough to care about their accommodation needs."

"So what do you think you could care about?"

"I don't know. I've never really thought about it. When I was younger I wanted to be an art teacher, but I was too busy earning money to go to uni."

"Why not study teaching now?"

"Well, because now I'm on a plane to Ireland in desperate need for some adventure."

"And adventure you shall have, young lady." Olivia shifted in her seat. "You should think about teaching when you go back home. I think you'd make a good teacher."

"How could you possibly know that?"

"I too have wisdom beyond my years."

Airlie smiled. They were whispering softly. Sleep wasn't far away.

"So you like art?" Olivia asked.

"I love it. I can't paint or sculpt or anything, but I could spend hours in museums and galleries. I can sketch a decent caricature, but the truly talented stuff just isn't in me. My aim is to decorate my house with all original art when I'm older. Nothing too expensive, but all original."

"But when you're older, of course? You must be what, twenty-six?"

"Twenty-eight, actually. It's depressing to know I'm already old enough. I choose to believe I need to be older still."

"Where are you staying in Ireland?" Olivia asked.

"We honestly haven't thought that far ahead." She and Hannah were keeping an open mind about where to settle. Galway or Dublin were their preferred options.

"You should come and stay with me and Gavin for a while. Only if you want to, of course." She hesitated. "I know I must sound like a right weirdo asking after I've only just met you, and I promise I'm not a psychopath—nor is Gavin, for that matter—but sometimes you just know people are genuine. You connect." She continued as if to hide embarrassment. "It's not terribly exciting where we live, no busy cities nearby to rock the night away or anything, although there is a disco every Saturday night in Westport."

Airlie laughed. "Discos aren't really my thing."

"So, you'll come and stay? Or at least think about it?"

"It's a kind offer, but I don't know. We wouldn't want to impose."

"It's no bother, honestly. I'll leave it up to you. We have plenty of room, and it's nice to have people in the house for a change. When we first arrived, we had visitors all the time, but not so much anymore now that everyone has settled down."

"I'd love to, and I reckon Hannah would, too. We'll discuss it and let you know." She felt like she had something to lose. "If Hannah doesn't want to, perhaps I could come on my own when we get settled. I'd love to see your place."

"Good, I'm pleased. I'd love to show you around."

Exhaustion washed over her. Olivia must have felt the same because she stopped talking, too. Within minutes, Airlie drifted off, but it was a disjointed sleep. Finding a comfortable position was difficult, and although she awoke to shift her position, she remained sleepy enough to fall back easily.

After what seemed like hours, although in reality she had no idea of the time, Airlie awoke to find Hannah's head resting heavily on her shoulder. Her left bum cheek had gone to sleep, she was too upright, and she desperately wanted to switch sides. Through a crack in the corner of her eye mask, she could tell that the status of the cabin had remained unchanged and there was hardly a light on. Resigning herself to an awkward, slouched position, she registered a gentle tap on her shoulder before lifting her mask to focus on Olivia patting her lap.

"You won't be able to sleep at all if I lie there," Airlie said.

"I've slept enough, here." Olivia shifted to elevate the armrest that separated them. "Pop your pillow there. I'll be fine. I'll tell you to move if you get too heavy." Smiling, she patted her lap again.

Too sleepy to argue, Airlie slowly did as suggested, and Hannah's limp body adjusted with her movement. She snuggled into a ball, her head in Olivia's lap.

The last thing she remembered was the soothing, rhythmic stroking of her shoulder by Olivia's thumb. This time, sleep came easily.

## CHAPTER THREE

Airlie squeezed Hannah's hand with a swell of emotion. "We're nearly there."

"Yep, Aerobar." This was Airlie's least despised nickname. "We are." Hannah was a little emotional, too. "I think we're gonna have the time of our lives."

"I hope so."

Hannah reached across to mess Airlie's already scruffy hair. "Ireland, here we come."

Airlie lowered her voice. "Olivia asked us to her place when we arrive. I didn't commit, said I'd check with you first. What do you think?"

"To hers to stay?"

Airlie nodded.

"For how long?"

"I don't know. We could play it by ear, I guess. I think it would be great. Apparently, she has a nice place near a beach on the west. I don't know." She shrugged. "It might be a good place to start."

Hannah's expression changed. "You don't think she's a nutter or anything, do you?"

"No, Hannah, I don't think she's a nutter."

"We hardly know her."

"True. But I've got a good feeling about her."

"You don't say? In that case, I reckon it's a great idea. You two did seem to be getting rather cozy during the flight."

"What?"

"I woke and you were cuddling."

"We were not." Airlie's dismissal was too quick. "You're full of crap."

"If you say so, but you were pretty close."

"Hannah, we were just trying to get some sleep. Your bloody head was just about in *my* lap. I had nowhere else to go."

"I'm kidding, Aerobar. You're so easy to wind up. So, we'll head straight to Olivia's when we arrive, agreed?"

She hated it when Hannah teased her like that. "Agreed."

The nearer the plane flew toward England, the cloudier the sky became. It wasn't until the end of the descent that Heathrow and its surrounds came into view as the plane burst through the white cloud. Determined not to let a little bad weather ruin their arrival, they remained excited beyond the realms of normalcy, until at last the plane taxied to the terminal.

"We're in England." Airlie was searching for words. "My God, Han, we're in the UK, on the other side of the world, in the northern hemisphere. Wahoo, we're here!"

❖

"Wow, great place." Airlie unearthed some enthusiasm as they pulled up after negotiating the long gravel driveway that climbed slowly through dense foliage. "Han, wake up. We're here."

After checking and double-checking with Olivia that it was no trouble to stay, all three had wearily made their way to Dublin's Heuston Station and onto a train across the country to Westport. Upon arrival, Gavin had met them on the platform, not at all surprised to see Olivia with two strangers in tow.

Gavin wasn't much taller than Hannah, and he wore brown cords, a cream T-shirt, and a dark green fleece vest. Airlie guessed his entire wardrobe comprised varying shades of green, brown, blue, and white—colors that legitimized a certain degree of anonymity and camouflage. She gained the strong impression that he preferred to blend into the background, and his gentle, soft voice would hardly command the attention of a fly. In contrast, his short gray hair and muscular physique implied a harsher, sterner type of man. His entire persona was a contradiction.

Earlier that morning in the departure lounge at Heathrow, Hannah and Airlie agreed that should there be even the slightest hint of weirdness at Olivia's, they would politely leave. After all, they'd only met this woman. She seemed nice enough, but they simply couldn't be too careful. They swore to stick together, no matter what.

Airlie stretched in salutation, carefully untangling from the confines of the car. Her hair was a tangled mess, and her skin felt grubby in her day-old clothes, but the magnificent view of Roaring Bay Beach, literally a stone's throw away, was breathtaking. Soaking in her surroundings, she smiled at the little white cottage looking quaint in contrast to the green and brown wooded hill behind. The gardens were immaculate—lush green lawn, as you would expect in Ireland, and neatly trimmed hedges. The smell of freshly cut grass enticed Airlie to inhale deeper.

"Hannah, wake up. We're here." Airlie knocked on the car window as Hannah jolted upright. "We're here."

"Best you don't sleep any longer anyway," Gavin said, unpacking the boot. "The longer you stay awake, the quicker you'll adjust to the time change."

Airlie had observed the reunion between Gavin and Olivia at Westport train station. Their embrace was comfortable, but fit for a sibling perhaps, not a lover. Her two brothers had been more animated and affectionate with her when she left Australia. Perhaps that's what familiarity bred after so many years together.

Despite his deceiving appearance, Gavin was sweet. He'd already prepared the second spare bedroom, and the coffee machine was primed to boost their caffeine intake just enough to help them through to a reasonable bedtime.

There was no doubt the house was a cottage, but to increase its size and comfort, they'd added a spacious conservatory to the far left to capture the sun and take advantage of the water views. Airlie fell instantly in love with Roaring Bay.

"Coffee's ready, ladies," called Olivia.

Airlie raised her eyebrows at the travel mugs on the counter.

"I know it seems cruel, but I find the best way to combat jet lag is some good old sea air. Half an hour on the beach with a coffee, and I guarantee you'll last until at least eight o'clock." Olivia ushered them out before further protest.

The pathway to the beach was rough and windy, but within

minutes, the rocky descent gave way to beautiful, white, coarse sand. The sun's warmth, while meager, was softly blown away by the crisp breeze, and they all agreed the sensation was heavenly upon their faces and through their limp, oily hair. Within seconds, the sound of a rather excited dog echoed off the rocks, and they turned to watch a little black and white terrier bounce along toward them.

"Ah, my little man, how could I have forgotten about you?" Olivia patted the excited dog. "Ladies, I'd like you to meet Ash." Olivia looked to the house and waved to Gavin, who must have let him out.

Airlie inhaled deeply. The salty sea air reminded her of home, but the fact that they were in Ireland energized her weary body. Hannah returned to the house complaining the sand was unbearable, and she was unable to cope a moment longer without showering. Airlie and Olivia remained, throwing sticks in the shallow waves for Ash to fetch. She desperately hoped that Olivia and Gavin weren't weirdos; she liked her too much already to be disappointed.

It took no time, after shepherd's pie and pudding, for the lounge room to fall silent. Airlie fought the urge to sleep, and when she glanced around, Hannah and Olivia were struggling, too.

It was seven thirty. "I can't make it until eight." Airlie stood and stretched. Jet lag after a long haul flight was like nothing she'd experienced before.

Hannah was next to move. "Me either."

Olivia kissed Gavin's forehead. "And that's a wrap. You're on your own tonight, Gav."

He shrugged and promptly changed the channel to hurling. A sport Airlie knew she had no chance to understand, let alone play.

At exactly 3:23 a.m., Airlie awoke, startled and disoriented, from a bad dream. Drenched with sweat, she floundered until her feet touched the ground. She sat on the edge of the bed, heart pounding as she recalled the final scene of her nightmare. During the flight to Dublin, the plane began to shrink, the walls turning into a jelly-like material that sucked the passengers through if they stepped too close. Airlie held on to Olivia and Hannah until her knuckles ached and she felt sure the bones would pierce her skin. Then, in the chaos, someone bumped Olivia, knocking her askew and causing her left hand to skim the side of the plane. Airlie battled, gripping Olivia's sweaty hand, to hold on to her, but she was unable to match the strength of the jelly walls. She had to let her go. She watched Olivia float from the plane, screaming for her. Airlie's chest burned. In desperation, she released her grip on Hannah, looked at her with an apologetic expression, and jumped after Olivia. As the ground drew nearer, Airlie woke.

She changed her T-shirt. There was little chance of falling back to sleep just yet. In the moonlit darkness, she negotiated her way to the kitchen for a drink. The house was quiet, and she listened so intently that the silence became a noise itself. She heard the sound of a distant car speeding on a nearby road, and this somehow reassured her.

Airlie gently eased on the tap, and the trickling water sparked a need for the toilet. A rustling sound beyond the kitchen alarmed her. *This isn't my night.* Her eyes were slowly adjusting to the dark, but it was virtually impossible to distinguish any movement in the shadows.

Nothing.

Outside, Ash barked enthusiastically in his kennel. Something, or someone, was setting him off, and the thought chilled her. Their first night with Gavin and Olivia would probably be their last. The silence was more than she could bear. Deafened by the sound of her own pounding heart, she poised to scream the house down when a glimpse of movement caught her eye. The scream froze high in her throat. She watched a silhouette move slowly from behind the antique rocking chair in the conservatory, a loud creak echoing through the kitchen.

"Couldn't sleep either?"

Airlie jumped before thrusting her hand between her legs for fear of wetting her pants. "Christ all-bloody-mighty."

With the simple flick of a switch, all the terrifying scenarios evaporated. Olivia stood illuminated in the doorway to the conservatory, smiling, clearly amused, while Airlie, squinting from the sudden bright light, stood stunned with her legs crossed.

"Sorry. I thought you knew I was there. I'd only just gotten up," said Olivia.

"You frightened last week out of me."

"Was it a good week?"

"What?"

Olivia shook her head. "Doesn't matter. Maybe you should go pee."

Airlie braced herself against the bench. "I had a bad dream. I came to get a drink and read for a while, but then I heard a noise and the dog started barking, and I was convinced we were all about to suffer at the hands of some homicidal maniac."

"I know."

"You know? Are you actually a homicidal maniac?"

"No. I mean, I know you had a bad dream. Obviously, I didn't know the rest."

"How did you know?"

"I heard you. But don't worry about that now. Would you like a hot—"

"What did I say?" The dream had certainly felt real. Even after nearly being scared to death, she could feel her cheeks flush. What had she said aloud?

"You mumbled something. I'm not sure."

"Mumbled?"

"Is there an echo in here?" Olivia patted Airlie's shoulder and smiled. "It was only a dream." She busied herself with hot chocolate. "Go to the loo or you'll wet yourself." She eyed Airlie. "Go on."

When Airlie returned to the conservatory, hot chocolate, a blanket, and candlelight awaited her. Her embarrassment had faded, and Olivia didn't seem bothered, so she let it go.

"I thought the candlelight might entrance us and send us off to sleep. The blanket is in case that happens," said Olivia.

Airlie snuggled into one corner of the huge day bed, sinking deep into the cushions, tucking her feet in the blanket. Olivia occupied the other end, and for a long while, the only sound was slurping hot chocolate. They both stared transfixed, into the flickering candle flame.

"Fewer people marry in their twenties these days," Olivia said.

Airlie wasn't sure if it was a statement or a question. She opted for silence.

"Look at you, nearly thirty and single."

She didn't need reminding.

"You are single, aren't you?"

By four a.m., Airlie had relayed the story of her breakup with Sam. It hadn't been difficult; talking with Olivia was easy, mostly because she was a good listener. "You probably know more about it than Hannah, now," she said.

"So why do I get the feeling that you just told me the abridged version?"

"It's my truth, what I have to live with, I guess."

"So far as you're willing to admit?"

Airlie smiled. "Yep. It's my story and I'm sticking to it. It's fairly accurate." The missing bits were the pieces she didn't yet understand. She knew blanks existed, missing thoughts and feelings she couldn't yet identify, but her life was too busy and fulfilling to delve into it all yet. Something told her that to dig deeper would be painful. It was easier to pretend it wasn't there.

She changed the subject. "So, I take it you two never wanted children?"

Silence filled the darkness. "I can't naturally have children. Gav still wants to try."

"I'm sorry." Airlie coughed to clear her throat. "It never occurred to me it wasn't a choice. I just assumed you both didn't want children. This is awkward. I'm sorry."

"Don't apologize. There really is no need."

Airlie waited. She sensed there was more.

"If we speak about this, you must promise never to tell Gav we had this conversation. This is between you and me, okay?"

Airlie felt out of her depth. "Look, it's okay, you don't need to explain anything. It was rude and insensitive of me to bring it up. I'm not usually so tactless." She glanced toward the hall door. "Plus, Gavin could get up at any moment, and I'd hate him to think we were talking about him behind his back."

Olivia smiled warmly, but with a hint of sadness. "He won't be awake for at least another hour—you'll know he's up because the plumbing from the en suite toilet will rattle. It's an old house. He always goes to the toilet as soon as he wakes. He has for as long as I can remember, no matter where he is, and besides, we won't be talking about him. We'll be talking about me."

Airlie shifted uncomfortably but nodded.

"I can't conceive a child naturally. To the outside world, this failing appeared to be the most devastating development for us. And maybe for Gavin it was."

"But not for you?"

"Initially, yes. As were the first two attempts at IVF. The third failed attempt was…" She stalled. "In all honesty, it was such a relief that it didn't work. I realized I'd lost any longing for children years ago. All I was left with was an unfulfilled husband and an unrelenting guilt."

"But it's not your fault you couldn't have kids."

"I wish that was all it was."

Airlie waited.

"My guilt wasn't for my inability to conceive; it was because I didn't want to, and because Gavin did. I refused further IVF." She shrugged. "Many marriages wouldn't survive that."

"But yours did."

"It's not that simple."

Airlie didn't understand. "Maybe not. Sorry." Having children had never really been on her radar. When she was with Sam, she'd tried to imagine their life with children and maybe a dog, but the thought refused to form fully. She was about to suggest another drink when Olivia continued.

"Everyone assumed I was grieving when the last round didn't take, but I was so happy I made myself ill with guilt. If we'd had children, our sabbatical in Ireland would have ended. I couldn't bear the thought of that. Gavin would have loved to raise our children in Australia. I didn't want to go home. All my friends are here. This is a special community, and I love being a part of it. I didn't want my life to change, and in my mind, having children would have ended the magic, not enhanced it."

"I'm sure Gavin understands."

Olivia shook her head. "I watched his heart break a little more with every failed IVF. I watched him cry more than any man should have to. Unfortunately, he doesn't understand how I feel, because he doesn't know."

Airlie couldn't hide her sudden intake of breath. Olivia turned to her. "I'm not a very nice person, am I?"

"It's not for me to judge, but after knowing you less than two days, even I can tell you would never deliberately hurt Gavin."

"These days, it's just easier to tell people that we didn't want children, and for my part at least, it's more the truth than a lie." Her shoulders sank. "For Gavin, not so much."

Airlie didn't know what to say, so she said nothing.

The candle flickered, and they both stared at the dancing flame.

"I can't believe I told you all that." Even in the dim light, Airlie could see Olivia had blushed. "There aren't that many people who know. I feel a bit silly saying it aloud really. Please don't repeat it."

"You can trust me, I promise." Airlie shrugged. "Although we've only just met, I hope you believe me."

"It's weird, isn't it? We've only just met and I told you my darkest secret?" Her eyes fixed on Airlie as if trying to work it out. "I feel like I've known you before." Olivia reached to touch Airlie's cheek. "I feel like I know you now, like you're an old soul I've met in a past life or something. It's quite odd really."

Airlie felt it too. A long silence surrounded them as they both relaxed against the back of the day bed, eyes closed. There was no need to speak.

At nearly seven o'clock, a dull light seeped through the curtains, and the night was over. Exhausted, Airlie suggested they try for another hour or two of sleep, and Olivia didn't argue.

"Sorry my dream woke you." Airlie crept through the kitchen door and into the hall.

"That's okay, no harm done."

"You said I screamed, but you didn't say what I said?"

Olivia gently touched her shoulder. "You screamed. Then you called my name, followed by the word no."

Airlie nodded. It was just as she remembered. The light was too dim to reveal her embarrassment.

The sound of a flushing toilet came from the direction of the en suite. It was followed by the loud groaning of ancient plumbing.

Olivia sighed.

Sleep caught Airlie almost immediately, and by the time she woke hours later, a beautiful crisp sunny Irish day awaited her.

## CHAPTER FOUR

Any reservations Airlie and Hannah harbored about their newfound friends, or the possibility of them perhaps being axe murderers, soon dissipated. After a day of rest and fresh sea air, Olivia declared it was time to shake off any remaining jet lag.

"Fancy a night out?"

Airlie and Hannah exchanged an approving glance.

"I'm not offering much, just a night out at the pub."

"Tell us more," said Airlie.

"I'm in the church choir at Finbeigh. Practice is tonight. I can drop you at Bridge End and join you afterward."

Their first Irish pub experience seemed like a great idea, and Hannah declared she was going to try a pint of every beer she could find. Airlie knew better than to boast such claims.

Nearing seven thirty, Olivia pulled up outside Bridge End bar and promised to be no longer than an hour or so.

"Don't worry about us," Airlie said. "We'll be fine. You take your time."

The bar was charming in a rustic way. There were plenty of lights, mostly glowing on photographs decorating the walls, and the bar had a cozy, moody atmosphere. Airlie gravitated toward the fireplace filled with glowing candles. The lack of cheap tourist paraphernalia—nothing branded "Traditional Irish Pub"—indicated that the clientele seemed to be local. It took her fancy immediately.

"Ladies." A small man from behind the oak bar greeted them with a complete lack of enthusiasm. "What can I get you?"

"A pint of cider and a pint of Smithwicks please."

The little man's eyes popped open. "I beg your pardon?"

Thinking it was a straightforward request—the taps for the two drinks were right there in front of her—Airlie repeated, "A pint of cider and a Smithwicks please."

The annoying little man laughed. "It's not *Smith Wicks*." He took great care to separate the two words. "You say Smithicks. It's a silent w." A hum of laughter rose and fell from the locals.

Wanting to direct this arrogant twit to shove his Smithwicks up his rear end, Airlie simply repeated her request, this time emphasizing the correct pronunciation.

The curly haired bartender, oblivious to his ill manners, continued smugly, deftly filling two pint glasses. "So, ladies, you just on your way through or will you be about for a while?"

Hannah jumped in, eyeing Airlie, obviously fearful of her response. "We're staying with a friend in Roaring Bay for a while."

"Oh right, who's that then?"

"Olivia Swanson," said Hannah.

Airlie refused to meet his beady little eyes. She never knew the Irish could be so nosy.

"Oh right," he repeated. "Choir tonight, is it?"

Ignoring him completely, Airlie took her drink to a table at the far corner, leaving Hannah to answer and wrap up the conversation.

"Christ, you'd think they'd hire someone with a bit more personality to work in a place like this, wouldn't you?" said Airlie.

"Maybe he's just filling in for someone."

"Maybe he should just stop being a complete twat."

Hannah took her first sip of Smithwicks.

"So, what's the verdict?"

"Not too bad, actually." She took another mouthful. "I could certainly get used to this."

Before they knew it, Airlie was at the bar ordering another round from the ignorant little man, who was even shorter than Airlie. His name was Ross. This time, she ordered Hannah a Harp. The more cider Airlie drank, the more she enjoyed it, and Hannah simply consumed anything that came her way.

Rather abruptly, the crowd seemed to grow with what appeared to be the after-dinner drinkers—mostly men who announced to Ross that they were only popping in for a quiet one. Just as Hannah merrily plonked another round on the table, Olivia walked in with four ladies. The youngest, who Airlie guessed to be about forty, was carrying a guitar case, and within seconds, they rearranged the table to accommodate the five extra people.

"Airlie, Hannah, this is Sharon." Olivia pointed to the shortish lady with the guitar, and Airlie smiled a greeting. "And this is Grace," she continued, introducing a tall, slender woman with dark shoulder length hair, wearing cumbersome gold jewelry that Airlie could only assume was not the real thing. "This is Marion." A shorter lady with mousy brown hair, she smelled of smoke, and Airlie thought, by the wrinkles in her skin, that she had perhaps lived a hard life. "And last but certainly not least, this is Siobhan."

"You have to watch those two." Siobhan nodded toward Grace and Marion at the bar. "They'll lead you astray as soon as look at you. You pay no attention to them."

It was evident that the tradition of a drink at the pub after choir practice had long been observed by these five ladies. Ross knew them so well, he'd have the drinks poured not long after someone gave him the nod for another round. Within an hour, Grace and Marion had consumed as many pints as Airlie and Hannah managed in more than twice the time. The filthy jokes Grace told gave justification to the conservative singers who never came for a drink, and between them all, including Siobhan, they all paid out on Ross at every given opportunity.

"There certainly are some people about tonight, so there are," said Grace. "Great for the local B&Bs," she explained. "Great for everyone in the village really."

"Grace used to run her house as a B&B," said Olivia. "That was until she started her famous toenail collection and her husband shut it down."

They all laughed, especially Grace. "Gerry O'Shea did not shut down my B&B, I'll have ye feckers know. And I'll guarantee those nails belong to exactly who I tell ye they belong to." She slammed her fist on the table in an attempt to silence the laughter. "I meticulously hoovered those rooms daily, and I'll not be called a liar when I tell you they belonged to none other than Richard Harris and some other famous fellow, whose name I can't recall right now."

"She has them labeled, you know," said Sharon. "They're in those little containers you pee in at the doctor's, and she has them labeled with their names so she knows whose is whose."

"I might sell them on the Internet, make a fortune."

"Or you might just throw them out because they probably belong to Gerry O'Shea," said Olivia.

Well after midnight, last drinks were called and the bar lights dimmed. Slowly, the place emptied until only Airlie, Hannah, and the choir ladies remained. They made no move to leave.

Still without a smile, but in a less abrupt tone, Ross looked over. "Same again, ladies?"

They glanced at one another before agreeing to have one last drink. Ross obliged, shut and locked the front doors, and dimmed all the lights except for where they sat. Sighing, he dragged in a stool to join them.

"You working all week, Ross?" asked Olivia.

"I am. Callum is on holidays until next month, and I can't be fecked going through all that shite getting someone new. I might as well do it meself."

Horrified, Airlie and Hannah exchanged glances; this arrogant little man was the *owner*.

The telephone rang, piercing the air with its intrusive clangor. This didn't appear extraordinary, until everyone fell silent. All they heard was Ross's tired, expressionless voice as he stood behind the bar, the ancient black phone to his ear.

"Yes. Right. Just now was it? Okay. Good man yourself." He replaced the receiver with urgency.

"It was old Jim O'Reilly, back down the road. The fecking guards are on their way."

The antics that ensued were quite exceptional. Suspicious that it might be a subject that was taught in school, Airlie observed what appeared to be some sort of *Emergency Illegal After-Hours Drinking Procedure.* Sharon rushed to switch off the TV, Grace cleared drinks from the table, and Marion gathered everyone's coats and belongings while Olivia propelled Hannah and Airlie into the toilet.

Within moments, everyone besides Ross, who was on the lookout, huddled silently in the dank ladies' toilets. Almost an entire minute passed before the stupidity of the situation struck them all, more or less, simultaneously.

Hannah developed the giggles and could barely talk. "When the police come in, won't they think to look in here?"

"They probably won't come in," said Sharon.

"They won't? Then what are we doing in here?" asked Hannah.

"Well, they might," Olivia said. "But usually they don't."

Hannah headed for the door. "Let's just go back out and have our drinks then."

In a whispered chorus of "No," everyone lunged to seize Hannah and pull her back.

"The guards should pass, they usually pass, but if we get caught, Ross will be in the shite altogether. We'll just stay in here until we get the all clear."

Before the *Emergency Illegal After-Hours Drinking Procedure* was initiated, Airlie had desperately needed a pee. Now, in the toilet with an audience, the thought of breaking the silence was off-putting and the urge had passed.

Everyone's cars were parked in the square directly outside the pub. They were the *only* cars parked in the square outside the pub. Really, at nearly two in the morning, who else did the guards think the cars belonged to?

Grace switched off the toilet light and pushed open the window. Everyone crowded behind her to see outside.

Within a minute, a pale yellow glow from the headlights of the patrol car slowly weaved along the road that hugged the water's edge. The entire pub was in darkness now, and as the patrol car crept through the square, circling the cars, everyone except Grace withdrew. She nervously inched the window closed. Eventually, after parking directly outside for a few more moments, the patrol car sped off.

Grace watched and waited. Airlie assumed Ross was out the front doing the same, and within moments, he switched the lights on and he yelled, "Right, you lot. Out. They're at least past old Ed's place now."

Grace slammed the toilet window shut.

Airlie wondered who Ed was.

*The Getaway* was evidently the final component of the *Emergency Illegal After-Hours Drinking Procedure*. After a push from Olivia, they charged from the toilet and rushed to their respective cars, before speeding off home in all directions.

❖

"He'll be watching us," said Olivia.

"What? Who will?" Airlie barely had her seat belt secured before they rounded the first bend at speed.

"The guard. He'll be high on a long, steep driveway somewhere, hiding and watching."

Both Airlie and Hannah looked toward the hills and houses that sat scattered along the edge of Dunstrand Inlet.

"He'll be next to an old shed or wood pile, in the pitch-black watching as all our car lights zip away from the square."

"Is he waiting to arrest us?" asked Hannah.

Olivia laughed. "Hardly. He wants to go home to his wife. He's waiting to make sure we all bugger off."

"You're joking, right?"

"Nope. That guard will go to bed safe in the knowledge that there's no after-hour drinkers on his patch, and more importantly, he'll have not one skerrick of paperwork to complete in the morning. For that guard, it's been a good night."

❖

Driving along the windy, bleak road, the impressive landscape of Swords Lough Valley took on an eerie feel. The strong beam of the headlights sliced through the night, and because of the low-lying clouds, not one star or the moon could be seen. Airlie wondered what it would be like to be alone out there. In all her life, she'd never been surrounded by such intense darkness. It was oppressive, as if it had mass that could, in some way, be measured. Predictably, the urge to pee struck her again. "Can you please pull over? I don't think I can make it all the way home. My eyes are floating."

Olivia nodded and slowed the vehicle, eventually swerving into a small lay-by. Airlie jumped out and rushed a safe distance down the road before squatting. Her relief was enormous. Besides the sound of her pee hitting the gravel verge and Olivia's car idling in the distance, the night was silent. She whistled for comfort.

Airlie returned to the car before struggling with the door handle and eventually flopping onto the passenger seat. Hannah had been quiet for some time, and she twisted in her seat to see her fast asleep with her mouth agape.

"I need to go now too, damn it," said Olivia.

"I highly recommend it. You'll feel so much better."

Airlie peered out the window, trying to determine where the sky began and the mountains ended. It was useless. She caught a glimpse of something in the side mirror. Holding her breath, she stared in case she saw it again. Nothing. Where was Olivia? She hadn't even bothered to look which direction she went. She was on the brink of waking Hannah when Olivia came into view. She watched as a glowing pink Olivia, lit by the car's taillights, undid her trousers and squatted by the road.

Airlie looked away. It was rude and intrusive to watch, but a warm tingle shot through her, and she focused again at the tiny figure in the mirror. Airlie watched, a voyeur, transfixed by Olivia's slim figure as she pulled up her underpants and jeans. Embarrassed, Airlie scrambled for her mobile phone and began to fiddle with it as Olivia jumped back into the car.

"You certainly do feel better, don't you?" Olivia said.

Airlie had never felt better in her life, but she simply grunted in agreement, ignoring the lingering, tingling sensation between her legs.

## CHAPTER FIVE

The weeks that ensued were filled with laughter and countless good times. Olivia's holiday ended, and reluctantly, she returned to work. It was only Airlie who felt obliged to rise early and share a pot of coffee with her. It was the least she could do given the circumstances. Hannah enjoyed sleeping too much to partake in such pleasantries and would rise mid-morning for a run along the beach.

A visit to the local butcher was enough indication that Roaring Bay was a small town. "Ah, you must be the two ladies staying up there with Gavin and Olivia?"

"That's us." Airlie returned the smile of the handsome young man. His crew cut suited him somehow as a butcher. "Can I please have a kilo of steak and kilo of lamb chops?"

"You mean a pound, love."

"I do?"

"You'll confuse the old fellows round here altogether if you go asking for kilos and the like." He winked. "And heaven forbid you start talking about meters and centimeters; that would cause a right stir, so it would."

"I'll try to remember that."

"So, will ye be round long then?"

Airlie and Hannah exchanged glances. It was a conversation they'd put off.

"We're not sure yet," Airlie said.

"Well now, it is a lovely spot. You should stay for a little while longer at least." He flashed a cheeky grin.

"Is there much work around here?" she asked.

"That depends on who you ask, to be honest. There is that Skirmish Paintball place on the way to Finbeigh. They have loads of foreigners working there, but they pay them pure shite. It's the best time of year to be looking for work though, coming up to summer and all." He plonked the package of meat on the counter with his broad hand.

Airlie turned to notice that Hannah had already wandered outside.

"Colm. My name's Colm Geraghty." His cheeks turned a brilliant pink. "I'll be in the Lough Bar later tonight if you fancy a drink?" He removed his hand from the meat.

Airlie smiled. She felt hot, her chest constricted. "I'll keep that in mind, although I think I'm busy tonight."

"Sure, no bother, maybe another time."

Before she could respond, another customer pushed past her in the doorway, and she slipped out.

Hannah raised her eyebrows. "Busy tonight? Busy doing what?"

"We're cooking a barbecue." Airlie took off toward the grocer.

"What? All night?" Hannah hurried after her.

"Well no, but it's rude to eat and run."

"I'm pretty sure Colm Geraghty won't be in the pub right on six p.m., you know. You'll have time to eat dinner twice over before you'd need to leave."

"Well, maybe I don't want to go out tonight."

"When was the last time someone asked you out?"

"I don't know. That's hardly the point. I don't want to go out tonight."

"Really, Airlie? Some fine looking bloke asks you out and you turn him down for no good reason."

"You go and meet him then if you're so interested."

"He didn't ask *me*; he asked *you*."

"He's not really my type, and we've only just arrived in Ireland. I don't want to be going out with the first guy that asks me."

"You only have to have a drink with the man, not marry him. And anyway, what is your type?"

Airlie eyed her. "Just leave it, okay? He asked and I said no. End of story."

Hannah threw her hands in the air and mumbled a series of unintelligible phrases before plonking herself outside the grocer to wait in silent protest.

❖

Regardless of how the meat arrived at the table—dinner preparations had been plagued with long, often uncomfortable silences—it was delicious. The tender steak had been marinated, and although it was too breezy to eat outside, they dined in the conservatory, taking in the view of the beach in the early evening sun.

"Airlie passed up a date for this," Hannah said.

Gavin and Olivia stared at her.

"You really should learn when not to speak," said Airlie.

"It's not too late to go, you know?"

"Your lips are still moving. Why is that?"

"A date with who?" asked Olivia.

"No one," Airlie growled.

Olivia folder her arms and raised an eyebrow.

Gavin coughed awkwardly and began clearing the table.

"Colm Geraghty," said Hannah.

"Colm Geraghty?" Olivia frowned. "Oh, the cute butcher?"

"That's him."

Airlie watched this exchange with little enthusiasm. "I'm just here, you know. You can stop talking about me now."

"He seems like a lovely man," Olivia said. "I think he was seeing a girl who went to university and eventually took off to Scotland. It ended a while ago though." She smiled at Airlie. "So you took his fancy, eh? You could do worse, you know."

"Thank you for your thought and interest," said Airlie. "Your unwanted thought and interest that is, but I'm perfectly happy with my decision to stay in."

"So, when are you going out with him, if not tonight?"

"He's taking me to the nudist colony near Donegal next weekend."

Gavin returned for the last of the dishes. "There's a nudist colony in Donegal? Who knew?"

"So you didn't reschedule?" asked Olivia.

"Nope. I'm not going out with him tonight or any other night. The apparently charming Colm Geraghty will have to live without me."

"He's a genuine kind of bloke," said Gavin.

"He's not my type. End of story." Airlie grabbed the condiments and followed Gavin to the kitchen to lend a hand. She knew Olivia and Hannah wouldn't let up if she remained in the room. She could see them talking. They had lowered their voices, and it was obvious she was the topic of conversation. Airlie excused herself to the lounge, waiting for Gavin to join her.

Much later on, she met Olivia in the kitchen. Hannah had called it a night after a long walk along the beach.

"Come and have a drink with me?" asked Olivia.

"No, thanks. I think I'll get some sleep."

"Ah, come on, it's Friday night. I've got a nice bottle of red I'd love to open." Airlie hesitated. "Look, if you don't want to date the butcher, at least have a drink with me." Olivia winked and held the bottle aloft. "I've been waiting for a special occasion to crack this open."

"Okay." Airlie had been annoyed for long enough. "What's so special about the occasion?"

"You are."

"I am?"

Olivia sighed and poured two large glasses. "You've been here a while now, and I get the feeling you're almost ready to move on. I think we should make the most of it while you're still around."

Airlie wasn't entirely convinced she was ready to leave, but she knew Hannah was. The conversation they had so far avoided, revolving around money, jobs, and the big city, was just around the corner. "We really appreciate you letting us stay, you know?"

"I know, and to be honest, I've loved having you around." She quickly added, "So has Gavin, of course. It's just a pity there's so few jobs on the coast or you could stay longer."

"Colm mentioned there's a Skirmish place or something nearby, but they pay badly. Personally, I'd really like to stay, but I know Hannah is keen on the bright lights of Dublin. I can't let her down."

"Of course you can't, and you're more than welcome any time you like."

Airlie smiled. She knew when the time came to leave she would see Olivia again. Somehow, it just didn't make sense not to.

"So, Colm's not your dream man then?"

"I don't know. He might be. I'm just not that interested in seeing anyone right now."

"Fair enough. As long as you know you could certainly do worse."

"I get that, and he seems lovely, but the pressure I get from my mother about being twenty-eight and single is incredible. I really thought being ten thousand miles away would be enough to avoid this."

"Point taken. Sorry." Olivia smiled warmly and squeezed Airlie's hand.

Airlie looked down. Olivia squeezed again before withdrawing.

She wished it were the wine that sent an instant wave of heat through her, but she knew it wasn't. Under her arms was hot and damp. Her body had never reacted like this before. Jet lag, she told herself although she knew this was impossible. They arrived weeks ago. She could think of nothing but the uncomfortable inferno beneath her clothes. She blurted out the first thing that came to mind. "God, you're lucky. You have such a great setup here."

"It's nice, so it is. You take it all for granted after a while though. Gav says I'm never here to enjoy it anyway."

"You're here now."

"Yes, I am. And so are you because you rejected poor Colm Geraghty."

"Will I ever live this down?"

"You will, of course. Maybe in a year or two I'll have forgotten."

It might have been a flippant comment, but Airlie chose to believe that Olivia was insinuating they'd still be friends in a year or two. The thought left contentment deep within.

They stared out over the water.

"Is Colm better looking than the man you nearly married?" Olivia lit some candles and turned out the lights. It truly was a stunning evening.

"Yes. No. Different really. Why?"

"I don't know. I was just wondering what he looked like, I suppose. I just can't imagine you with someone short or fair. I have it in my head he would have been tall, dark, and rather handsome. Was he?"

"I suppose." Airlie avoided discussing Sam. "He had brown hair, was tallish, and nice looking. He was a nice man. Probably still is."

"Just not the nice man for you?"

"No." She twisted loose cotton through her fingers. "I wasn't in love with Sam, but I did love him. I agreed to marry him because I thought it was the next thing in life to do. It's what all my friends were signing up for."

"But you had doubts?"

"I just didn't get it. I thought the longing to permanently hitch myself to someone would come later. It never did. I waited as long as I could stand." She shrugged. "I don't feel like I lost anything I particularly wanted to keep." She sounded callous, as if she deserved someone better, but the truth was Sam *had* been good enough. He *was* a great man, but in the end, she just didn't fancy him. It was that simple.

"You've never missed him, have you?" Olivia asked.

"I tried to miss him, as stupid as it sounds. I just didn't. Why does everyone want to make me feel guilty for that? We broke up. I'm not miserable. I never was. Why should I be? Perhaps everyone would have preferred it if I'd turned into a dribbling mess."

"I didn't mean it like that. Please don't get upset." Olivia poured the last glass from the bottle. "It's just that, please don't take this the wrong way, it's just that you seem so reluctant to move on, or perhaps you're scared to let someone else in for fear of getting hurt. I don't know."

Airlie gulped. "I'm not scared. Not of that, anyway. I'm scared of a hundred other things. Maybe everyone should be glad Sam's one thing I'm okay with."

The candlelight flickered across Olivia's face, blurring her features in a way that caused Airlie to stare. "What other things are you scared of?"

"You want to know what scares me?"

"Sure."

"Flying scares me. Spiders scare me. But right now, you're scaring me. Why are we having this conversation?"

"Sorry. I didn't mean to offend. You've made your point." Olivia sighed.

"I know. How about getting mugged or raped or murdered? That scares me." Airlie struggled to contain her frustration. "Or perhaps drinking too much red wine. That's fucking scary as hell!"

"Airlie, enough." Olivia leaned forward and moved her wine to one side. "Look at me."

The silence was long and Olivia's gaze relentless. Slowly, Airlie lifted her head and met her eyes.

"What's really going on?" Olivia asked. "What are you really running from? Talk to me. Maybe I can help."

Airlie felt helpless. In the true sense of the word, she felt like she was unable to be helped. How could she be helped when she didn't know what was wrong? Olivia rose and moved toward her.

The conversation had gone too far. She wasn't emotionally prepared for what was about to happen. She stood before Olivia reached her. The room closed in, and her breathing became shallow. She needed to get out. Airlie leapt for the conservatory door.

"Airlie!"

They reached the door simultaneously, each firmly gripping the handle, Olivia's hand covering Airlie's.

"Airlie?" Olivia lowered her voice. It was soothing, her mouth only a short distance from Airlie's ear. She could feel warm breath blow her hair. "There's nowhere else to run, sweetheart."

Airlie refused to meet her gaze and released the door handle, sliding her hand from beneath Olivia's. Olivia moved closer, trapping her with her other arm across her shoulders.

"Airlie? Talk to me."

Airlie looked up. "I'm not running anywhere. I just want to get some fucking fresh air. Is that okay with you?"

"Honey, just talk to me."

"Please?"

Olivia sighed and stepped back, allowing her to pass.

Airlie slammed the door behind her. The calm evening was fresh and bitter, and she upturned her collar against the breeze, wishing she had a cigarette. She chanced a glance inside and saw Olivia slumped against the kitchen bench, her head in her hands, defeated.

Airlie huddled on the doorstep, wondering what had happened to their wonderful evening. Fucking Sam. Something told her Olivia wouldn't bring the conversation outside so she bunkered down, biding her time. Eventually, the door opened slightly and Olivia whispered good night.

Airlie remained outside for what seemed like hours. She arched her neck skyward. The beautiful stars appeared to bubble just above an invisible surface. She cursed Olivia for crossing a line.

# CHAPTER SIX

Airlie sat cross-legged on the bottom of Hannah's bed. "Maybe it's time to make our own way in the world."

"Really? You sure?"

Airlie feared if she waited to be sure, they'd be old and gray by the time she made a decision. "Sure, I'm sure."

"Dublin. Definitely Dublin." Hannah clapped her hands. "I mean, Galway is nice and all, but I think Dublin will be amazing."

Airlie didn't mind. She was delighted to see Hannah happy and enthusiastic.

"This last month or so has been great, but I think it's time to move on, don't you?" Hannah said.

Airlie did, and she didn't. For now, she focused on the part that knew it was time to go. "Our next adventure awaits. And Dublin is a good choice. More opportunity."

"More jobs, clubs, bars, and men. What more do we need?"

"What more indeed." Airlie sighed. "I'd better go break the news to Olivia."

"We'll go together."

"No, it's okay. I think I'd prefer to do it on my own." Something told Airlie the situation was delicate. It had only been a short friendship, as far as friendships went, but it was important she try to convey to Olivia that the decision to leave had nothing to do with last night.

She found Olivia sipping coffee in the conservatory.

"Morning. I thought I heard you two chattering," Olivia said. "Coffee?"

Airlie wasn't one to decline caffeine. She nodded. "We've got some news. Hannah and me." Her voice came out all wrong.

"By the sound of that, you've set my house on fire. What's up?"

"We think it's about time we left you and Gav in peace."

Olivia stalled, but only momentarily. She straightened. "Is this about last night?"

"No. Not at all." Airlie rushed toward her but pulled up short. "Hannah is keen to embark on the next phase of our journey."

"And what about you?"

Airlie couldn't look her in the eye. "If I don't go now, I may never leave."

"If there's one thing Roaring Bay can do, it's lull you into apathy."

"Is that why you've stayed?"

Olivia smiled, but it seemed sad. "I've stayed because I don't know where else to go." She patted Airlie's shoulder. "But you do. As far as I know, we only get one crack at this life thing, so you'd better get out there and enjoy it."

Westport train station was wet and miserable. Everyone huddled in the modest foyer as rain lashed on the poorly insulated roof. The noise was intensifying Airlie's alcohol induced headache.

"Now, you know you can come and visit any time you like?" Olivia said.

Airlie nodded.

"Together or alone," Olivia added. "I don't think you ought to wait until the other is free if you feel like a visit, okay?"

"And you'll be down to see us sometimes, right?" Airlie sought reassurance. They'd shared such a lovely final week, she wondered if her decision to move on was premature.

"Of course. And now I have a reason to visit Dublin more often. But I'll wait until you get a place first. Goodness knows where you'll be in the interim."

"The Ritz," said Airlie.

"More like a squalor," said Olivia.

The conductor blew his whistle. They exchanged hugs, gathered their belongings, and boarded the train. Airlie watched as Olivia stood in the rain waiting until the train gathered speed before she turned and walked away. Hannah was elated to finally be on her way to the city.

She appeared keen to plan their arrival and the ensuing few days, but Airlie's pounding head was heavy, and her eyes wanted to shut. She smiled at Hannah's enthusiasm and promised to talk about it later.

Airlie closed her eyes and rested her head on her hands, allowing her body to relax with the motion of the train. She felt a little empty, and although she wasn't feeling her best from too much cider, she knew over-consumption wasn't her ailment. She missed Olivia already. She told herself that the sense of loss was a result of sleep-deprived emotions and nothing else. A couple of unconscious hours on the train would lift her spirits, and she eventually gave in to exhaustion. A sense of longing to remain with Olivia nagged her as she drifted off. If she let herself succumb, it threatened to overwhelm her with a groundswell of panic. Without sensible rationale behind these feelings, she slipped into a dreamless sleep.

Mid-afternoon in Dublin was wet and cold. With the aid of a guidebook, they located the hostel *every* travel book apparently recommended. The Rest, as it was known, was near capacity, but they took a rudimentary room on the ground floor with three other bunk beds. The room was so depressing they dumped their bags and left immediately. They made it as far as the pub next door but were too exhausted to even attempt a logical conversation. In the end, they called it a night disgracefully early, a poor effort for their first Saturday night in Dublin. Even Hannah, who had initially shown promise, couldn't stomach the beer. Airlie declared that next Saturday would officially be their first *real* Saturday night on the town—tonight was simply a test run.

Thankfully, sleep took them without resistance, but as Dublin's drunken revelers took to the streets in search of their favorite drinking hole, the noise became impossible to endure, and they tossed and turned on the creaky bunks.

Airlie drifted off in the early hours, but was disturbed yet again by their roommates stumbling in at dawn. It sounded as if they literally fell through the door. Eventually, the noise died down, and Airlie breathed a sigh of relief, determined to catch another hour or two. Within one minute of silence, their roomies proceeded to have sex on the top of their respective bunks. Airlie was sure she'd heard two male voices, but the female voices sounded alike, and it was a mystery how many were actually in the room. The sex was quick. Thank God for alcohol and small mercies. With the first glimpse of daylight creeping through the cracks in the curtains, Airlie welcomed the silence.

Then the snoring began. She looked at her watch. It was seven o'clock.

Hannah appeared over the edge of the bunk. "I can't take this anymore."

"Shall we go?"

Hannah nodded, jumped from the top bunk, and switched the light on. A chorus of whinging groans echoed in the room. "Sorry, folks, but I'm sure you'll understand." Her voice boomed and oozed sarcasm.

"Can't you do that with the light off?" An American man, many years younger, glared over the edge of his bunk. His hair was wild and black, and the girl he was with pulled the covers over her head.

Airlie wasn't in the mood. "Look, asshole, if you hadn't woken me with the bloody light already this morning, had what sounded like the most pathetic attempt at sex I've ever heard, and then snored your butt ugly head off, I can assure you we wouldn't be having this conversation, so shut the fuck up and suffer like we did."

Hannah glared at her approvingly.

"Christ, lady, chill out. I think you're at the wrong place. The convent is just around the corner." He rolled over and joined his friend beneath the covers.

After showering in silence, they packed and left. Airlie went to switch off the light, but Hannah pushed her out the door winking. They heard cursing and a loud thump as one of their roommates jumped from a top bunk to dim the room again. Airlie wasn't convinced the security room was all that secure, but regardless, they left their packs and headed out onto deserted Dublin streets.

"At no age would staying in hostels appeal to me," said Hannah. "I now know why I've never gone backpacking. Surely, we can afford a cheap twin room somewhere just until we get sorted. It's gotta be better than that."

"It couldn't be worse," said Airlie.

"It sounded like a porno in our room."

"Don't remind me." Airlie spied some Golden Arches in the distance and pointed. "It'll be the only place that's open this early."

"If it sells coffee, it's good enough for me."

"If there's no one having sex, it's certainly good enough for me."

# CHAPTER SEVEN

The cost of accommodation, even in the dingiest corners of Dublin, was expensive. They rented a room for seven nights because it was the cheapest rate, but it was imperative they searched for a more permanent and affordable solution.

Their room at the Dublin Arms Hotel was surprisingly spacious, complete with saggy beds and deplorable water pressure, but at least it was better than the hostel. The decor hadn't been updated since the seventies. Airlie found it rather amusing and depressing all at once. The bathroom looked dirty, but the strong aroma of bleach indicated the ground-in dirt was probably as old as the place itself.

On Monday morning, Airlie rose early and met the day with a sense of excitement. After printing several copies of their résumés, they were armed and enthusiastically ready to find a job. The people they spoke with at the various agencies were confident that with their skills, they should be gainfully employed within a week or two. To expedite the process, they separated in search of more permanent accommodation, and for a couple of days were like ships passing in the night, usually meeting at the somber, and slightly damp, Dublin Arms bar in the late afternoon to discuss their respective days.

The initial shine on the process was beginning to tarnish, not only through lack of progress, but it turned out to be both physically and mentally demanding. The days were long, public transport was unreliable, and it was challenging. Neither had expected it to be so grueling.

Room 107 at the Dublin Arms became a mansion and the height of luxury. All the places Airlie inspected were barely a step above slums.

In one sordid apartment, you could use the toilet, shower in pure filth, and clean your teeth, all by remaining seated on the toilet. If the broom cupboard-cum-bathroom wasn't tempting enough, then perhaps the fact that your neighbor could watch you at it from only a meter away was more appealing.

To ensure their survival and to avoid catching poverty prone diseases, they would need to pay more rent. While the standard of accommodation rose, most prospective landlords were reluctant to rent a room to a pair of Aussies with no jobs and no guarantee of long-term tenancy. The Dublin Arms would have to do for another week. That week turned into another, and by week three, things were looking grim.

It wasn't until Hannah stumbled upon a stroke of luck that the pendulum finally looked like it might swing their way. Hannah had been called back for a second interview in a café she'd come across while on her way to an employment agency. They were advertising for an "Experienced Barista."

Hannah had marched straight into the café and announced she was there for the job. It was quiet at the time, and she suggested to the man behind the counter that he take a break while she prepared him a coffee. He complied, drank the coffee, and then invited her back the following day to meet the other owner. When she turned to check the name of the café, the little sign advertising the job was gone.

"Sounds like you've got it in the bag, Han."

"Fingers crossed. The bloke seemed really nice. Gay I think. Dresses too smartly for a straight man. The café has a lot going for it, and I know it's not what I wanted, I'm a bloody accountant for Christ sake, but it's a start."

"You're not an accountant, actually."

"Well, I'm just as good as one."

"But not *actually* one though, are you?"

"Oh, shut up."

"Your brother will be proud." It was in Hannah's brother's café that she learned how to make great coffee.

Airlie reluctantly returned to the Arms at the end of another fruitless day and lay awake contemplating the future. The familiar smell of bleach wafted beneath the bathroom door, and Hannah snored lightly, falling to sleep easier than usual with the prospect of employment.

Airlie crossed her arms behind her head and contemplated

changing her résumé to reflect she used to be a porn star. She wondered how long she could keep a straight face while prospective employers blushed.

Reluctant to face another day of rejection, she thought she might accompany Hannah to the interview. It could be fun, pretending to be a customer while Hannah charmed her way in. It would be nice for them to both hang out and celebrate if Hannah was successful.

"Hey, you still awake?" asked Hannah.

"No. I'm fast asleep."

"Something will turn up. You'll see."

Hannah could read her like a book. "I hope so. Look, I might come with you tomorrow. Job hunting is doing my head in. One day off won't hurt."

"Great idea. I'd like you to come along. I could use your support."

Airlie appreciated how, in the face of adversity, Hannah liked to try to make her feel useful. When they were at school, Airlie had attended the trials for the soccer team because Hannah had asked her to, and when she was trialed for less than a minute on the pitch and obviously failed to make the team, Hannah tried to cheer her up by having a T-shirt printed that said "Team Physio." Halfway through the first match, she forgot she had Deep Heat on her hands and rubbed her eyes. She spent the second half in the emergency room having it flushed out. Airlie had conceded her physio days were over. It made her love Hannah more, though.

"Try and get some sleep, and try not to worry about it, okay?" Hannah added.

"Me worry? As if."

"Airlie, I can practically hear your brain ticking over."

"At least it proves I have one."

"Just try."

"All right, I'll try."

Hannah rolled away. "Night, Air-Porter." She pulled the covers high around her ears.

"Night, Han."

Airlie turned toward the wall, away from the streetlight seeping through the curtains. From Monday until Saturday, she'd been flat out trying to find work. The process was tiring and frustrating. All angles were covered, from checking the Internet, signing on at temp places, ringing numbers on notice boards, to physically fronting up with résumé in hand, trying to fluke anything that may be available. There simply wasn't much else they could do. They often inquired after spotting a "Help Wanted, Apply Within" sign, but most looked thoroughly dodgy, or the uninterested person behind the counter informed them that the position had already been filled.

Airlie was not having fun. Her desperation was yet to reach the critical stage, but she wanted something positive to report to Olivia soon. They had spoken only a few times since arriving in Dublin, and the more miserable she became, the more she longed to be back in Roaring Bay where she seemed to fit in.

Airlie imagined what it would be like when she eventually found a job. Top of the list was to move into a nice flat and have a room each. They would travel around the rest of Ireland, attend concerts, and eat out at all the restaurants they'd been walking past in the last while. It all seemed so far away, and she certainly had the goal to work toward, but patience was eluding her, and she was becoming increasingly frustrated at her lack of progress.

## CHAPTER EIGHT

With only minutes to spare until Hannah's midday interview, they arrived at Sean's For Coffee, a stylish little café, only slightly off the beaten track, along a trendy alleyway on the Grafton Street side of Dublin.

"Looks promising." Airlie pressed her nose against the window.

"It's not bad, is it? I hope they're ready to be impressed." Hannah was on a mission.

The beautiful, strong smell of coffee drew them in when Hannah swung the door open. "Wish me luck," she said.

"You'll be fine. See you when you're gainfully employed."

Airlie sat at a table with her back to the wall, gaining full view of the café. She relaxed while Hannah ordered her a cappuccino from a handsome, ginger haired fellow. He proceeded to point toward a door that said Staff Only, and in a flash, Hannah disappeared.

With little else to do Airlie, picked up a copy of the *Irish Times*, opened it to the crossword, and smiled as the handsome man delivered her coffee. In no time, the crossword consumed her.

Three-quarters of an hour passed before she began to worry. First, because she had already drank three cups of coffee, and that was approaching a dangerous level of caffeine for her, and second, because it couldn't possibly take that long to have an interview simply to work at a café.

She closed the newspaper and became aware the place was empty; even the handsome man behind the counter was gone. A hint of panic welled inside. What if this was a cruel setup? A complicated conspiracy to knock Hannah unconscious, beaten by a frozen panini, and thrown into the back of a butcher's van with box upon box of pork sausages. Just as she rose to investigate, the handsome man from behind the counter bounded through the Staff Only door, followed by Hannah and two other fellows, one of which, she assumed, was Sean.

"Great news," said Hannah. "Start next Monday."

Airlie dismissed her wild abduction scenario. "That's fabulous." She rushed to embrace Hannah. One job down, one to go.

One of the men who followed Hannah through the door was glowing. "And *you're* gay too! My God, this was meant to be. Dan said you were the one to hire, and look at you two, such a lovely couple."

Airlie chocked on words of denial. Hannah jumped in. "We're not together. Although I'd be a pretty good catch." She winked. "This is my best friend, Airlie Porter. Airlie, this is Sean, Dan, and Liam."

Airlie's brain was slowly sending the message to her mouth to smile. Hannah nudged her. "You know, the Sean from *Sean's For Coffee.*"

Finally, Airlie beamed. "Nice to meet you, Sean. Great place you've got here." His trendy beret was tilted to one side, and now that she was breathing normally again, she found him likable. He was a tiny man, not only rather short, but also lean and upright. Although sporting a French beret, he was wearing an outfit one would expect to see on the canals of Venice—perhaps on a hairy Italian man deftly steering a gondola.

"And how about the coffee?" He smiled broadly. "It's an Ethiopian blend. You look like you know coffee."

"I know a smooth talker when I see one." Airlie smiled and stepped away from the arm Hannah had left draped over her shoulder. "The coffee was lovely, thank you, but to enhance the experience, to make a truly sound judgment, I'd have to try it with some of that carrot cake first."

"Takes a smooth talker to know one," said Dan. He filled a container with an enormous slice of cake.

In contrast to Sean, Dan was a solid specimen. His pale green shirt left nothing to the imagination, and Airlie doubted his jet-black hair was naturally so dark.

"Don't be offended." Dan's piercing brown eyes met Airlie's. "Sean thinks that just because he's gay, everyone else is, too."

Airlie was in a state of caffeine overdose. Did people really think she and Hannah were a couple?

"Why don't we go for a drink later?" Dan said. "Things are starting to get busy here again. We can welcome our new staff member over a pint."

They arranged to meet that night.

Lunch was celebratory, but Airlie was distracted.

"Earth to Airlie. What's up? Hannah asked.

"I can imagine someone who's known me for years *possibly* mistaking me for a lesbian, but really, he'd only just met me."

"Why would people who have known you for years think you were gay?"

"I guess the fact that I'm single, and happily choosing to be, might lead people to believe that I'm in the closet or something." Airlie knew she was trying too hard to be cool about this. "And the clothes. I hardly dress like Audrey Hepburn."

Hannah frowned. "Who does?"

Airlie stuffed another guacamole-laden corn chip into her mouth to shut herself up. She failed. "Plus, I don't even own a dress. That's a dead giveaway."

"I know gay boys are good and all, but I doubt they can tell just by looking at you that you don't wear dresses."

"Or even own one."

"Whatever. Either way, since when does it mean you're gay if you don't have a boyfriend? I don't have a boyfriend and I'm not batting for the other team."

Airlie almost itched in agitation. The fact that she didn't *have* a boyfriend didn't bother her at all. The fact that she didn't want one worried the hell out of her.

## CHAPTER NINE

That evening they left for the pub early. It was a much-preferred option to their room. It was timely that Hannah had secured work; their funds were dwindling, and things were tight.

They arrived just a little past eight. The Bartender was a trendy nightspot Airlie imagined would be packed with equally trendy and sweaty people, dancing to throbbing, nauseating music all night long. An unvarying beat of modern jazz filled the funky room. They were lucky to find a shiny red vinyl couch that sat behind a stained glass-topped table. Airlie sat down and almost immediately slid back off again. She pushed her bum to the rear of the cushions and fell in love with the bar and all its curved, rounded, albeit slippery, surfaces.

Amazingly—for the Irish aren't known for their punctuality—Sean, Dan, and Liam arrived at exactly nine o'clock. With them was a stunning woman with long, dark hair to the middle of her back and the deepest brown eyes and fair complexion.

"Well done, ladies." They bounded toward them. "You found a table."

Sean and Dan acquired extra stools while the unknown woman and Liam squished onto the couch next to Hannah and Airlie. Sean introduced the woman as Rachel, Irish born and bred from somewhere on the east coast. Her day had been terrible until now because apparently a formula she had been working on in the lab was a dud, months of work down the drain. Judging by the subsequent conversation, Airlie guessed she must be a chemist for a pharmaceutical company. She was usually terrible with ages, but aged Rachel in her early to mid-thirties. She must have come directly from work because she was still wearing a fancy business suit. Until Rachel gulped her first drink, she appeared haggard and deflated. Airlie was surprised to learn she wasn't Liam's girlfriend.

Six people at the table meant six rounds and six drinks. Airlie wasn't capable of competing with the well-seasoned Irish drinkers, and with finances tight until Hannah's first pay packet, their near empty wallets would also struggle. Airlie thought it best to stick with half pints.

"Bollocks to that. Two young Aussie lassies like yourselves should be well able to keep up with the likes of us," said Liam.

"This, my new friends, is a celebration," said Sean. "It is a celebration in your honor." He smiled warmly at Hannah. "So, we'll hear nothing of this half pint rubbish. Hannah here has just joined the best, and soon to be most famous, coffeehouse in all of Ireland."

Airlie wasn't usually one to converse with God, but she said a silent prayer that the night would end before they all had a chance to buy a round.

Conversation flowed easily, and as the fourth round of drinks disappeared, Rachel tapped Airlie on the leg, requesting her assistance to carry the next round. By now, the place was heaving with people, and as she followed Rachel through the dense crowd, they became separated. Standing on tippy-toes, she craned her neck searching for the long brown hair.

From nowhere, soft, warm fingers linked through hers. Rachel leaned close. "I thought I'd lost you there for a moment. This place gets so crowded."

Airlie sensed she should release Rachel's grip, but as she relaxed her hand, Rachel tightened hers and deftly weaved them through the masses. Rachel leaned over the speckled orange bar top to order drinks from a beautiful girl sporting a Mohawk. Rachel's smart black suit was not at all out of place, and as she leaned over further, Airlie couldn't help but glance at the crisp white shirt that gaped to expose a dark, claret colored bra. Her heart quickened, and she rubbed her hand where Rachel had held it.

"This place is fabulous," said Airlie. She wasn't sure why, but even though the room was thumping with music and people chatting, she needed to fill the silence between them. She attempted to maintain focused on Rachel's brown eyes and nothing lower.

"It's great, isn't it? We should come one weekend and have a dance. That's when it really goes off."

"Would there be any room to dance?"

"Well." She smiled. "It can get fairly intimate. You wouldn't be shy about that now, would you?"

"You're kidding? The more people tightly squeezed around me, the less anyone notices my dancing."

There was an awkward pause.

Rachel smiled. "So, Sean said you and Hannah aren't a couple, although he mistakenly thought you were."

"Just best friends. Although Hannah thinks she'd be a good catch."

"Hannah's not gay though, is she?"

Airlie was relieved this conversation was only about Hannah. "God no, but I'm sure she'd try anything once. In fact, I'm surprised she hasn't yet."

"But you are?"

"What? *Gay*?"

Rachel's cool demeanor cracked, replaced with confusion. Before Airlie could set her straight, the bartender delivered the drinks then awaited payment. Airlie gulped half her pint. She couldn't understand why everyone thought she was gay today. Perhaps she'd need that sixth drink after all.

As the night wore on, their discussions gradually sunk to gutter level. They all appeared to enjoy the smutty conversations, with perhaps one exception. Airlie.

"Okay," said Liam. His eyes were beginning to look heavy with alcohol. Thankfully, they were on the last round of drinks. "Name, and I mean actually name, the best shag you've ever had. First and last name."

Dan leapt in. "Sean, of course. I'm not daft enough not to know who I'm going home with." Sean then proceeded to tell him if he behaved, he'd remind him of his prowess later.

Liam said his best shag was a blond Scandinavian girl he only saw once while on holiday in Spain, but he couldn't pronounce her name, nor could he spell it. Hannah thought carefully through the throngs of men she had been with and came up with Scott Giovanni.

"Really? Scott Giovanni?" Airlie wouldn't have picked him in a million years. "He was so hairy. I reckon his arse would've had more hair on it than his head." It was news to Airlie that he had been so good in bed.

"Yes, well, he had hidden talents."

Rachel, who was now sitting close to Airlie on the couch, rested her head on her shoulder, laughing.

"How come you dumped him then?"

"Because he farted all the time!"

"But *you* fart all the time."

"I do not. Well, not as much as he did and…" Now Hannah was in fits. "And he'd only have sex if we were both covered in baby oil. We'd slip about all over the place. It was just too much hassle."

"So what about you, Rach?" Liam asked.

"Okay, I would have to say Niamh Burke. Although I think the only way she could cope with being gay was to take speed. So, it's really Niamh Burke-On-Speed as the best sex ever for me."

"And you, Airlie, lucky last, who was your best, babe?" asked Sean.

Airlie's body stiffened. Rachel was stunning and not fitting her idea of a lesbian in the slightest. She remembered the conversation at the bar. Rachel had assumed *she* was gay, but Airlie hadn't even considered that Rachel might be. With all the jokes and laughter that night, she'd inadvertently slid close to Rachel on the slippery couch, practically snuggling. She felt a knot of anxiety grow in her stomach as she realized Rachel's arm was over the back of the couch around her shoulder, prodding her. "Airlie? Christ, you must have a few if you have to think about it for that long?"

Hannah tapped her knee. "Airhead, snap out of it, who's your best root?"

"Um, okay, let me think." Airlie had only slept with two men, and Sam was the only sober encounter. She'd hated having sex with him, but she couldn't remember sex with the other person. "Sam, Sam Washington."

"Is that a boy or girl?" asked Rachel.

"For Christ's sake. He's a fucking boy!"

Rachel removed her arm from behind Airlie and held her hands up in surrender. "Sorry. I was only asking."

The knot in Airlie's gut tightened. She slipped off the shiny red couch and made a dash to the toilet. By the time she returned, they would have changed the conversation and no one would even have noticed she was gone. The cubicle began to spin the moment she sat down. In a complete state of relief, she finished one of the longest pees ever. She cocked her head and read aloud the message on the back of the loo door. "For a good fecking time call Sumo on 09100987." Odd name, she thought, and doubted Sumo had picked up much business from the scribbled advertisement. "Peep shows only 4 euro," she continued.

"Is that an offer?"

Airlie froze. She recognized the voice. She buttoned her jeans and hesitated briefly before flushing the toilet and emerging from the cubicle. Rachel peered into the mirror, wiping smudged mascara from beneath her eyes.

"It is an offer," said Airlie. "But not from me. Sadly, my pen name isn't Sumo. It's on the back of the loo door." She stumbled to the washbasin, and Rachel followed her every move.

"Pity." Rachel raised her eyebrows and disappeared into a cubicle.

Back at the table, the conversation had indeed taken on a lighter tone, and Airlie provided the next topic of the funniest thing they had ever read on a toilet door. As the final drink was knocked back, it soon became time to "crawl home to your feckin scratcher" as Liam eloquently put it. The good-byes were long and provided amusement for other not-so-drunken revelers on the street. There were kisses all round. Sean and Dan delighted they had finally found some good hired help in Hannah. When reminded she hadn't even completed five minutes work yet, they hugged everyone again in honor of themselves and their amazing ability to make such a sound decision with such little evidence.

By chance, Rachel hugged Airlie last. She kissed Airlie's cheek and gently pushed a floppy strand of hair from her eyes, drawing her close. Caught off guard, Airlie returned the embrace, and with her head buried in the hollow of Rachel's neck, she became engulfed in a waft of sweet perfume. Airlie's pounding heart quickened, and her legs began to give way.

"I know you don't know, honey, but I do," whispered Rachel in her ear. "I'm here if you want to talk about it when you work it out." Rachel kissed her cheek once again, and then she was gone.

Oblivious to the exchange, Hannah continued to Riverdance along the footpath with strangers. Airlie's world had turned deathly silent. She was barely able to stand, move, or speak. The silence was interrupted only by the sound of rapidly flowing blood throbbing through the veins in the side of her head. She had no idea what Rachel was talking about or what she needed to work out.

Dan, Sean, Liam, and Rachel stumbled in the opposite direction. She assumed they must be laughing and joking about her, but she couldn't hear anything. Fury rose slowly from her feet and consumed every cell to poison her entire body with rage. She was drunk and she was about to explode.

"Let's go." Her harsh tone was undeservedly directed toward Hannah, and when she didn't respond, Airlie raised her voice. "I said, let's go, Hannah. Now." When Hannah ignored her, she stormed across the road to drag her away. "I need sleep. We've wasted enough time here tonight."

Drunk and tired, they trudged silently along the streets of Dublin before reaching the Arms and the solace of their respective beds.

If Airlie never saw Rachel again, it would be too soon.

# Chapter Ten

Airlie's anger had barely subsided by the time her head hit the pillow, her annoyance amplified by the room's endless spinning. She tossed and turned; eyes open, eyes closed. Her stomach lurched with every movement. When flinging her leg out of the bed in an attempt to stop the head spins failed, she got up to throw up. She swallowed three paracetamol, which she also threw up.

Sleep was a long time coming, and she recounted the exchange with Rachel. Airlie was unable to accept Rachel's offer of help as genuine. She didn't need any help. She chose instead to believe Rachel was an interfering bitch who should keep her thoughts and opinions to herself.

Finally, sleep took her.

The following morning produced the most intense hangover. Airlie woke with a throbbing head and a churning stomach, enough to make even the most seasoned sailor seasick. The acidic taste of vomit remained on her tongue, and she scratched crusty remnants from the corners of her mouth. Her pounding head dragged her down as if it weighed more than her entire body, and yet somewhere inside her, this dreadful hangover was the exact sensation she needed. She deserved to feel this way.

Hannah was gone, but a fresh glass of water rested on the floor beside her. She drank it in one gulp, rubbed her eyes, and held her forehead for fear it might fall off should she let go. She took more paracetamol and refilled the glass, then returned to bed to relish her painful, miserable state. She gave in to the nausea. *I deserve this. I fucking deserve this.* She pondered how on earth Hannah could have felt well enough to actually leave the room.

Mid-afternoon, the phone rang. The ringing pierced her skull until her ears felt numb. She hated the phone and smothered her head beneath the pillows. When the ringing stopped, she was thankful. Seconds later, the phone rang again, and again, and again. Airlie threw the pillow across the room. Pain engulfed her head. She tossed her clothes around in search of the source of the racket before realizing the phone was next to the glass. She was poised to throw something when she saw it was Olivia calling.

"Hi there." Airlie attempted to sound far better than she felt.

"Jaysus, what's wrong with you? You sound like shite. Are you not well?"

Airlie didn't know how Olivia could tell from just two words that she was in pure agony, but she didn't mind. There were many things Olivia just knew about her.

"I'm as well as can be expected given the amount of cider I drank last night." She gulped more water. "Hannah scored a job yesterday, and we went out for a quiet night with her new employers." Airlie finished the rest of her water and flopped back. Her head clouted the edge of the bedhead, and she swore. She stared at her pillow across the room. "I'll tell you one thing, I'm never drinking again."

"I've heard that one before."

Airlie was sure she meant it.

They exchanged small talk for a while. She was reluctant to let Olivia know that the lack of job success was disheartening. It was enough that she thought of herself as a failure; it certainly wasn't how she wanted Olivia to regard her. She'd have liked Olivia to invite her over next weekend, but she didn't mention it. The refuge of the west was an easy way out, but if she went, she would probably stay for a few nights longer than a weekend, and it was imperative to be in Dublin to search for a job sooner rather than later. As if reading her mind, Olivia urged her to hang in there; a job would turn up eventually. Airlie hoped so. She whispered, "I miss you," after the line disconnected.

She sighed. *Hang in there.* Things couldn't possibly get any worse, and with the comforting thought of making a trip to the west as soon as she landed a job, Airlie succumbed to another fitful sleep.

In the early evening, Hannah returned laden with hangover treats.

A strong cappuccino, orange juice, cheeseburger, and chips—Airlie's favorite stomach settling hangover remedy. Never in her life could she remember being so happy to see Hannah. The timing was perfect; she was just out of the shower, feeling almost human again. Her mood had improved somewhat.

"You, my dear, are a lifesaver." She stuffed herself with a handful of chips. "How on earth do you feel good enough to have been out and about half the day?"

Hannah shrugged and grinned. "Three pints."

"Pardon?"

"You drank about three more pints than me." Her smile widened. "And I might have vomited pretty much as soon as we got home last night."

Airlie felt slightly redeemed. She pulled on her coat.

"You're heading out?"

"Just for fresh air. You deserve some peace and quiet."

"I won't argue with that." Hannah was already under the covers.

On the busy street, the air was bitter cold and the grimy city smell seemed to latch on to her. Spring had been mild this year, and tonight was possibly the coldest Airlie had experienced in Ireland, although perhaps her poor condition was contributing to the chill infiltrating deep into her bones. Undeterred, she pulled on her woolly hat, zipped up her army green jacket, and dug her hands deep in her jean pockets. She began to walk. There was no destination; she didn't need one. This was Dublin, Ireland, and the fresh Irish air, cold on her cheeks, was exhilarating. After a few blocks, confident she could stomach it, Airlie bought a pack of cigarettes and lit up. Since arriving in Dublin, she found herself smoking with alarming frequency and hiding it from Hannah, who would be mortified. After crushing out the first, she lit another.

The encounter with Rachel consumed her. Now, standing on the Ha'Penny Bridge over the steadily flowing Liffey River, her attention was dominated less by what Rachel had said and more about the way she had touched her, how her arms tightly secured their bodies together, rendering her motionless. And they were tight; her cloudy recollection told her they felt strong and safe. She recalled Rachel's lips lightly brushing against one cheek, and her hand gently stroking the other.

The memory sent tingles down her spine, or perhaps it was the penetrating breeze. It was all so vague, or so it seemed, and while this close, almost intimate contact governed her thoughts, she became extremely annoyed at the lack of clear memory surrounding the embrace. Why couldn't she remember *exactly* what it felt like, and why did she want to? Why couldn't this inexplicable desire to savor the embrace just leave her alone? There was something wrong, Airlie knew that, but the familiarity surrounding her sense of dread held no comfort.

She flicked her cigarette butt into the Liffey. She imagined throwing herself in there, too. She wondered if she'd be able to float downstream on her back and watch the dirty lights of Dublin pass her by as she washed out, lonely and alone, into the Irish Sea.

Airlie tramped through the streets for hours, her head low, enjoying the anonymity a foreign country offered. She ventured through dangerous alleyways she knew she shouldn't chance where gatherings of young men simply stared at her. She passed a place called the Dungeon, and plastered on the front door was a poster of two men kissing. Puzzled by her feelings again, she hunched further in the cold, still wandering aimlessly until she came across a pub where the temptation of a hot cup of coffee enticed her.

As if her brain was wired to do so, she found herself automatically ordering a pint of cider. She promised herself to drink just the one.

It was during the third pint when Airlie's mood began to improve. Her spirits had lifted and she'd found a friend. He was a man in his late thirties, she guessed, from Dun Laoghaire, southeast of Dublin. He was going through a shit time as well, or so he said. Something about his mother dying, and him trying in vain to help a friend who was in jail. It all sounded a bit too deep and complicated, and Airlie deliberately chose not to listen to the details. It was his shoulder length gray-flecked hair that first caught her eye, and he was good-looking enough, a bit rough, prominent cheekbones, but what harm was there in talking to him and having a drink or two? As the night wore on, Airlie had a job to remember how she had arrived, not the means of transport, but the route she had taken, and she had no idea how she was going to get home.

Halfway through her sixth pint, her new friend covered her hand with his and whispered lustfully, "I think you know where this is headed."

Airlie stared at her half empty cider. After she finished this one, the only place she wanted to head was home.

"We have something, you and I. I can feel it."

Airlie could barely feel her legs. This bloke was okay, but why did all men have to get weird?

"I just live five minutes from here. Come on, let's go fuck."

"Do you think that's what I need right now?" she asked.

"Yep."

"Think you'll satisfy me?"

"Too easy."

Airlie considered it. She stared deep into his eyes, or perhaps just tried to focus, while his hand suggestively slid up her thigh. He squeezed, and she thought, why not? She couldn't remember the last time anyone had touched her like this, the last time anyone paid her any sexual attention at all.

He leaned in close, about to kiss her, but she blinked and broke the spell. She thought of his scrawny, sweaty, naked body on top of hers—her legs spread wide—banging her hard for his pleasure, mystified as to where her enjoyment would come from. The familiar clench of rage gripped her insides. The suggestion of fucking, and the fact that she gave it even a fleeting thought, was indication enough that it was time to leave.

"Go fuck yourself," she told him, slipping off the stool.

He grabbed her arm. "I'd really rather fuck you."

"I'm sure you would."

"Don't be a tease. Come on, you'll enjoy it. I promise." He grinned and his teeth were perfectly straight but stained from smoking. "You've not had a man go down on ye until you've had me." He poked out his revolting tongue.

Just before shoving him violently off his stool, she called him a filthy little prick and tipped his half-full stout all over him. She had underestimated her own drunken strength, and he fell hard on his backside, cracking his head on the tiled floor as the stool crashed beside him. Before she could react, two enormous men with arms the size of tree trunks, scruffed her by the back of her jumper, dragged her across the floor, and promptly threw her into the street. With no balance, she fell hard, grazing her hands in a failed attempt to break the fall. Her coat and hat followed a second or two later when one of the security men threw them at her, telling her to fuck off and never come back.

Onlookers walked past, stepping over her, staring as they went about their business. Were they intrigued, disgusted, or pitying? She attempted to stand but fell back down. Concentrating with all her being, she coordinated her drunken limbs enough to ungracefully struggle to her feet. With the aid of a rubbish bin, Airlie regained her balance and took a few minutes to orientate herself. Blood dripped from her palm. She lit a smoke and made a completely uneducated guess about which direction home was. It was late, and not surprisingly, she felt like shit.

Again.

## Chapter Eleven

For the next week, little changed. Airlie continued a downward spiral, and although she knew Hannah was worried, nothing she did improved her foul mood and appalling attitude toward absolutely everything. Hannah was worried she would become so despondent that the only option was to go home. Airlie had no intention of going home. The way she was feeling now, returning to Australia, to a sense of feeling trapped and suffocated, was the last move she was contemplating.

In the nick of time, and after negotiating a reasonable month-long deal on their room at the Arms, Airlie acquired data entry temping work for a large IT company. All it really required on her part was punctuality and accurate work. Nothing she couldn't handle.

Hannah was over the moon. "Well done, you."

Airlie shrugged. "It's about time."

"Could you not just be happy for yourself for a change?"

"It's only temporary."

"And sometimes temporary things lead to more permanent things. Although, I hope that's not the case with your shit mood."

Airlie released hold of the growing anger inside. "Sorry."

"Don't be sorry, be happy." Hannah hugged her.

"I am happy. And now I'm relieved. So tell me about your first week?" Airlie pushed herself to delve into the details of Hannah's first week of shifts at the café.

"Put it this way." Hannah beamed. "I'm no longer looking for an alternative." Airlie knew Hannah had only seen the café job as a stopgap or supplementary income to something more substantial, but obviously, things had changed.

"Wow. That good."

"I can't explain it. It's a great place to work. The thought of leaving is just shit. I don't want to."

"Then you should stay."

"I've learned so much, even in the space of a week. They trust me with everything, and now they're talking about ditching their accountant and increasing my wage to cover the extra financial responsibilities."

"You're not actually an accountant, remember."

"I wish you'd just forget that tiny detail, plus it doesn't matter anyway. The laws are different over here so they're sending me on a course to learn what I need to know for a small business."

"Fabulous. And does all this excitement have anything to do with a tall, handsome, ginger chap by any chance?"

"He's not made of wood." That was Hannah's favorite saying when Airlie marveled at how easily she roped men in. "I've let him know I'm interested and available. The rest is up to him. Plenty of fish in the Irish Sea, I'll just wait to see which way he jumps."

Airlie wondered how long Liam had to make a move before Hannah did. She wasn't buying her patient routine at all.

Airlie wanted to stay in the mix of things, keep in the loop with Hannah and her new friends, but she just didn't have the energy to engage with them. She hoped now that she'd have money coming in, things would change. She guessed everyone noticed her distance; she just couldn't find the best method to change her circumstances. The fact that Rachel evoked nervousness and excitement in her all at once was a foreign sensation best ignored. She fought hard to process her emotions, but it was hopeless; something blocked that pathway in her brain. She preferred instead to dismiss her restlessness and subsequently, her friends. They were really Hannah's friends, she reminded herself frequently.

On one particularly clear evening, Airlie returned home after another long day at work. Her two-week temporary job had stretched to three, and she was looking at being offered a six-month contract that might even extend further. Exhausted, and as usual alone—Hannah had left a note to say she was at the Derry with the others—Airlie craved a cigarette. She dashed to the corner shop, only to be greeted by a sign offering an apology for the inconvenience, but the store was closed indefinitely due to fire. Airlie remembered the vending machine in the front bar of the Arms.

"I thought you must have taken off." The bartender beamed in her direction. "You've not been in for a while."

"No, not much spare time now." Airlie sighed. "I finally got a job."

"Good for you, love."

"Thanks. It's not that good," said Airlie. "But it'll do for now."

"Aye. Any job these days is better than a kick up the arse, so it is."

Airlie nodded, fishing in her pocket for change.

"So," he said. "You get a job, but you don't come in for me to shout you a drink to celebrate?"

She smiled, pulled the smokes from the machine, and joined him at the bar. "You must be a mind reader. I'm here to do just that."

With a cheeky wink, he poured a pint of cider, poured himself a small whiskey, and then toasted. "Here's to this beautiful young Australian lass, working at last." They touched glasses and drank.

"Thanks for the drink." She savored the mouthful. "But I don't know your name."

"I'm Martin. Martin O'Grady. Not the O'Grady on the plaque outside, mind, that's me father, God rest his soul, but I am an O'Grady nevertheless."

"I'm pleased to meet you, Martin O'Grady. I'm Airlie."

"Ah, what a lovely name. Delighted to make your acquaintance, young Airlie." He paused, studying her intently over his small oval spectacles. "There ain't nothin' in the world as bad as you think, you know?"

"I'll take your word for that, Martin."

"Aye, you should, although no one else does." He chuckled to himself and turned his attention to a new customer.

That night was the beginning of many new things, few of them positive. The Dublin Arms Bar—Martin's company in particular—soon became preferred above Hannah's and her new friends. Martin was funny, a gentleman in the true sense of the word, and she enjoyed his little riddles of encouragement and words of wisdom. What began harmlessly soon developed into a web of lies and deceit. Airlie avoided contact with the others, waiting patiently until Hannah left before throwing on a coat and heading downstairs for a pint and a chat.

Her timing became impeccable. She could visit the bar and sneak back, all snuggled in bed, before Hannah returned. Her jaunt was just long enough for three or four pints, half a packet of smokes in the adjoining alleyway, and a chat with Martin between serving customers. She began despising the nights when Hannah stayed in, sometimes making excuses to go out on her own, but other times she'd stay and retire early to avoid conversation.

To her great surprise, she enjoyed her new job. Even more alarming, she was beginning to enjoy the long hours. Concentrating all day meant her mind rested during the evening, and she welcomed that sense of exhaustion. Every day, she woke at six a.m., showered, and left for work, buying breakfast on the way. Her work was accurate, the tasks monotonous, and it suited her.

Airlie was thankful for all her distractions, and she was again able to assert a degree of control over her life, but more importantly, her emotions. She pushed the unsettling business with Rachel to the back of her mind—she'd only seen her on a few occasions since that night and intended to keep her distance. She also called Olivia less frequently, determining that if they spoke less, she might not miss her as much.

Airlie had become the master of denial and the queen of pretend, but the only person she was fooling was herself.

## CHAPTER TWELVE

Now that Airlie and Hannah were earning decent money, they were eager to establish a more permanent living arrangement. She longed for a comfortable place that felt like home.

When the phone rang, she jolted from her reverie. Propped against the bar in her usual spot, she instinctively went to answer but gathered herself at the last minute and shot out the back where it was quiet.

"Hey, Hannah, how's it going?"

"Good, thanks. Look, sorry if I woke you, but I have some great news. Are you in bed yet?"

"Um, no, I'm not far from it though, why?" This wasn't exactly a lie. She was on her last drink. "Where are you?"

"I'm on my way home now. We've got something amazing to run by you. I reckon you'll love it. See you in ten, okay?"

Before Airlie had a chance to object, the phone disconnected. She shoved the phone deep in her pocket and returned to the bar to gulp the remaining cider. Moreover, who was the "we" in "we've got something to run by you"? She shook her head and waved good-bye to Martin, who was busy serving another customer. In less than a minute, she'd returned to their room and changed out of her clothes and into her pajamas before brushing her teeth to hide the smell of alcohol and cigarettes. She attempted to look as relaxed and tired as possible.

Within thirty seconds, she heard a key in the lock.

"Have we got some good news? Great news in fact." Hannah charged through the doorway, Rachel on her heels.

Airlie and Rachel smiled at each other—Airlie awkwardly, Rachel naturally. Hello seemed redundant now that Hannah had launched into an excited diatribe about how their luck had changed, and from that day forward, everything would get better.

Airlie inhaled slowly and deeply to conceal her shortness of breath, although not before absorbing the way Rachel's jeans slouched comfortably around her slim waist. "You've won the lotto?" Airlie asked.

"No, better than that. We're going to ditch this shit-hole and move out," said Hannah.

"You know winning the lotto would actually be better than that, right?"

"Well, we have won the lotto, in a way. Well, Rachel has really, I suppose, but we're all winners here tonight." Hannah was rambling so fast she might hyperventilate.

Airlie shook her head. "You're not making sense, Han."

Rachel took control. "I can explain. My aunt has a house in Rathmines. It has three and a half bedrooms and has been rented for years by my aunt's husband's parents, who have recently moved out due to ill health."

"It's a great place, Airlie. You'll be delighted when you see it," said Hannah.

"Anyway," Rachel continued. "It's empty now, and to cut a long story short, my current lease has expired and my aunt is offering the place to me to live in and sublet. I thought you two might want to come and rent a room. Each."

The emphasized word *each* didn't go unnoticed. It deserved emphasis. Separate rooms would be amazing, and Airlie could tell Hannah was already on board, but the thought of living with Rachel was confusing. Airlie needed time to think.

"So you've seen it then?" she asked Hannah.

"Of course. We'd be paying the same as here, but we'd have our own space. Plus, it'll be an actual home, not just a bed in a shit box like this is."

Airlie needed to buy some time. "Can I see it first?"

"Sure you can," said Rachel.

Hannah frowned. Airlie knew she was pushing her luck. "Airlie, just take my word for it, it's better than this, and to be honest, I think I'm going to move there with or without you. I know once you see it you'll understand, but really, we need to make this move. What's with all this procrastination?"

Hannah was right. Rachel wouldn't live in a hovel, and Hannah wouldn't say it was great unless it was. But living with Rachel? It was too complicated to think about. She looked at them, both staring expectantly back at her.

Something had to give. A small flashing light, buried deep in the pit of her stomach, fluttered. It was the same light that twitched with excitement when someone mentioned Rachel's name, creating a sense of stimulation that prickled her skin whenever she saw her. She wanted to despise this light, this exhilaration, but she didn't, couldn't. Like a silent, solitary bubble in a champagne glass, it rose to the top and popped at the surface.

"All right." She smiled. "I'll take your word for it. I'm in."

❖

The house was amazing. It was set on a lovely, tree lined street, where all the houses were attached and looked the same with the exception of various brightly painted front doors. Theirs was faded orange that would have been bold and eye-catching once.

The moment Airlie stepped over the threshold, she experienced a strong sense of belonging. The house covered two and a half floors. The lower floor only five steps to descend into the kitchen, bathroom, and one of the double bedrooms. The ground floor was the lounge room; virtually fully furnished with an open fireplace, a formal dining table, and a beautiful old grandfather clock. Airlie smiled. At least there was one man in the house. Adjacent to the lounge room was a small room the size of a study, furnished simply with a wide chair, side table, and lamp. Airlie assumed the chair folded out to become a sofa bed of some sort, handy for visitors who may have over-indulged, but the room was no bigger than a broom cupboard. The first floor was home to two other bedrooms. The master bedroom and a single room. There was also a toilet on the first floor.

Overall, the place was perfect, far superior to any rentals they had looked at and couldn't afford. They left the Arms without any hint of a teary good-bye.

Hannah and Airlie were already inside making coffee when the first van load of Rachel's belongings arrived. Rachel remained behind packing and cleaning while Liam periodically delivered her things. Airlie observed, with interest, the playful pushing and shoving between Liam and Hannah. They would openly exchange sweet, lustful grins, and she found it endearing how they couldn't manage, for love or money, to agree on anything. Although, according to her calculations, Liam capitulated more than Hannah did. Airlie hoped they would become a couple, if for nothing other than to end their sickening love dance. It was obvious that Hannah really liked him—not that she'd elaborated since that first discussion about him.

Airlie realized how little they had communicated recently. She hadn't been to the café in weeks. She was proud of Hannah, without question, and delighted she'd landed on her feet, but she couldn't help feeling a hint of jealousy. She needed to get her shit together. She promised to do this, starting right then and there.

"I'm in, girls, we're all in," shouted Rachel from the kitchen. "Let's crack open the bubbly and toast to new beginnings." She poured the champagne. "Here's to the three of us, our new home, and here's to our friendship."

"Sláinte!" they all said in unison, clanking glasses.

It was thrilling how things had unfolded for them, and Airlie, in a peculiar way, tingled with excitement. The sentiment caught her off guard, but for some curious reason, she felt less intimidated by Rachel's presence, and strangely, she felt quite lucky to be sharing a home with her.

"So, have you two sorted out the sleeping arrangements?" Rachel finished her glass and refilled.

Airlie and Hannah stared blankly at each other.

"Jaysus. I thought that would have been the first thing you organized after living in each other's pockets for so long."

Talking over the top of each other, they both started to say they didn't mind where they slept, before turning to each other and saying, "You choose," also at the same time.

"You two sure do need to be separated," said Rachel. "How about we draw straws?" She looked around for something resembling straws. "Okay, that may take some time. Here, one of you flip this coin." She pulled a euro from her pocket. "Heads or tails."

Airlie let Hannah call, she was the oldest after all. Age before beauty and all that.

"Right. I can do this," Hannah said, bracing herself for the toss. "Heads."

The coin flew high in the air, landed on the couch, bounced onto the floor, and rolled under the dining table, where they all scrambled to see.

"Tails. I guess you're upstairs," said Rachel.

They slid out, dusting themselves off.

Hannah looked disappointed but smiled regardless. "You get the double bed, Airlie, you lucky thing."

The double bed would be fabulous; the thought of a spacious room all to herself, and in such a fabulous house, was satisfying indeed. That was until Liam bounded in, looking at the three of them.

"Is this a bad time?" he asked.

The penny dropped. The downstairs room for Hannah meant privacy, a double bed, and hopefully, Liam.

"Hold on," Airlie said. "I think you should have the double room. I'm happy to go upstairs; in fact it will be nice and quiet up there."

"That's what you think," said Rachel.

"No, it's okay. You won the room fair and square. It's fine really." Hannah's eyes didn't match her sentiment.

"Hannah." Airlie flashed her a look that indicated she knew exactly what was going through her mind when it came to Liam. "I insist you take the downstairs room. Don't make me tell you why."

Hannah mouthed a heartfelt "Thank you." "Downstairs it is then. Thanks, buddy, I owe you."

"Right, kiddo, it's you and me upstairs then." Rachel slapped Airlie on the back and disappeared with an armful of bed linen and towels. "Did you bring some beer?" she called over her shoulder to Liam. "The champagne's all out."

"I certainly did not," he replied. "You ladies have some serious unpacking to do and ye all need clear heads."

Hannah raised her eyebrow.

He grinned. "The lads are about fifteen minutes away. They've got the beer."

Hannah loaded him with bags and sent him to her bedroom. "Thanks again, Aerobar." She quickly kissed her on the cheek before skipping away.

Airlie smiled in the middle of the messy room before hauling as much as she could upstairs. "The lads are bringing the beer," she called into Rachel's room, dumping the stuff on her bedroom floor and launching herself onto her springy bed.

"You seem happy," said Rachel.

Airlie looked up to see her leaning in the doorway. "I'm very happy. This place is great."

Without invitation, Rachel entered and crossed to the window, opening the curtains before turning to Airlie, whose eyes remained fixed on her. "Fair play to you for giving up the double room. This room is small, sure, but it's cozy, and it'll be warm in winter when the heat from downstairs rises." Airlie nodded. "We haven't seen you around the traps much lately. Hannah's been a bit worried, to be honest."

"Work is busy. I'm trying to make myself indispensable." This wasn't exactly a lie. "It took so long to get this job, I want to keep hold of it for long enough to save a bit of cash in case it all hits the fan and I'm unemployed again. Nine- and ten-hour days don't leave much energy for much else, I'm afraid."

"You know what they say, all work and no play makes for a boring Airlie."

"Is that what they say, is it?"

Rachel smiled. "So, Hannah's all loved up. Any love on the horizon for you? A fine thing such as yourself should have no problem picking up in this fair city." Rachel meandered out again. "Just depends what you're looking for, I suppose."

Airlie ignored her. Her secret drinking at the bar would end now anyway. She no longer lived upstairs, and she'd vowed to make a concerted effort to spend more time with Hannah and her friends. Her feelings for Rachel were a concern, but she attributed that to a simple case of intrigue; she was an interesting person, and her attraction was purely on a friendship level. The strange niggles were just a phase. It had been quite a while since she'd had sex, a very long while, but she was normal. Everybody had weird feelings about their friends one time or another. What did it matter, anyway? Regardless, she knew how to fix the problem. She resolved to find a disposable man and break the drought.

Airlie pulled out her mobile and called Olivia. She missed her. It felt like they hadn't spoken in so long.

## Chapter Thirteen

Moving had extended Airlie's journey to and from work by at least twenty minutes, and although she didn't mind, it was a long, exhausting day. She learned to embrace the tiredness, ensuring a sound, though often dreamless sleep. In the last few weeks, she'd thought little about escaping to the Arms bar, or any other pub for that matter.

Friday evening found Airlie alone, and she was delighted at the prospect. Rachel was in Sligo attending a work conference, and Hannah and Liam were spending time at his place. They were now lovers in a cute, yet disgustingly gushy way.

She turned on the radio and took her time preparing an omelet before devouring it with a smooth glass of red that she'd left to breathe on the windowsill. Her next indulgence was a relaxing bubble bath, and when the water became too cold, and the wine bottle empty, she heaved herself out and wrapped one of Rachel's huge bath sheets around her. She ran naked upstairs to retrieve her robe before giving in to an urge to lounge on the front step and observe Irish life in Rathmines.

Memories flooded her of nights drinking with Olivia. It seemed like it was *their* thing to do, and she hoped, when she visited soon, that the tradition would continue. She looked on as people of all ages passed the house—groups of single girls, couples, young and old, joggers, all sorts really. Airlie was happy the world was turning, satisfied to be a part of it and not an observer.

As the folk in the street dwindled, she retreated inside and curled on the couch under a blanket before flicking through the channels—sport, movie, annoying sitcom, more sport, and another movie, until she stopped on a scene in which two women were kissing. Mesmerized, and instantly aroused, Airlie quickly gathered her thoughts and flicked the remote again. She gulped more wine and stared blankly at a boring advert.

*Fuck it!* Surely it was normal to watch that stuff. Thousands of normal, probably married, women were watching it right now.

She switched back. If they could watch it, she could, too. The credits were rolling, and her heart sank until she realized they were the opening credits. Airlie watched, holding her breath; the entire cast were lesbians, their lives intertwined with couples and relationships and sex. So much sex.

A seduction began between two women—one younger, the other considerably older. Airlie's heart pounded as if she'd run a marathon. The scene was a dimly lit lounge room with candles and hypnotically sexy music. The lovers cuddled on a couch, the older one gently caressing the younger one's breasts, her tongue darting in and out of her mouth. Writhing beneath the touch of the older woman, the young woman moaned. They undressed to the waist, exposing breasts and erect nipples.

Foreign emotions and physical sensations overwhelmed her. She'd seen naked women before, of course she had, but they were always with men. She'd never even seen a porn movie with two women. She knew she wasn't watching porn, but she felt unclean, tainted somehow, but the thought of changing the station was unimaginable.

A faint throb developed in her crotch. She was wet and she couldn't look away.

On the screen, the young woman pulled away from the kiss, leaning down to take a nipple in her mouth. Airlie swallowed. The woman sucked the nipple. Gently at first, and then more passionately before kissing her mouth again. The older, dominant woman, pushed her young lover back on the couch and unbuttoned her pants before lying on top of her. Her hand plunged deep between her legs as the young woman cried in pleasure. They moved rhythmically together.

Airlie's mind was a foggy haze, and her ears rang incessantly. She was aroused like never before, and any attempt to resist would have been futile. The older woman was in control, the younger in ecstasy. The older one pulled off the young one's trousers and knickers before pulling her close to thrust her head between her legs, her hands reaching for supple breasts. Airlie was enthralled, her heart pounded, and she was hot, so hot under the blanket. The camera shot became wider, the moaning louder, the camera shot blurred. Airlie held her breath, the moaning more urgent with the wild thrusting of the young lesbian. Sweat dripped between Airlie's breasts, and then the young woman cried out in complete satisfaction as the screen went black. When the picture returned, it was an advertisement, bright, annoying, and loud. The spell was broken.

Airlie trembled, withdrawing her own hand from between her legs. Her filthy actions repulsed her. She experienced an element of excitement, but she felt sickened, rotten to the core, and disgusted with herself. *Fuck, fuck, fuck!* She threw the remote at the couch. *What am I doing?*

She attempted to drink the remainder of wine from the bottle but spilled it down her robe. Her mind was racing. She didn't know what to do. An idea came to her, and she stormed upstairs, threw on some clothes, and within minutes, rushed away from the house, lighting a cigarette and hurrying to the nearest pub.

The Shamrock was half-empty when she rushed in. A lifeless, old-man pub wasn't what she needed. One man nodded to her in greeting, but she ignored him and left, striding in the direction of the city. Lighting another smoke, she kept a brisk pace and neared the next pub. From across the street, she heard a raucous din seep out as the door swung open and a group of jovial patrons stumbled out, sprawling onto the street. It was perfect. Without even checking for traffic, she crossed the road and entered the pub.

Inside was packed. Hot, loud, and sweaty. She ordered a pint and then called after the barman for a whiskey on the side. The whiskey disappeared in one gulp and the pint not long after.

She wasn't thinking of what had just happened in the house. Thinking was impossible; she was *doing*. Becoming drunk was her priority, and she wanted to have sex—with a man. The subsequent whiskey disappeared like the first, and she savored the burn in her throat. The barman eyed her when she ordered the same again, but she ignored him.

A middle-aged man muscled in next to her. He was pleasant looking enough, not that it really mattered, and she thought he'd do the trick, but Guinness in hand, he muscled his way back out as quickly as he had arrived.

*Fuck him, anyway.* Her pint reached the lower half.

Airlie moved to the beer garden and lit a smoke the instant she crossed the threshold. Her stomach churned. The wine, whiskey, and beer were an unhappy mix, and nausea settled in her stomach. What did she care? If she was going to do this, it had to be soon.

From across the garden, she locked eyes with an older man. She only looked twice at him because he reminded her of Gavin. He gave her a wink, but when she ignored him, he turned away. She resumed scanning the room. Sucking in the noxious smoke from yet another cigarette, the memory of the lounge room flashed in her mind. Disappointment overwhelmed her. She shouldn't have allowed the events of the evening to transpire, and her self-loathing refused to abate as the liquor took hold.

Airlie reminded herself with increasing frequency that she was straight and she liked cock. So disturbing was her rage that in her mind the most appropriate word to use was cock. Never in her life had Airlie referred to a penis in that way, and certainly never fueled with such utter contempt. Faced with less extreme circumstances, her filthy mind would have repulsed her, but tonight she was a stranger to herself. Her present actions should have been more disappointing than masturbating while watching two women have sex on the television.

She lost patience and pushed her way through the crowd of smokers in search of a man. Quite deliberately, she brushed against any man near her, hoping for some attention, and lucky not to have unhappy wives or girlfriends take offense. Fortunately, most just ignored her or, falsely believing they had stepped in her way, politely apologized and moved aside. It wasn't until she deliberately burned a hole in a roughly handsome, dark haired, thirty-something's jacket sleeve, that she gained the desired interest.

"Shit, I'm so sorry."

"What the feck are you doing? Jaysus," he said in a broad Dublin accent. He brushed frantically at his sleeve to stop the burn from spreading.

People around stopped and stared.

"Look, it was an accident." She lied without flinching. "I'm really sorry."

"It's gone right through. I can't believe it. Are you fecking blind or what?"

This man was drunk. It was unlikely he could have focused clearly on the burn, let alone been able to determine its extent. Airlie wasn't sure if he would be able to perform, but she was determined to try her luck.

"I really am sorry." She made every attempt to sound genuine. "Look, I'll make it up to you. I'll buy you a drink or something. What can I do to make it up to you?"

He sighed and stared at his sleeve, calming down. Onlookers relaxed and returned to their business. "I'll have a Guinness." His tone was harsh, but his mock snarl and dark brown eyes indicated he wasn't entirely put out.

Airlie ordered two pints before inhaling deeply and turning to entrap her victim. In doing so, her palms became clammy, and she suddenly felt awkward. Not because her actions were those of a complete idiot, things had progressed well beyond her capability of recognizing that, but because she had absolutely no experience in seducing a man. How was she to progress from buying this bloke a drink to having sex with him? Subtlety wasn't the best option. He was as drunk as she was. She crossed her fingers and produced what she hoped was charm. "Are you sure there isn't anything else I can help you with?" She scanned over his chest to his crotch.

Perhaps not as drunk as she first anticipated, he immediately understood. "Let's find a nice quiet spot for you to make it up to me then, shall we?" He smiled, more than likely thinking it was a game, but he played along regardless.

"Lead the way." She motioned for him to make a move.

"What?"

"I said I'd make it up to you, didn't I? So get on with it."

"You're not fucking joking, are you?"

She shrugged.

Without speaking, he took her hand and directed her through the crowd. When they encountered a bottleneck near the bar, he pulled her hand to his crotch. He was hard. There were so many people jostling for a position at the bar, no one noticed. The thought of his penis repulsed her. She pushed the visual from her mind. He guided her toward the toilets, but the disabled toilet was occupied. Gently, he pushed her against the wall and kissed her as they waited. Stale smoke and Guinness was all she could taste. His teeth were crooked and yellowing, but he was tanned and handsome in a weathered kind of way. She reminded herself that this was what she wanted. She needed to get it over with so she could go home as straight as the next person.

"Are you sure about this?" he asked.

No, of course she wasn't sure, and she gave him credit for asking, but swapping pleasantries wasn't what she was here for. Ignoring his questionable breath, Airlie kissed him hard as reassurance, her hand cupping the front of his jeans.

The disabled toilet door swung open, and a woman stumbled out, ignoring them. He pushed her forcefully, but playfully inside. It was cold and damp, and it reeked of urine. He locked the door as he undid his trousers. She stood back and watched, reminding herself that this was what she wanted and she could get it anytime she liked.

"So," he said, obviously still unsure if this was a nasty setup. "I get to choose how you make it up to me, right?"

"Within reason." She hesitated before reminding herself why she was there, and cutely added, "You're the boss."

He crossed the room and they kissed again; he mumbled in her ear that she was fucking hot.

It was in direct contrast to how she felt.

"Take them off." His breathing was shallow and his voice crackled. He fumbled with the buttons on her jeans. "Take them off." His tone became urgent.

After she pushed her jeans down, he pulled her knickers off, groping deeply at her crotch with probing fingers before pushing his own jeans over his ankles.

Airlie was not aroused and she knew she wasn't going to be. It was probably going to hurt without lubrication. Undeterred, she reminded herself that this is how it should be. A man wanted to fuck her, and she was going to let him. Obeying his orders, she removed her top and bra. She stared at his hairy, naked body. It disgusted her.

She wished he'd just get on with it.

"Do you want to sit on the loo or will you be all right on your knees?" he asked, fondling his erect penis. She stared blankly. "I suppose I get to choose seeing as though I'm the victim here."

Grabbing her, not roughly, but firmly, he pushed her to her knees onto the cold, wet floor in front of him. With a sense of urgency, he gripped her head, clawing at her hair as he pressed her face toward him. Airlie's mind numbed, and her body stiffened with the horror of what she was about to allow to happen. Without protest, she parted her lips. She took him inside her mouth and performed the act she despised more than anything in the world. With no desire to see his dark, hairy crotch thrusting repeatedly toward her, she closed her eyes and let him slide back and forth, as he directed her head. Her neck ached from the tension that gathered there. She wanted to gag, but told herself this was what she had to do. Airlie concentrated on shutting down her emotions. There was no sense of pleasure or thrill, no arousal, just violation, and although she wanted to stop, it simply wasn't possible; his grip was tight, thrusting her head back and forth, as he moaned in pleasure. When he surprisingly released his grasp, a sense of relief filled her, and she was thankful he didn't come in her mouth.

Repulsed and ashamed, she began to utter that her repayment was over, that she'd paid her dues. He just laughed at her, thinking they were still playing, and besides, he wasn't finished. He stood her up, turned her round, placed her hands on the basin, and bent her over.

Panic overwhelmed her. Airlie knew she was making a mistake. She wanted it to stop, but she couldn't find the words, it was all happening so quickly. She felt his penis near her bottom. "Please, not up there. I don't like it."

"It's okay," he huffed. "I'm not really an arse man."

He entered her.

Frozen with fear and dread, Airlie at last understood. She didn't want this man, or more importantly, any man, inside her. She didn't want a man to touch her this way. Not now, not ever. Never again in all her life did she want to feel so dirty and wretched, but it was happening too fast. He was strong and he thought he was playing his role in a game she had enticed him to be a part of. He thought she'd said no to anal sex. He wasn't to blame. Softly, she began to cry, giving him no chance to hear her silent pleas to leave her alone. Ultimately, he grasped a breast forcefully in one hand, pulled her head back by the hair with his other, and thrust hard until he came. He finished in a matter of seconds. The whole thing took no longer than a few minutes from the time she was on her knees to the end. Semen dribbled down her inner thigh.

Airlie crawled to gather her clothes while he stood hunched over the basin, panting like a dog. "Hey, I'm the one dishing out the punishment here. I might want to go again in a few minutes." He wasn't serious, but she felt little comfort.

She continued dressing, tears streaming onto her bare chest.

"You're crying," he said. "Are you okay? I was kidding about going again. Honestly, couldn't even if I wanted to." Dressing, he continued, "You're amazing. You know that. Amazing. That was fucking awesome. I'd really like your number." Confusion quickly replaced his elation as he buttoned his jeans. "What's the matter? I didn't hurt you, did I?" He looked mortified. "I've never done anything like this before. That was what you wanted, wasn't it?"

"I'm fine." She attempted a smile. "That was just what I needed, but I won't be needing it again."

"Aw, come on. Let's meet again. I'll be the one being punished next time if you like?"

His genuine proposal repulsed her. "Thanks for the offer," she said. "I know where to find you." Her smile was halfhearted. She left, suppressing a strong urge to vomit at the bitter taste left in her mouth.

Airlie smoked and cried all the way home. When she arrived, she lit one last cigarette and slumped on the front steps, sobbing shamefully. The night had changed, the world had changed, and the street no longer looked alive and vibrant as it had earlier. Now, it was cold and empty, and she felt frightened and alone.

# CHAPTER FOURTEEN

Sleep was impossible. Her mind wouldn't rest, so she froze in the cold night air, smoking, or she lay huddled in her room, shivering. Predominantly, she grieved. She grieved for the person she was yesterday; that person no longer existed. She grieved for the person she wouldn't be tomorrow; she would be someone else. She grieved not for what happened last night, but for the unwanted revelation that exploded in her mind during the sex she had sought with a man she didn't know. Airlie unwillingly accepted she didn't like having sex with men; she was attracted to women, and unless this was a phase, she was probably gay. For this, she grieved the most, and she hated the word.

There was nothing to feel except the lack of feeling itself. Numbness. She was shattered, broken, and crushingly defeated. The blame of the night before lay squarely on her shoulders. It was not the fault of the drunken man. The night could have ended far worse. It was sheer luck he hadn't taken her back to his place or worse still, a dark, dingy alley somewhere, and made a complete mess of her. The thought of what happened with him, and what could have happened, caused her to be physically ill on more than one occasion. She was devastated by her own stupidity. There was alcohol in the house, but she didn't touch it. She'd had enough, and her stomach and mind simply couldn't take any more.

The stinging hot water from the shower pounded her throbbing brow and washed away the tears as though they were never there. She brushed her teeth for so long the toothpaste burned her mouth, yet the taste of the man remained. She buttoned her pajamas to the top and covered her bed in the thickest of Rachel's blankets. She wanted to be warm and needed to feel safe in her little cocoon.

Slowly, Airlie's thoughts began shutting down, saving her from further pain. She didn't fight it, letting the deadness consume her and settle like a dense fog. She would deal with it eventually, but for now, all she knew was that she was gay.

Airlie didn't want to be gay, and perhaps the thing that she loathed most was that this was not her choice. Nobody had asked her if she wanted this. Nobody asked was it okay to do this to her. The issue wasn't homophobia. *She* was the issue. Being someone she didn't want to be was the issue.

Airlie was confronted with the slow process of acceptance. Choosing to ignore it, or trying to pretend to be something else, were the only remaining options. It wasn't much of a choice.

As daybreak neared, the reality of the previous evening began to sink in. She had been stupid enough to have unprotected sex. The mere thought of contracting a sexually transmitted disease or, heaven forbid, HIV was almost more than she could bear given the circumstances. Then there was the real risk of pregnancy. She would need the morning-after pill, which she hoped was available in Ireland, although she wasn't sure, given its stance on abortion.

She showered, yet again, and then dressed to search for the nearest pharmacy. There were things to attend to, and she went about them as one would go about posting a letter or collecting laundry. The nearest pharmacy wasn't far, only a couple of streets away, and asking for some advice about sexually transmitted diseases and the morning-after pill was, in a way, her last hurrah in the straight world before she had to process being gay.

She wanted to scream at the little Catholic blond girl behind the counter that she'd had unprotected, premarital sex with a man and was probably gay. The thought disappointed her. She felt ashamed. The young woman was kind and helpful, handing her the pill and explaining where the local medical center was. Grateful for her assistance, she took the paper bag and turned to leave, colliding head-on into Rachel.

Rachel reached out, grabbing Airlie's shoulders to steady them both. The silence was awkward. It was clear from Rachel's horrified expression that she'd heard the entire conversation with the pharmacy girl.

"Hi, Rach."

"Hey, Airlie." She frowned. "Are you okay?" Rachel stared.

She knew she looked rough. Her eyes were puffy and sore from crying all night, and her hair was damp and fell limply on her shoulders.

"I'm fine, thanks."

"You don't look it."

"Well." She shrugged. "I will be." Halfheartedly, she waved the bag containing the pill. There was no use pretending, but she had neither the energy nor the inclination to explain or defend herself. She looked at Rachel's hands, still on her shoulders. "So, how about you? You okay?"

Rachel released her. "I'm fine. Bloody headache though. Too much champagne."

"I'm sure you'll get it sorted," said Airlie vaguely before making her way to the door.

"We'll talk later, yeah?" Rachel called after her.

"Sure, see you at home."

Airlie knew that Rachel would call Hannah before she even made it out of the pharmacy. She stepped over a large splattering of vomit on the footpath. It saved her the trouble of telling Hannah. Rachel wasn't one to gossip; the call would be out of concern, not malicious intrigue. In a weird way, although she wished she could continue her life without feeling any effects from the night before, she was glad at least one person knew she was struggling.

Airlie's visit to the clinic was uneventful. Because of the state she was in and the tests she required, many questions were directed toward sexual assault and rape. The elderly female doctor soothingly asked would she like to be examined, but Airlie assured her she hadn't been raped, the sex was consensual, and she didn't wish to be poked and prodded. The doctor took blood to detect any diseases or HIV, and she was advised the results would be available in due course. Against the better judgment of the doctor, Airlie declined the offer of counseling, but took the brochures anyway. There was a chance the man had a disease, but the odds were in her favor, and she could do little about it now regardless. It was a waiting game. When the doctor suggested she abstain from unprotected intercourse until her results were known, Airlie nearly laughed out loud.

A lazy afternoon with Dublin City to explore would have been a wonderful way to spend the day, under normal circumstances. However, today was far from normal. One might have argued that it was a monumental day, the first day of the rest of Airlie's life as a lesbian. But she wasn't in a celebratory mood. Her only desire was to go home and shut out the world. Drinking wasn't the answer to her problems, but she wasn't convinced she could manage sober for long.

Last night had been a disaster. Her actions would eventually require analysis and dissection, but right now, and for the immediate future, it felt easier to let these next few days pass. She needed time to digest the possibility of being gay and to allow the relief of her abandoned burden of denial to grow into something positive.

Airlie unlocked the front door, heard the TV, and quickly rushed past the lounge and up to her bedroom. She needed to think, but there was so much to absorb, she barely knew where to start. A knock at the door broke the silence.

"Come in."

Rachel held a steaming hot coffee. The situation was awkward. She moved to sit, but hesitated. With thanks, Airlie took the cup.

"I heard what you needed at the pharmacy," said Rachel.

"I know."

"Do you want to talk about it?"

"I don't think so. Not yet."

Rachel occupied the far corner of the bed. "Please just tell me if everything was okay at the doctor's?"

Airlie's composure faltered, and she began to cry. Through tears, she explained that she didn't know if everything was okay yet; she had to wait for test results. Rachel took the cup from her trembling hands and wrapped her tightly in her arms.

"Were you raped last night, Airlie? You don't have to tell me anything else, but if you were, I think you should call the guards and get some professional help. Is that what happened to you?"

Airlie shook her head. "I wasn't raped."

"Okay." Rachel exhaled.

"I'm sorry. I don't think I can talk about it."

"It's okay, sweetheart. I know I don't know the circumstances, but when you're ready, you can talk to me about anything. I'm a good listener. I'm here if you need me."

The embrace ended. "I know. And I appreciate it. Thank you."

Rachel offered to make lunch and bring it to her, but Airlie was sick of the sight of her four bedroom walls and realized she felt better with Rachel around. Together, they prepared lunch and lounged on the couch all afternoon and into the night. They watched movies, snuggled beneath Rachel's big blanket, hardly spoke a word, but at least Airlie wasn't alone.

# CHAPTER FIFTEEN

It was important that Airlie maintain a routine, so come Monday, she returned to work, much to the objection of Rachel, who thought a few days off wouldn't hurt. Airlie was determined. She had her reasons. Routine meant control, and control was something she had little of these days.

The thought of running away to Olivia's was an attractive alternative, but it felt too soon for that. Their friendship was new, and to visit someone with the possibility of falling apart in the process wasn't exactly polite. So for the time being, Airlie chose to remain in Dublin.

For many days, she allowed the numbness to linger without resistance. She knew Rachel had recounted what she knew to Hannah, and Hannah tried to talk, but it just wasn't what Airlie needed. So, after reassuring Airlie that her shoulder was for crying on, Hannah left her alone.

The following Friday, Airlie received a phone call from the clinic. It was good news; her tests had been negative. Her relief was so immense she cried at her desk and was sent home early.

As a result of her denial-driven rampage, three problems presented themselves. Airlie systematically eliminated two of those problems—she took the morning-after pill to avoid pregnancy, and she was now cleared of any sexually transmitted diseases. This left one issue, and it couldn't be fixed with a pill or any blood test. Airlie had to come to terms with the realization that she was gay. Feeling she owed Hannah and Rachel an explanation for what happened, Airlie recounted an abridged version of events, omitting all reference to her sexuality, explaining she foolishly talked herself into a situation with a man she couldn't back out of.

The power of Airlie's denial and how deep-rooted it had become astounded her. Bedtime was when unwanted thoughts troubled her. She looked back on her life and pinpointed situations, places, and emotions where she had blatantly ignored moments of truth. She first noticed she was different when all her friends actively sought a boyfriend, and she actively fended boys off. Where was the thrill in holding hands, and progressing to kissing at lunchtime when the teachers weren't looking? It was now clear that her reaction to a lesbian kiss or storyline on television wasn't necessarily normal for a young girl. It seemed that all Airlie had ever wanted was to be normal. It wasn't a bad thing to be gay, but it wasn't what she was brought up to believe was normal. Normal was easy. Normal was stress free with a mapped out future. Airlie felt abnormal, and the uncertainty terrified her.

Her sexual preference should have been obvious a long time ago. It would have certainly made her current journey less painful. All the barriers she had built to feed her denial and protect her true self were falling one by one. There were so many of them. She knew it would take time and there was no hurry, but she wanted to keep up with her new feelings and not let them overawe her to a point where she might lose control again.

Airlie continued to work long hours and spend considerable time at home. She remained sober and avoided clubs and bars. Her unbalanced emotions left her feeling like she was walking a tightrope; it was a long way down should she fall, but her mind had settled considerably. Although she was still processing thoughts about what being gay would mean for her, she allowed this progression and considered it necessary to improve her state of mind.

Airlie lay face down on the floor in the lounge room, fruitlessly fiddling with the cords of the failing DVD player when Rachel and Hannah bundled in.

"Let's go to Edinburgh," said Hannah.

"Edinburgh? But I have a lamb roast in the oven." Airlie was organized these days, a by-product of maintaining control.

"On the weekend."

Airlie sneezed through the unsettled dust. "Who's going?"

Rachel and Hannah loomed over her. "Just us," Hannah said. "It'll be great. We can fly out Friday morning, stay a couple of nights, and return Sunday afternoon."

Rachel jumped in. "We can drink and shop and just get away from here for a weekend. C'mon." She nudged Airlie with her bare foot. "It'll be great old craic."

"What about the café? I thought you were rostered on all week?" Airlie asked Hannah.

"I changed my shift. Dan thinks it's a great idea, and Rachel is taking Friday off, aren't you, Rach?"

"It's all sorted at my end."

"We won't take no for an answer."

"I don't know." Airlie was torn. "I really should be going over to Olivia's if I go anywhere at all."

"Why?" asked Rachel. "You can go there anytime, but a trip to Edinburgh isn't something we'll be doing every weekend. Say you'll come. Don't make us have to make you."

"If you make us have to make you, it'll hurt," added Hannah.

Airlie hesitated before rolling over and peering at them staring down at her. Olivia wouldn't mind, but then there was the whole drinking thing, which she'd managed to avoid by being a hermit.

Rachel put her hands on her hips. "You know what, Hannah? I believe she needs persuasion."

"I believe you're right."

With that, they dragged Airlie from the cabinet, grabbed as many cushions as they could, and proceeded to bash her, sit on her, and tickle her until she gave in.

"Okay, okay, I'll come." She tried to curl into a ball. "I'll come!"

Hannah and Rachel ceased at once with high-fives all round.

"Can you two get off me now?"

Rachel and Hannah gave one last lash with a cushion before sitting back to discuss the trip at length.

❖

Edinburgh was bathed in sunshine and buzzing with enthusiastic tourists wearing thick winter coats. They toured the usual attractions—the castle and the Royal Mile—before eagerly shopping. By early evening, they were famished and exhausted. As luck would have it, they stumbled upon a quaint restaurant where they ate pasta and drank champagne without a care in the world.

That evening, Airlie relaxed in bed, her mind in tune with her body. She was tired, but satisfied with the wonderful day shared with friends. She was pleased with her moderate alcohol consumption, and even more pleased with the lack of desire to overindulge. They all woke early the following morning in full holiday mode, with just a hint of craziness.

It had been Rachel's suggestion to make a bus trip to the highlands and the Lough Glenn whiskey distillery. All three behaved like naughty school kids released from a convent for the day. They joked and messed about the entire journey, leading a sing-along, inventing ridiculous stories about local landmarks, and just as the distillery tour was about to conclude, the handsome young guide requested volunteers.

In one slick, seamless motion, Airlie elbowed Rachel, Rachel grinned, and they both raised their hands in a desperate bid for selection. Airlie, Rachel, and three older men were the lucky volunteers, sitting in view of everyone in the tasting bar. The tastings began in a civilized manner, but it soon became evident that the quantity of alcohol they consumed was far more than anyone had expected.

The tour group appeared to enjoy the entertainment, especially Hannah, who, when Airlie glanced at her, was in stitches. The other three volunteers began swapping drinks with Airlie and Rachel until soon all five were in fits of laughter, as were the sober onlookers. Airlie and Rachel were a stumbling, giggling, drunken mess.

The return drive was a rowdy affair. Airlie spent considerable time attempting a headstand in the aisle, and Rachel led a chorus of the rude and crude version of "Seven Drunken Nights." Not to be outdone, the bus driver had them all falling over each other when he drove around a roundabout no less than half a dozen times. Almost everyone was bursting for the toilet when they finally lurched to a halt, signaling an end to the tour.

It was mid-afternoon, and Airlie and Rachel were weary. Hannah, whose sides were aching from constant laughter, was not at all tired, reminding them she was the sober one. She energetically bounced off to explore while Airlie and Rachel snoozed to gain their second wind.

Their room was sizable, a double bed and a rollaway trundle that Airlie was sleeping on. Hannah and Rachel seemed happy enough to share the big bed, and thankfully, no one snored, although with a gut full of whiskey, it was becoming a possibility.

Airlie's stomach churned incessantly. She took some paracetamol, hoping to keep any hangover at bay so she could start over again that evening. They both flopped like rag dolls on the double bed.

"God, I'm fucked." Airlie's head was spinning.

"Well now, you're not, but you could be if I had the energy."

Not so long ago, such a comment would have sent Airlie into a confused rage, but today, she simply laughed and said, "Good one," before ineffectively flinging her arm, playfully slapping Rachel.

"You just hit me."

"Yes, I did."

Rachel plucked a pillow from beneath her head, and with an amusing lack of coordination, thumped Airlie across the chest.

"You just hit *me*."

"Yep, sure did."

Airlie retaliated. The pillows proved an effective weapon before wrestling took over. As they both fought to hold the other down, Rachel took the upper hand and pinned Airlie on her back, unable to move except to hiccup.

"Do you give in?" Rachel panted.

"*Hic*."

"Do you admit that I am the champion?"

"I think I'm gonna—hic—wet myself." Airlie giggled. "You're sitting on my—hic—bladder."

"You're just saying that so I'll let you up. Do you succumb to the might of the almighty Rachel?"

"The might of the almighty is not—hic—how I'd put it."

"Perhaps, but you're not the one on top here, I am, and that makes me almighty, all righty?"

Airlie laughed hard again. "Like it—hic—on top, do you?"

"You're not making this any easier on yourself, and yes, as a matter of fact, I very much enjoy being on top. In fact, I'm enjoying it right now."

A moment of silence passed between them. Their eyes locked, and all traces of playfulness dissolved. Airlie was sure she wasn't alone in her feeling. The tension was unmistakable and almost tangible. Rachel leaned down and kissed Airlie full on the lips, slowly and gently.

Airlie's brain went into sensory overload before a satisfying sensation of warmth and arousal leached into her core, before settling with an insistent tingling between her legs, moisture soaking her knickers.

Rachel pulled away. "But I don't want to be this person to you." She released Airlie. "I'm sorry. I'd rather be the next one, or the one after that."

Airlie lay in shock. "The next what?" she asked, propping herself on her elbows.

Rachel looked her in the eye. "Your first love will be great, and I'd love to be that person; share with you all the new things you'll want to feel and experience, but it probably won't last. It hardly ever does. I think I want to be with you when you're happy being you. I'll give up this," she shrugged, indicating the current situation, "to be that person." Without another word, Rachel rushed to the bathroom.

There was no mistaking where the kiss could have ended, but Airlie wasn't convinced she was ready for the next step. Until that exact minute, she'd been unaware she was ready for the first step. It was all so confusing. She needed time to think. Right now, and for the remainder of their holiday, she would pretend the kiss never happened.

She wasn't angry, hurt, or disgusted. Gone were the negative thoughts that would have plagued her in the past, and this breakthrough was a welcome change. A weird sense of elation engulfed her, and she felt flattered by the unexpected kiss.

Rachel knew she was gay. She didn't have to say it.

# CHAPTER SIXTEEN

The journey home proved an arduous mission for everyone. They had rolled into bed at four a.m., caring little that their flight was scheduled for eleven fifteen. They fell asleep on the plane—each leaning on the other's shoulder. That afternoon was good for nothing except sleeping. Liam dropped by, but left soon after arriving. Hannah was only fit to tell him she'd had a great time, but really needed to rest.

Airlie had grown desperate to dissect the kiss she shared with Rachel, but her mind was beyond tired and her thoughts were a jumbled mess. As far as she could tell, nothing between them had changed. There had been no awkwardness, although with such fierce hangovers, it was difficult to move beyond the headache and nausea.

The following week proved that they weren't teenagers any longer. All three declined offers for a midweek dinner with Dan and Sean. Airlie and Rachel chose instead to have a night in front of the TV, and Hannah was "resting up" at Liam's.

By the end of the week, Airlie relaxed in a hot steaming bath and reflected on her actions and emotions. She pondered what it all meant. Since the disastrous encounter with the man in the toilet, she'd taken stock and attempted to regain control of her life and her emotions. It was no longer acceptable for her to feel angry all the time, and she understood that the incident in the rank toilet had somehow set her free, but it had also left her extremely confused.

Airlie leapt out of the bath, an idea evolving. She rushed to her room and searched for pen and paper. She sat cross-legged on the bed and asked herself how she felt while messing about with Rachel. She concentrated on writing the first thoughts that came to mind. She wrote that she was aroused, happy, excited, and that it was extremely enjoyable. In capital letters, she added that she felt completely flattered. She had no idea Rachel had any feelings for her at all. Ultimately, she scribbled that she was scared, conceding that in a completely sober state she might have felt uncomfortable, vulnerable, and utterly terrified.

Airlie then asked herself what these feelings meant. She flicked the pen nib in and out. She wrote the question, "What do these feelings mean?" She drew an arrow toward her previous responses. *Think.* She continued flicking the pen. *Think.*

A drop of water from her hair slid down her back, and she rested her brow in the palm of her hand. When she opened her eyes, she wrote the words, "I'm GAY." Airlie placed the pen neatly below those words, as if to underline them. She stared at the paper. *I'm so gay.* The words stood out like beacons. She wasn't shocked at seeing them. She wasn't shocked while writing them or saying them. She wrote, "I'm a lesbian."

Airlie screwed up the paper and threw it in the bin. Her written words echoed in her mind. *I'm gay and I'm a lesbian.* There were no tears; she didn't feel like crying. That time had passed. *Shit.* She didn't know how to be a lesbian. There was only one way to learn.

The weeks that followed were a time of discovery, but they were also Airlie's loneliest. She had wanted to visit Olivia more than she could express or understand, but she needed to be ready to talk before she made the journey.

For whatever reason, the distance between Airlie's brain and mouth became so vast, she wondered how she conducted conversations at all. The words "I'm gay" computed adequately in her mind, she just struggled to say them aloud, and until she could speak the words, any conversation was terrifying.

"I'm here if you need to talk," Rachel said.

It wasn't the first time Rachel had offered.

Airlie felt ridiculous. Of course she needed to talk. There was so much she wanted to know, wanted to say, but the remnants of denial were ruling her head. "I know I'll be ready one day. I just don't know when that will be."

"I'm not going anywhere." Rachel hesitated. "Would you like to talk about what happened in Edinburgh?"

Would she? She wasn't sure that would help. It would probably only intensify her confusion. It terrified her to think that a conversation might somehow invoke a repeat performance, and without cocktails for courage, there was no way she could let that happen.

"I think I'm doing okay." Her hands were shaking. She hoped Rachel didn't notice.

"You're doing fabulously. Just know I'm here if you need me."

The first significant change Airlie observed was a newfound interest in looking at women. Not in a leering, perverted way, but now she took pleasure in admiring women without experiencing the usual wrench of guilt and shame. She'd wasted so much time and energy ignoring the beautiful women around her to such an absurd extent that to even admire a pair of jeans or a nice top on a woman had sent irrational rushes of guilt through her.

Unfortunately, this was only a single breakthrough, and it required no open recognition of her sexuality.

Many nights, Airlie lay in bed fantasizing. She welcomed the solitude of her room, and bedtime, when she would allow her mind to wander through various scenarios involving women—their touch, their soft lips, and their sexy bodies. The amazing sensations this awakened were new and exciting. Sadly, her new fantasy world was simply that, a fantasy. It was becoming increasingly difficult to reconcile her real life with her fantasy life. No matter how good she felt in the solitude of her room, the reality was that although she had begun to accept her sexuality, it was all too difficult. The rest of Airlie's world began to take on the familiar spiral of discontent and self-destruction. There was no way for her to be happy about being gay when the only happiness surrounding it was in her mind. Talking about it would make it real. If she said it, just once, she knew she'd never be able to take it back. She was scared. People only know for sure when they were told, she reassured herself. So, while she felt gay in her own mind and in the solitude of her bedroom, for all intents and purposes, she remained straight. Until the day came when she chose to reveal her secret, she felt protected and normal, but her own betrayal ate away at her like a parasite.

With denial creeping back into her life, and no avenue to positively move forward, Airlie withdrew, preferring to spend time alone in her bedroom, rarely interacting with anyone. She began drinking to excess, and she knew both Hannah and Rachel noticed.

One lazy evening, as rain lashed against the windows, Airlie descended the stairs on her way to the kitchen. Voices from the lounge room caused her to stall. She assumed the conversation had been going on for some time.

"I thought she was coping okay." Rachel's voice was laced with concerned. "She said she was."

"I thought so too, but she's not. I know her well enough to know she's not right," Hannah replied, barely louder than a whisper. "Can't we just sit her down and have a good talk to her? *You're* gay. Why won't she talk to you?"

Airlie edged toward the door and peered through the crack.

"I'm not sure. I guess she doesn't feel comfortable talking to me, and anyway, I don't know if I'd be the best person to help. My struggle was different. I fell in love with a girl first. It was an amazing revelation for me, quite the opposite of Airlie's experience. She's got years of denial to sort through. She was engaged to be married, for Christ's sake."

"I just hate it when she's so hard on herself. Should I talk to her?"

"You might have to," Rachel said. "I fucked it up in Edinburgh. I shouldn't have kissed her. I've tried to talk to her. I don't want to drive her further into herself."

Airlie had no idea Hannah knew about the kiss in Edinburgh.

"And she let you kiss her, right?"

"No, because kissing people without permission is my thing. Of course she did, but God we were drunk."

"And she knows she can talk to you if she wants to get it off her chest?"

"Yep, I've mentioned a hundred times that I'm a good listener."

"God, I don't know then."

"She's a complicated person, Hannah, you know that, and that's one of the things I like about her, but she just isn't ready to be gay yet."

"And she knows you don't want her until she is."

"That's not exactly fair, and it's not exactly the truth either."

Airlie froze. Not only did Hannah know about the kiss, she knew about the conversation that followed it. She felt stupid. Everyone was talking about her behind her back. How did they think that was helping her?

"I just want her to go out and have a good time before she settles down with someone. I really like her, but I don't want to be her first and then watch her want to play the field. I'd rather be the person she wants last, after all the mucking about is over," said Rachel.

"Fine. But how will you feel when she brings girls home and it's *you* who really wants to be with her?"

"I don't know. I'm trying not to think about that."

"If your plan succeeds, that *will* happen, and what if she falls in love with someone along the way and that someone isn't you? I'm worried if we let this go on any longer, the Airlie you want will be lost forever."

"I know that too, but the real Airlie is deep inside the Airlie we have now, and I want her. Don't get me wrong, I really like the Airlie we have now. Sometimes it drives me crazy. And I do want to guide her through this, but as her friend, not her lover."

"But if you love her—"

"I never said I loved her." Rachel firmly interrupted.

"Okay, if you *like* her so much, don't you want to be the one that shares those first intimate moments with her?" Hannah paused. "Or would you rather have her go and get fucked out the back of a nightclub by some butch-dyke-lesbian to rack up her first experience? She's not coping with this and she's losing herself in the process."

"Of course I want to be the one to share all her first times, but I've done it before. I've *been* that person, and I fell in love to the point where I was convinced we would spend the rest of our lives together, then one day she woke up and wanted to fuck around. She was out of the closet and she wanted freedom."

Airlie observed her friends deep in conversation. She had no idea there had been such hurt in Rachel's past, and evidently, neither did Hannah, who appeared lost for words.

At last, Rachel sighed. "I don't want to have her later because she'll be better in bed or broken in or whatever. I want her then because the chances of her wanting someone else will be less. I really think she's worth the wait."

"I'm sorry, Rach. I had no idea. It's a gamble though."

"It's fine, and I know it could backfire, but it's not addressing the problem we have now, is it?"

"We can't just sit back and watch her destroy herself though, can we? That's just shit. I'm gonna go talk to her."

Airlie panicked and turned as if to hightail it back to her room until Rachel spoke. "She's not ready, Han." Airlie paused and inhaled deeply. Rachel grabbed Hannah's arm as she rose from the couch. "You force her now and she'll run a mile. She knows we're here to help. She knows she can talk to us any time. She's just not ready. I really don't think we should push her."

Hannah slumped on the couch. "Sometimes I just want to shake her and tell her it's okay to be gay. Be out and proud!"

"It's okay to be unemployed too, Hannah, or left-handed, or have eleven toes, or whatever, but if it's not what you want to be, then it's the worst in the world. It's okay to be single or married, but you know yourself, if it's not what you want to be, it can drag you down. Being gay is a big thing for Airlie. It's not what she wants to be, so it's hard as hell for her right now."

Airlie had heard enough. She returned to her bedroom, infuriated to have been the subject of their discussion and enraged to hear they knew exactly how she felt. Beyond all that, she was livid with herself.

It became apparent there was a long way to go before this process would be complete. After waiting until they had retired for the evening, Airlie crept to the bathroom. She began to cry as she cleaned her teeth, tears and toothpaste dripping from her chin. Why was it she could lie in bed at night and have the most amazing, erotic fantasies about women, yet she couldn't bring herself to admit, not openly, to being gay?

Airlie's life was a mess, her emotions were a disaster, and she had set free a beast in her mind and heart that wouldn't let her rest. Nothing could stop her transformation now. Staring intently at her distorted, anguished features in the mirror, she made a decision.

Airlie returned to her room and made a call.

"I thought you'd lost my number," Olivia said.

They hadn't spoken for over two weeks. "I know. I'm really sorry about that."

"It's late. Are you okay?"

Airlie choked back tears. She should have known that Olivia would see straight through her. "No, I don't think I am."

"What's wrong, honey? What's happened?"

"I think I really need to talk to you."

"Okay. Do you want to talk about it now?"

"No, I don't think so. Not over the phone."

"Do you want me to come down? I can leave now and be there in a few hours?"

"No, no, that's okay. I'll come over to you, get out of Dublin for a while. Is that okay?"

It was Thursday evening, and they decided Airlie would call in sick the following day, catch the early morning train, and stay in the west for the weekend. Olivia agreed to work a half day and collect her from Westport train station.

"Are you sure you'll be all right until tomorrow?" Olivia asked.

"I promise. I'll be fine." She felt better already. "I'll see you in Westport around twelve."

"I'll be there. I've missed you."

Hearing those words set Airlie off crying again, but she held it together long enough to say good-bye. She was relieved to have made the call and pleased that Olivia knew she needed to talk. There was no backing out now. Olivia's offer to come to her was reassurance she was doing the right thing. Airlie pulled the covers tightly around her and cried herself to sleep.

## CHAPTER SEVENTEEN

Airlie woke to the sound of her nagging alarm and immediately felt sick with nerves. The word she needed to say was so small, only three letters, but it carried enormous repercussions. She called a cab, showered, and left a note for her housemates by the kettle. The last thing she wanted was for her friends to worry.

She arrived at the train station far earlier than necessary, and her first thought was how expansive and clean the bitterly cold Heuston Station appeared with so few people around to litter the gleaming tiled floor. She bought a coffee and welcomed the strong, hot hit of caffeine. With her ticket secure in her coat breast pocket, she waited nervously to board the seven thirty a.m. train.

It was a long enough journey to Westport, but Airlie felt as if it might take days to reach her destination. Sitting opposite her were some sprightly lads who, as far as she could tell, were heading to the west for a paintballing weekend at Irish Skirmish, near Finbeigh. She wished her weekend would be that simple.

For most of the journey, she closed her eyes, her head resting against her fleece on the window. She attempted to concentrate on the conversation of the lads and their impending weekend, but her mind drifted back to thoughts of how she was going to tell Olivia she was gay. She knew Olivia wouldn't mind, she had other gay friends, but once she spoke the words, it would be one hundred per cent true. No taking it back, no more denial. She presumed there would be a sense of relief, but all she could register was her heart pounding with dread.

She wasn't expecting to see Olivia waiting on the platform as the train pulled into the station, and her nerves heightened at the sight. This journey felt right, like coming home.

The train seemed to take forever to reach a complete stop. Passengers gathered their belongings, or stretched, or hurried to the nearest exit. When the train eventually stopped, Airlie jumped off, weaved her way through people, and leapt into Olivia's open arms. Their embrace lasted many moments. Neither of them had been particularly affectionate in their brief friendship. Airlie savored the sweet smell of Olivia's perfume. Olivia's strong arms wrapped tightly around Airlie's shoulders. It was the only place on earth she wanted to be.

It was a sunny and relatively mild afternoon in Westport—that is to say, it wasn't raining for the first day in three weeks—and the town seemed alive and cheerful as they drove out of the car park and along Altamont Street. Under normal circumstances, they might have stopped at Hannigan's Café for lunch, but today they drove directly to Roaring Bay. The thirty-minute car ride was full of small talk, largely concerning Airlie's job, the new house, and her recent drunken trip to Scotland. She elected to omit her encounter with Rachel. She figured it might surface later. The familiar sight of Gavin and Olivia's home reassured Airlie that her instincts were accurate. This was the right time and place to share her secret.

They sat awkwardly side by side on the couch in the conservatory, a fresh pot of coffee steaming on the table and the sun streaming through the windows. It provided little warmth.

Olivia raised her eyebrows. The small talk was over. "You're not okay, then?"

Airlie felt claustrophobic, as if she were trapped in a sauna. She wiped her clammy hands on her thighs in an attempt to control their trembling. She couldn't make eye contact with Olivia; her courage had all but disappeared. Instead, she fidgeted with the zipper on her jacket. "I don't know how to say it," she said.

"Are you sick?"

"No, I'm not sick." Airlie took a deep breath. "You know how sometimes you think you're something, but you're not?"

"How do you mean?"

Airlie could feel Olivia's eyes on her and imagined the worried look creasing her brow. "You know, you grow up to be one thing, but you realize you're not, only you don't want to be the alternative, so instead you just be nothing?"

Airlie desperately looked at Olivia.

"Are we talking about what I think we're talking about?"

Airlie sobbed. She hadn't even uttered the words, but it was out. She was out, and things would never be the same again.

Olivia held her. Her sobbing, convulsing body deflated, eventually relaxing as the weight of her secret lifted. Olivia reassured her that it was going to be okay, the difficult part was over. She urged Airlie to let it out, let it *all* out, and when the tears ended and Airlie gained composure, Olivia opened a bottle of red.

"You have a lot to get off your chest. I don't know if I can say all the right things, but I'll try, and I'll listen, so for that, I think we need a drink."

The relief was yet to hit Airlie, but she wanted to rid herself of the burden shouldered by years of denial, and she needed to start from the beginning.

"I used to want to do everything my dad did. I wanted to shave, trim my beard, and dismantle my BMX, only to put it back together again. And I did. We had a man come to our primary school to show us how to service our bikes. I had mine done and dusted before the others had even thought about it."

"That sounds like you."

"It is me. Or it was me, until Alicia Castlemaine teased me relentlessly. She used to shove me in the boys' loos and tell me I couldn't use the girls'. I wore my brother's old shorts for the athletics carnival, not those daft knicker type things, and she started again. In the end, it was just easier to be like a girl."

"Airlie, I'm sorry."

"So am I because I should have stood up to her. I shouldn't have bothered so much about being different. It sounds so cliché, but I just wanted to fit in. I wanted to be left alone. That's how I got into art and drawing. Looking back, I guess I needed to create things. I consciously stopped myself from tinkering with bikes and building with the old stuff in Dad's shed. I was miserable until I realized I could draw."

"All those feelings are perfectly natural. It's difficult being a kid," Olivia said.

"I wonder if I'd stayed that confident kid who could build stuff for another few years, would the teasing have bothered me."

"You know what they say about hindsight."

"And I know firsthand how damaging an accomplished bully can be."

"Where's bloody Alicia Castlemaine now?"

Airlie laughed. "I've no idea. God, I wish I knew then what I know now. None of the popular girls at my school amounted to much. Sure, the boys loved them, they had an entourage of young, drooling groupies, but where did that get them? The real world goes far beyond school."

For a moment, Airlie was disappointed in herself, but then she realized that kind of disappointment—the kind where you beat yourself up—was what landed her in this mess in the first place.

"Do you think your friends ever guessed? Does Hannah know?"

"Hannah was the only friend I kept in touch with when we left school. I don't like making new friends."

"Gee, thanks."

Airlie smiled. "You know what I mean. I felt comfortable making friends with men when I first began work. I was frightened women might think I was coming on to them if I made an effort to become friends."

"But weren't you in denial about being gay?"

"Yes. But something's always been there. A niggle, an attraction, a flirt. It's easy to justify anything when you really want to."

Olivia raised her eyebrows.

"Well, the niggle was just a feeling. A glimpse of a sexual desire. We all have those, right? And an attraction to women, well, that's just a normal part of sexuality isn't it? It didn't mean anything. Straight girls hug other straight girls all the time. The fact that it stirred something in me was just a normal part of getting older, of maturing."

"And the flirting?"

Airlie thought of Rachel. "The fact that I enjoy flirting with women far more than I ever could with any man is certainly an obvious sign."

"And?"

"And I guess I chose to ignore it. I shoved it to the back of my mind and moved on. Easily done."

"Did you sabotage your relationship with Sam?"

What happened with Sam still felt raw. She shut her eyes to lessen the pain. "I never lied when I said I didn't feel bad for ending our relationship, but I was terrified about what that meant. I knew what I didn't want. I just wasn't ready to accept what I did want. He was a kind, decent man who I hated having sex with, who I faked every orgasm with. He did nothing to deserve that."

"You set him free, Airlie. That day you broke up with him and set yourself free, you set him free, too."

Airlie had never looked at it that way.

Olivia patted her knee.

There was one other burden Airlie needed to set free. "I did something stupid recently."

"How stupid and how recent?"

Airlie explained her disastrous judgment on the night she had sex with the man in the pub. She explained the trigger that instigated her madness and the subsequent consequences of her denial. Tears came again as she described in detail the encounter in the toilet.

"Jesus, Aerobar." It was the first time she'd used one of Airlie's nicknames. "He could have done anything to you. What were you thinking?"

"I wanted it to stop, but I couldn't get the words out."

"And the tests are all clear?"

"Yes, thank God."

"That's some way to realize you're gay. Promise me you'll never put yourself in danger like that again?"

"I don't intend to. I promise. It wasn't my finest hour."

Olivia pulled her close again and squeezed. "I wish you had called me, just talked to me. I would have come down. I knew something was up, but I thought you wanted to work it out for yourself. I didn't think you'd want me interfering."

"I dialed your number so many times. I just didn't know what to say. It wasn't until that stupid moment in the toilet that I realized who I was. I was so stupid. I can't believe it took that to make me see who I really am."

"I think you've known, Airlie. I just think it was in that moment when you accepted it." Airlie rolled her eyes. "This is a start. I know you're not comfortable with who you are yet, and it will take time, all the time you need, but at least you know that here with me, you can be yourself. If you want, I'll tell Gavin, and anytime you need to just be yourself, you can come here, just until you're happy being yourself around others."

"Thanks. You don't know how much that means to me. I'm not ready to tell anybody else. Christ, I can't even say the word *gay* and refer it to myself yet."

"It'll come. It's a process."

"I just know I could have saved myself a whole load of stress and heartache if I hadn't ignored the signs. I mean, how did I expect to be married for the rest of my life if I hated having sex so much? I could have conceivably gone the rest of my life without having an orgasm. Shit, I still could if I don't sort myself out."

"I've never had an orgasm either," Olivia said softly.

"Really?"

"Really. I don't know why. I've never been a really sexual person, I guess." Olivia stared out the window. "I've given up trying now, to be honest."

"How old are you?"

Olivia frowned. "Forty-one."

"And I'm twenty-eight, so that's…" Airlie quickly calculated. "Sixty-nine years between us and not one orgasm."

"Jesus." Olivia took Airlie's glass from her. "I need another fucking drink."

## CHAPTER EIGHTEEN

Early the following morning, Airlie awoke with a dry mouth and a throbbing headache. Her queasy stomach gurgled.

Her exhaustion was emotional, and this morning she felt awkward facing the day a new person. The truth had at last been spoken. Her awkwardness extended to Olivia. She didn't know what she'd do if Olivia felt differently about her or abandoned her. It crossed her mind that Olivia hadn't meant what she'd said, that she'd been saying the right things just to get through the weekend until Airlie left.

"Ah." Olivia glanced from the paper when Airlie entered. "She lives."

The aroma of freshly brewed coffee filled the kitchen. She wondered how long Olivia had been up. She was showered and dressed, her short dark hair looking a bit flat, in need of some product, but besides that, she appeared annoyingly normal.

"How come you don't have a hangover?" Airlie asked. "You're older than me. You should feel as shit, if not shittier, than I do." She let her throbbing head slump to rest on the table.

"You're young and inexperienced, my dear."

Airlie ignored her.

"I thought we might go to Galway today. Shop a little, do lunch, check out some galleries. What do you reckon? Plus, I have choir practice tonight. We can call into Finbeigh on the way home. Sound like a plan?"

Airlie lifted her head and smiled.

"I thought that might spark some interest from you." Olivia slid a steaming hot cup of coffee under her nose.

"I haven't been to Galway for ages. *We* haven't been for ages. Definitely sounds like a plan."

Olivia patted her on the back. "Get that coffee into you. You look like you need it."

Airlie sipped the coffee. Olivia seemed normal. A combination of relief and caffeine hit her stomach, and she felt better. The last time they'd traveled to Galway together, they'd left early and hadn't returned until nearly midnight, exhausted, thirsty, and carrying nearly a dozen shopping bags between them.

They danced around further talk of Airlie's sexuality until they neared Galway, over an hour into the journey. Olivia spoke first. "So, besides a bit dusty, how are you feeling today?"

Airlie wasn't sure how she felt. It was still sinking in. "Good, I think. I feel a bit weird though, to be honest. I just hope telling people becomes easier. I don't think I could go through this every time."

"I'm sure it will get easier."

"I can't imagine telling anyone else will be as hard."

"As telling me?"

"Yes, as telling you. I was shitting myself."

"Because you told me first?"

"I'm not sure. Maybe." Airlie thought she had more to add, but couldn't find the words, and even if she could, the courage to speak would probably have deserted her.

"What about Hannah? She's your best friend. Surely telling her will be easier."

"She already knows. I overheard her talking with Rachel. She knows about the bloke in the toilet. The only thing missing from the story is why I was in the pub in the first place. She won't be surprised in the least. I told you, that's the hard part over. I feel a bit more relaxed about it now."

"I'm not that scary, am I? What did you think I'd do, put you on the next train back to Dublin?"

Airlie looked away.

"Seriously, c'mon? I'm your friend, a good friend, aren't I? Telling me couldn't have been that bad?"

"No, I guess it wasn't, but you're always so together. I didn't want to disappoint you." She hesitated. "I care what you think and what you think of me. That made it complicated."

"Well, I *think* I'm extremely proud of you. It takes a lot of courage to accept who you are and make positive steps toward being that person. *And* speaking of positive steps, I've taken on board your words of wisdom, and just the other day bought my very first G-string."

Airlie laughed. Olivia wasn't quite in the loop, as it were, when it came to skimpy underwear, and convincing her of the benefits had proven almost impossible. Vowing never to wear one, Olivia had made fun of Airlie's that were drying in a row on the mantelpiece over the fireplace.

"So, how's it working out for you?"

"Bloody uncomfortable, to tell you the truth. Honestly, I don't know how you do it. Where's the fun in having a piece of cloth stuck up your arse if it hurts?"

"You'll get used to it. Pretty soon they'll be more comfortable than your normal bloomers."

Olivia shook her head, unconvinced.

After an hour strolling through shops, Airlie's stomach began to grumble, and they entered the first restaurant that looked half-decent. What they found was a lovely, cozy place with a vast menu. A dreadlocked young waiter with tattoos and a most handsome smile took their order and was barely walking away from them before Olivia excused herself. Upon her return, she appeared flushed.

"Are you all right?"

Olivia's body heaved beneath the strain of laughter. She took something from her pocket and swiftly snuck it into her handbag.

"What was that?"

Tears streamed down Olivia's cheeks.

"What's so funny? Was there something in the toilet?"

Olivia took a deep breath. "That was my G-string."

"Your what?"

"My knickers."

"Did they break?"

Olivia laughed out loud, gaining attention from other diners. "No, they didn't break." She gathered herself. "You know how I said it was uncomfortable?" Airlie nodded. "Well, I had it on the wrong way round."

"What? Back to front?"

"I had a leg hole round my waist." Olivia's mascara streaked her cheeks.

They laughed, holding their stomachs while other restaurant patrons remained clueless to the source of their amusement.

The joke of the day was justifiably on Olivia. Airlie found herself holding aloft granny undies at every opportunity, asking Olivia in a rather loud voice if they were more suitable than the G-string she had removed earlier.

"I bet Gav would love you in a pair of granny undies."

"I reckon he'd be grateful to see me in any undies at all."

Airlie covered her ears. "Too much information."

"You started it."

"I must really cramp your style when I'm in the house then. I had no idea you were such a naturist."

Olivia didn't laugh and kept walking. "On the contrary, I should imagine he'd like to see me either way."

Airlie jogged to catch up. "You must get undressed in front of each other. Isn't that what married people do?"

"Not so much anymore." Olivia quickly looked away. "I'll give the G-string another go next week." She paused. "That's if I don't hang myself with it or cause any permanent damage down there."

"I'm leaving that one alone."

"Wise decision, young lady." She linked her arm through Airlie's, something she'd never done before, and they strolled contentedly down High Street and Quay Street in the mild afternoon sun.

The entire afternoon drifted away, and as the sun descended, a cool, crisp breeze weaved its way through the streets of Galway. As if by magic, people quickly transitioned from relaxed shoppers to harried workers, busily negotiating traffic and each other on their way home. They shared a quick bite of Indian before making the long journey north toward Finbeigh.

Airlie knew that choir practice was usually a quiet affair, and on a good night, the hymns could be selected and practiced all within an hour. On a bad night, this process seemingly took forever. It was amazing to think that in a village the size of tiny Finbeigh, the gossip surrounding the events of the week could take an hour or more to discuss.

Practice on this particular evening was animated, and not at all as serious as singing hymns should be. Airlie and Olivia had shared a fantastic day and were not fit to concentrate on much at all. Grace was in fine form, her mind not straying far from the gutter as soon as she arrived, passing on the latest filthy email joke. Her son, Seamus, home from Greece where he worked as a builder, had already been to the pub for a quick pint, so he was keen to get practice over with.

There were many factors that contributed to after-choir drinks being either a big event or an early night. Not every night at the pub was magic, but every time Airlie settled in with a pint, she hoped something special would happen. Some nights would just see Olivia, Airlie, Grace, Marion, Siobhan, and Ross sitting by the fire, chatting over a solitary pint before heading home. While other nights, such as this night, Airlie felt the planets align, and she just knew that there was potential, in this tiny pub on the west of Ireland, with these amazing people, for something special to happen.

The size of the crowd inside Bridge End could usually be determined by the cars parked in the square, but tonight was deceiving. They met the clamor of hordes of people, and Airlie recognized the lads from the train. The Skirmish crowd were out for the night, and heaven help them tomorrow, when they were seeking cover with hangovers, dying of thirst.

Their usual table by the fire was already taken, so they squeezed their way to the far corner to the only remaining empty one. In no time at all, a small sing-along gained momentum, and people from all corners of the pub were approaching Sharon, asking the whereabouts of her guitar. A few of the rowdier lads became aware that the majority of the local choir was in attendance, so they requested a hymn.

Sharon retrieved her guitar and the choir sang the last hymn they had rehearsed. The crowd clapped and whistled, so Sharon launched into a well-known Irish tune, and the entire pub united as one in song. Other musicians maneuvered their way through to join them. A worn, elderly woman played a bodhran, and another a tin whistle, and much to Airlie's delight, the night was poised to be special for sure.

For the next two hours, they drank and sang. Airlie never ceased to be amazed at the talent of the Irish and their bold confidence to sing in front of a bar full of strangers, even if most of them were drunk.

To everyone's disappointment, at exactly midnight, the bus arrived to collect the Skirmish crowd and deliver them home in preparation for shooting each other the following day. The revelers cheered and jeered, trying to persuade the driver to stay for "one more ol' song," but he was tired and grumpy and having none of it.

Even though the crowd had cleared and all the other musicians had gone home, for the members of the choir, the night was young. They took a break from singing to move and chat by the fire, and by one o'clock, they were the only ones remaining. Aside, of course, from Ross, who was flitting about the place cleaning to keep busy on account of his latest attempt to quit smoking. His cranky mood was almost unbearable.

Only minutes after he had poured another round of drinks and delivered them to the table, something he only did when the place was empty, the phone rang.

"Right, you lot, out!"

"Ah no, Ross, not the guards again?"

"It is, yeah, the feckers. All of you, out."

Everyone attempted to finish their drinks—another skill obviously taught as part of the *Emergency Illegal After Hours Drinking Procedure*—while walking toward the door. Ross was in no mood to harbor illegal drinkers in the toilets tonight. They discarded their half-empty glasses on the end of the bar, Ross yelling at them to hurry up. They threw a terse barrage of insults at him as he slammed the door leaving them in the quiet, freezing car park. Marion and Siobhan reluctantly took off in the opposite direction from Olivia and Airlie, who intended to call into Grace's for a cuppa.

In the black of night, with no moon visible, Olivia and Airlie followed Grace and Seamus as they cautiously negotiated the potholed road that wound endlessly along the edge of Dunstrand Inlet. Dark mountains rose high on one side, and a thickset dry stone wall provided the only barrier to the often sheer drop to the water on the opposite side.

Upon arrival at Grace's house, Seamus spotted the light still on at old Mikey's place next door and headed over there to lock up. This wasn't unusual; Mikey was becoming forgetful in his old age, so Seamus, or one of his sisters, would regularly pop their head in and make sure they could hear him snoring before switching off the light, flicking the lock, and leaving him in peace. Seamus had only been gone a few minutes when they poured four large glasses of red wine. So much for having a cup of tea. The lounge was comfortable and warm, and they sank into the huge leather chairs, a welcome alternative to the unforgiving wooden seats in the pub.

They had only taken one mouthful of the smooth Argentinean Shiraz when Seamus crashed through the front door, then burst into the lounge room.

"I think Mikey's dead."

They rose from their seats.

Seamus was trembling and pasty. "I touched him and he was so cold. I don't think he had a pulse, but me feckin' hands were shaking so much, I couldn't really tell."

There was a moment of shocked silence before Grace calmly took charge. "We'll go over and take a look," she said, eyeing Olivia. "I'll get the torches."

Olivia turned to Airlie. "Why don't you stay here? I don't know if you'll want to see this."

"I'm not staying here on my own, thanks." The evening had taken on a sinister feel, and she didn't fancy being left in the house alone.

"You'd better call the guards," Grace said to Seamus. They shrugged on coats and tramped back up the driveway, past the horse stables, and over the knee-high stone wall into Mikey's place.

They entered through the front door, the door they had seen open, and the place reeked. The stench was a sickly sweet odor of a man who cleaned the house little, and himself even less. The sitting room was to the left of the entrance hall, the main bedroom to the right. The bed was empty. Grace strode directly to the sitting room, the others followed, and there, sitting in an old green armchair, the filthy upholstery worn through on the arms, was Mikey, eyes peacefully closed and mouth agape. Grace went to him to check for a pulse. "Ah, Mikey," she said, crossing herself. "You poor old devil."

Olivia and Seamus crossed themselves too. Airlie stood, not knowing where to look or what to do. She dug her hands deep in her pockets. The silence was broken by Seamus phoning the guards to inform them that no ambulance was necessary; Mikey was certainly dead.

They all stared at each other. A tear or two slipped from Seamus's cheeks and fell on his jacket, the shock of discovering Mikey beginning to sink in. Olivia comforted him with an arm around his strong, broad shoulders. No one thought to leave the sitting room. They simply didn't want to leave poor Mikey on his own. He had died alone, and the least they could do for him now was stay with him until others could care for him.

As soon as the guard, Sean Duffy, arrived, Airlie slipped out the front for a smoke. The stale air inside clung to her like a film of dust, and the need for the crisp breeze to blow off the stench overcame her. Drawing the smoke slowly into her lungs, she heard the guard say he reckoned he'd been dead a few hours now, although it was hard to tell because he might have been colder than expected, due to the front door being wide open. His body was already stiffening.

There was nothing suspicious about Mikey's death. Nobody suggested otherwise. It was just a terribly sad and lonely way to pass.

Ross Sweeney was also the local undertaker. Sean Duffy summoned him to come, collect the body, and deliver it to Castlebar morgue. Father Ryan was on his way.

Airlie and the others, including Sean Duffy, waited outside when the priest arrived. It was a sobering occasion, but the irony of the evening wasn't wasted on any of them. Here they were, Airlie, Olivia, Grace, and Seamus, standing outside a dead man's house with the guard who had been patrolling earlier in the evening, ensuring their timely exit from the pub. The publican and undertaker, Ross—who no one was particularly happy with for kicking them out with half-full drinks—had been called, hopefully out of his bed, to come and collect a body for delivery to the morgue.

There was some more chat and a discussion in the lounge room about what clothes to dress him in for the funeral. Grace chose a brown suit, while Olivia ratted around the grubby little kitchen for a plastic bag to put it in and send with Mikey to the morgue.

Seamus and Airlie were outside smoking when Ross arrived with his van. He appeared a shorter man in the darkness, and he walked quickly, with purpose. He reminded Airlie of a rat ferreting for food.

"Seamus, Airlie." He nodded his acknowledgment as he entered the house. Moments later, he was back outside, and he and Sean Duffy pulled a wooden box from the van. Even Airlie could tell that to fit Mikey in that skinny box was certainly going to be a squeeze.

Seamus was obviously thinking the same as he threw his cigarette away and took some weight of the box. "Jesus, lads, will he fit in this thing?"

"Well now, he'll have to, Seamus," said Ross. "It's the only one I've got."

They all huddled against the sitting room walls as the box was placed in the middle of the floor, devouring any free space. No one was confident Mikey would fit. Ross removed the lid, and as gently as possible, he and Seamus pulled Mikey down into the box. It soon became apparent that due to the onset of rigor mortis, the only way he could even remotely fit was in a sideways fashion, so everyone helped as they tilted him halfway onto his side. Ross placed the lid on the box, but before he could push down, Mikey's arm fell out, giving Olivia and Grace an awful shock. Flustered, he glanced apologetically at them both before removing the lid. Sean Duffy tucked Mikey's arm back in, holding it in place while Ross and Seamus made adjustments. It wouldn't close. Mikey's arm and shoulder were too high. They all stared blankly at each other, Ross sweating profusely.

"I've no other box." He began to pace in the small room.

"Is the lid on his head?" asked Father Ryan.

"Pardon, Father?"

"I mean, when you put the lid down, is it his head that's preventing it from closing?" Father Ryan was softly spoken and calm.

"Oh, right. I see what you mean." Sean Duffy peered beneath to check. "No, Father, it's not his head in the way. It's his shoulder, really."

"Well." Father Ryan thought deeply while the others waited expectantly. "I don't believe it's in the best interest of poor old Mikey, God rest his soul, to be left in this house alone until Ross can arrange delivery of a larger box." Everyone mumbled agreement. "So I think we should try to fit Mikey in the box as best we can, so he can be looked after by the good folk in Castlebar first thing in the morning." Everyone agreed again, and as if given the blessing of God himself, they all pushed heavily on the box to ensure the lid shut tightly. Ross secured the lock with an elaborately large silver key.

Within minutes, the box was in the van, and Ross Sweeney was carefully winding his way toward Castlebar. Airlie thought it would almost kill Ross Sweeney having to drive so slowly.

Father Ryan and Sean Duffy politely declined a cup of tea, preferring to go home to bed. Airlie needed sleep too, so it was decided that she and Olivia would stay at Grace's. Adrenaline still pumping, Olivia and the others felt it appropriate to have a drink or two in

Mikey's honor. Airlie took a small whiskey, to be polite, but was falling asleep when Seamus put her out of her misery and showed her to a bedroom. The guest room was small and welcoming, and because of the awkward shape, two single beds were pushed together. With no pajamas or toothbrush, Airlie stripped to her knickers and top, and was asleep only moments after her head hit the pillow.

## CHAPTER NINETEEN

Airlie felt like she'd only been asleep for a minute when she stirred from the door opening. She listened to Olivia's attempts to whisper good night to Grace and Seamus before the door shut.

"You okay?" Airlie asked.

"Oh fuck, sorry, did I wake you? I was trying to be quiet."

Airlie looked at her watch. It was nearly five a.m. and Olivia was more than a little tipsy.

"That's okay."

"Shit, what a night, eh?" Olivia began to undress.

"Sure was weird. I've never seen a dead body before, let alone helped to squeeze one into a box like that."

Olivia giggled. "It was a first for me and all." She yawned. "I hope you don't mind, but I have to crash in here. No other beds are made up."

"I don't mind. We can't push the beds apart though. They don't have separate bedding."

"Oh, whatever." Olivia sighed. "God, I'm wrecked." Her outline silhouetted against the curtain. Airlie watched her remove her jeans. "Do we have anything on tomorrow?"

"Not that I know of." Airlie's voice rose an octave as reality set in. Panic, followed by an unwanted excitement, ripped through her. They were about to sleep in the same bed.

"Good," Olivia said, almost to herself. "We can have a lazy day."

Although she attempted to relax, Airlie remained rigid while Olivia disappeared into the en suite. Without a care in the world, Olivia opened the door while peeing and asked why she had even thought that the beds needed moving.

*What?* Airlie couldn't think straight. "I don't know." She shifted to the far edge. "I thought you might not want to be in the same bed as me or something?"

Olivia stood beside the bed, removing her top, then her bra, before replacing her top. She bounced under the covers. "You worry too much, my dear."

Airlie *was* worried, very worried. Since acknowledging her sexuality, she'd been fighting increasingly inappropriate thoughts about Olivia. Until then, for the short time they had known each other, she'd been able to convince herself that the infatuation was just a phase, and now, alone in a bed with Olivia, she was attempting, more strenuously than ever, to convince herself of that again.

What she longed for, she realized, was Olivia's arms wrapped tightly around her. Her thoughts drifted to how little Olivia was wearing, and when she began to imagine her with nothing on at all, her heart raced. Airlie rolled over to savor the thought and develop it into a full-blown fantasy. She knew it was wrong, but she couldn't help it. She visualized Olivia coming to her, snuggling behind her, and whispering in her ear all the erotic things she wanted to do to her.

She felt beset with guilt and desperately attempted to extinguish the fantasy. It was impossible to deny, however, that her feelings were addictive, both in her heart and between her legs. She struggled to substitute Rachel for Olivia, but it was hopeless. She wanted Olivia to want her. The fantasy gripped her again—Olivia progressed from an innocent cuddle, to touching her, caressing her breasts and removing her top and knickers before forcefully rolling her onto her back.

Airlie leapt out of bed and rushed to the toilet. *What are you doing?* The reflection staring back at her looked horrified. She had no idea what she was doing.

"You all right in there?" Olivia called.

*Shit, shit, shit.* She thought Olivia was asleep. "I'm fine. Just need to pee."

"I guess it's a bit of a shock, really." Olivia sounded groggy, the alcohol slurring her words as Airlie flushed and returned to bed.

It was a shock. Only one day after she'd come out to Olivia, she was sharing a bed with her. Shock wasn't a strong enough word. Horrified was a better term.

"I mean, you've never seen a dead person before. You must be a little upset?"

Airlie's heart slowed. Olivia had no idea what was going through her mind. She played along. "I guess. It's sad that he was all alone." Airlie lay on her back, so close to the edge that barely any blankets covered her.

"Hey, you're freezing," Olivia said. "Come here, you poor thing. It's probably the fright of it all." She shifted closer, lying on her back, arms outstretched for Airlie to move in and be comforted.

In an instant, all the blood in Airlie's increasingly aroused body rushed to her head, with perhaps the exception of some that sought other parts, causing a throbbing sensation. She froze. In light of what she had just been fantasizing, this should be a dream come true, but she was terrified. Olivia couldn't console her. It was wrong. She forced herself to think of mundane things. She came up with tractors, muddy boots, sheep, and Olivia naked in the barn. *Shit!*

On one hand, she wanted Olivia to touch her, comfort her, and just be close to her. On the other hand, she couldn't believe she was betraying her friend and their friendship.

*Oh my God.* She moved her head onto Olivia's shoulder and cuddled beside her.

*Oh my fucking God.*

❖

Airlie awoke with a jolt, disappointed to find she was no longer in Olivia's embrace. It was light outside, and the sun edged through the few gaps available between the dark curtains. As far as she could tell, there was no one up. The house appeared silent and still. Sighing, she rubbed her eyes. Today wouldn't amount to much.

She rolled over to watch Olivia sleeping. Olivia lay on her back, one arm resting above her head. As Airlie's eyes drifted from her perfect lips, she was drawn to Olivia's chest rising and falling in a slow rhythm. A stray tuft of hair stuck out on one side of her head. Airlie became aware of how beautiful she was.

She tightly shut her eyes. It was wrong; she knew, to be thinking these thoughts about Olivia. She was married and it was crazy, but such whimsical daydreams filled her with such joy. She opened her eyes and stared again, realizing she had probably felt this way for some time. Airlie had opened the floodgates to a completely new world of emotions and sexual fantasies. Loving Olivia was one of these feelings, and she didn't know what to do. For now, however, she would watch her sleep.

Airlie's eyes grew heavier and her resolve failed. When later she woke, it was she who was being watched.

"Morning, sleepyhead."

"Hey." Airlie stretched, pleased she had woken before Olivia was up. "How did you sleep?"

"I slept like a log. I reckon that's the first night in ages I haven't been woken by Gav's bloody snoring." Olivia pushed the pillows back and sat up, her chest now exposed, although wearing a T-shirt. Airlie couldn't help notice the outline of her small breasts beneath it. "You and I should sleep together more often."

A nervous, ridiculously high-pitched laugh escaped so inappropriately, Airlie had to disguise it with a cough.

"And how did you sleep?" Olivia continued, oblivious. "You okay about last night?"

For a brief moment, Airlie misunderstood and thought she was referring to their cuddle, but she recovered and realized she was talking about poor Mikey.

"You were in a bit of shock. I remember you shivering rather badly," Olivia said. "Did you get to sleep okay in the end?"

"I did, thanks." Airlie was annoyed for thinking Olivia would even give their cuddle a second thought. "I think perhaps I was already hungover. You know how sometimes you can get a bit cold and stuff, and it's a pretty emotional thing: death. Although, I didn't really know him well...or at all, actually." She rolled her eyes. *Shut up, you idiot.*

"You sure you're okay?"

"I'm fine, honestly." Airlie composed herself. "You knew him, though. How are you doing?"

"I'm okay. Tired. We might skip breakfast here and go home for a fry-up, perhaps watch a movie or something this afternoon. What do you think?"

"Sounds good to me." *Or we could just stay in bed together all day.*

## CHAPTER TWENTY

As autumn arrived, so did a sense of belonging. Airlie had spent the past couple of months commuting between her job in Dublin and weekends on the west. She was using this time to adapt to being gay. She and Olivia would often joke about it, and although she hadn't told anyone else, there was a tiny glimmer of contentment creeping into her life.

"So, the way I see it, our options are the pub, the cinema, or a quiet night in."

Airlie, Olivia, and Gavin sat drinking coffee in the conservatory. It was early Saturday evening and they were yet to make plans.

"I vote for the pub," Gavin said.

Olivia snapped her head toward him. It was rare that Gavin offered an opinion. It was even rarer that it involved leaving the house.

Olivia turned to Airlie. "How about you?"

"Let's stay in." The words spewed from her before she had time to catch herself. It hadn't been obvious until now, but this wasn't the first time that, regardless of what Gavin said, she knew she'd say the opposite. The truth was she wanted to go to the pub, but not with Gavin. The infrequent times she had been out with both of them, she'd felt like a spare wheel. Olivia was different around Gavin, more conservative, and frankly, boring.

Airlie and Gavin looked to Olivia. She held the deciding vote. "Pizza and red wine in front of the fire it is."

Airlie smiled.

Gavin silently took his coffee cup to the kitchen before disappearing to the lounge room.

"What sort of pizza do you fancy?" Olivia called after him.

"You two decide," he called back.

Airlie was already opening the wine and pouring two glasses. She tried to convince herself that she was absolved of any wrongdoing because staying in had ultimately been Olivia's decision. Until she'd finished the first glass of wine, she felt guilty that perhaps Gavin was missing out. After that, she didn't think about it again.

"Eggs?" asked Rachel.

Six a.m. was hardly the time Airlie expected to see Rachel in the kitchen, especially on a Monday. Airlie had returned from her usual weekend with Olivia and had slept well. She was up early to get a head start on a data and mail-merging job that had arrived late Friday afternoon.

"You're cooking eggs?"

"If you'll have breakfast with me, I will."

Airlie looked at her watch and then looked at Rachel smiling warmly. "Sure. Sounds good."

"Can I leave you with coffee duties?"

"I think you should. I make a better coffee than you."

"That's an unsubstantiated claim." Rachel nudged her. "You can always cook breakfast and *I'll* make the coffee."

Airlie kissed her cheek. "Now, that would be a disaster."

Rachel starred at her.

She realized what she'd done. "Sorry."

"What for?"

She wasn't sure. It was a natural, friendly reaction to some early morning banter. "Maybe I'm not sorry, then."

Rachel shrugged. "Good. Nothing to be sorry about."

"Why are you up so early, anyway?" Airlie changed the subject.

"Driving to Cork today. We're cutting some research funding to one of our subsidiaries. I predict the rest of my day will be shit. I'll be stuck in the car with my boss for six hours of my life I'll never get back, and then I'll have to tell someone their funding has been halved. Great day all round."

"I'll save you some dinner."

"And run me a bath?"

"You're pushing your luck."

This time Rachel kissed *her* on the cheek. "But you'll do it, right?"

Airlie smiled. "Of course I will."

That evening, Rachel returned home shattered and disgruntled, and as promised, Airlie looked after her. As was Airlie's customary evening routine, her mobile rang and she left Rachel to enjoy her dinner while she retreated to her bedroom to talk to Olivia. The conversation didn't go as planned.

"Gav and I are going to Paris on the weekend." Olivia's tone was light, but her voice conveyed little excitement.

Paris was the city of lovers. Gav and Olivia were married, but they were hardly romantic. The tightness in her chest released as she quickly convinced herself it must be a work thing.

"Gav's arranged a second honeymoon," Olivia said.

Airlie felt the air suck from her lungs. She forgot to breathe until it became uncomfortable. "Fabulous." She forced the words out. "You'll have a great time."

"I'm sure it'll be fine," said Olivia.

Airlie thought it would be as boring as fuck, but she remained silent.

"It's just for the weekend. He's been saying it for years, and well, I suppose he's finally got round to it." She laughed, but it sounded false. "Hannah will love having you home, I'm sure."

Airlie might never have been home on the weekends, but she knew Hannah wasn't either. She spent most of her spare time with Liam. Regardless, being at a loose end for the weekend wasn't what was annoying her. It just showed how little Gavin knew his wife, how completely off the mark he was with his surprises, and how he thought he could make a difference with just one lavish weekend. Airlie made Olivia laugh all the time; they shared fulfilling time together *every* weekend. Gavin was like a wet blanket at a slumber party. Airlie shut the call down before she said something she might regret.

"What's up?" Rachel asked when Airlie returned to the living room.

"Nothing. Why?"

"No reason. You just normally talk on the phone longer, that's all."

"Not tonight."

"So everything's okay on the west, is it?"

Airlie shrugged. It didn't feel okay.

"And you're going up on the Friday train again this week?"

"Nope. Not this week."

Rachel sat forward. "How come? Just can't be bothered?"

"Olivia has something on this weekend." Airlie didn't want to talk about it, but Rachel appeared more interested than ever.

"You two are just about joined at the hip. I thought she included you in all her stuff?"

"She can hardly include me in her second honeymoon, can she?"

Airlie saw red, many shades of red, all of which were fueled by one other color: green. She stormed out. She'd never been jealous in her life. When other girls flirted with Sam, she'd felt nothing except a sense of validity or reassurance that even though she had never felt complete with him, he must be okay because other girls thought so. She inhaled deeply and calmed herself. It had to end anyway. She was young and single and shouldn't be spending so much time with a happily married woman. There were probably loads of women that were just as much fun as Olivia, and some of them would surely be gay.

Airlie fetched a glass of water. Rachel was loading the dishwasher. "Sorry. I didn't mean to snap."

"That's okay." Rachel put the kettle on. "Did you have something planned this weekend? Is that why you're so upset?"

"Not really. She's been meaning to do the second honeymoon thing for ages." Saying the words left her feeling empty. "I hope they have a good time. They deserve it."

"So, you'll stay in Dublin then?"

"Looks like it. Actually, it's worked out well. I've had a few things to do here for a while, so it will be nice to stay home." There was nothing Airlie needed to do in Dublin that she couldn't have done elsewhere. A weekend without Olivia in Dublin was a lonely prospect.

"Do you fancy going out then?" Rachel blurted it out so quickly, Airlie barely understood.

She stared at her. Sweet, attractive Rachel. A hollow pit of jealousy grew in her stomach. "Sure, I'd love to."

Rachel's eyes popped open. "Really?"

"Sure. Why not."

"Right. Okay then. Do you trust me to organize something for us?"

"Of course. I trust you and I'll be at your mercy." Airlie regretted saying yes already.

"Excellent." Rachel smiled. "Keep Saturday free from about five. Will that give you long enough to do your stuff?"

Airlie nodded, knowing she'd just be in a café somewhere passing time to cover her stupid lie. "Should be plenty of time."

"Great." Rachel stirred her tea.

"What will I wear?"

"Whatever you're comfortable in. Nothing too fancy. I'm sure you'll look good in anything."

Airlie felt better, but the mood was short-lived. She thought of Olivia and Gavin in Paris, romantic evenings, countless beautiful cafés, and incredible food. Then there was the honeymoon component. The sheer thought of them having sex was more than Airlie could bear; the thought of Olivia lying there while he did his business and she faked an orgasm made her cringe. Olivia didn't like sex. She deserved better than that.

Saturday came sooner than anticipated. Olivia left for Paris with Gavin on Thursday, and Airlie attempted to block out all thoughts of them. When they did enter her mind, it was usually a visual of them in bed together, and that sparked an anger she simply didn't want to confront.

With nothing else to do, she lazed about the house, prolonging her time at home and shortening the time she would need to be out on her pretend errands. She cooked a bacon roll for breakfast, watched some TV, read in her room, and come lunchtime, she showered and made herself scarce.

As it turned out, Airlie enjoyed a lovely day pottering around Dublin. It had been such a long time since she had spent time like this on her own. As a light drizzle fell, she made her way to her favorite coffeehouse. It felt like a lifetime ago when she first sat in Sean's For Coffee. She saw the boys during the week occasionally, but because she hadn't been around on weekends lately, they had lost touch.

"Look who it is." Dan rushed over for a hug. "The prodigal friend returns."

Airlie returned the embrace, and they kissed on the cheek.

"Where have you been?" Dan held her at arm's length, looking her up and down.

"I've been around."

"I hear you've been finding yourself in the west."

"Maybe. I guess so."

"Well," he said, kissing her again, "I'm glad you've found yourself here today. Latte?"

"Yes, please." She took a seat near the counter so they could continue chatting while he worked.

"So, a little birdie tells me you've got a hot date with Rachel tonight?"

"I have?"

"That's the rumor." He winked. "You know she likes you, don't you?"

Airlie wasn't sure if this was a question or a statement. She caught his expectant gaze. "Rachel likes everyone." She shrugged.

"Perhaps. But she *really* likes you."

"Should you be telling me this?"

Dan frowned and pulled out the chair opposite her to sit. "I'm not going to ask you if you're gay. I don't have to." Airlie began to interrupt. "Let me finish." His voice was low and possibly the least gay she'd ever heard him speak. He commanded her undivided attention. "This self-discovery you're going through can be as hard or as easy as you want to make it. In one way or another, we've all done it. We've all questioned who we are and who we want to be. There's no right or wrong way to be gay, Airlie. If you strip it down to what it really is, at the end of the day, all that's different is that you're attracted to women, not men. It doesn't make you a bad person—no matter what the hypocritical Catholics think. You're still you. Do you understand me?"

She nodded. She understood perfectly, and in Dan's position, she would probably give the same advice, but she just couldn't relate it to herself. Not yet. She'd spent so long denying who she was; it was taking longer than she expected to accept the truth. Her internal struggle continued, and it was wearing her down.

"Sure, Rachel breezed into being a lesbian. She fell in love with a girl, and it just all made sense. But like everyone else, she's had her moments. I don't know if you've noticed she never talks about her folks. They haven't spoken a word to her since she told them she was gay."

Upon reflection, it was true; Rachel had never mentioned them. "That's awful," Airlie said.

"If nothing else, go out with Rachel tonight and have a good time, but if you like her at all, then lower your guard and let her in. You can trust her with your life. I would. She won't hurt you."

It was good advice, and Airlie was smart enough to take it. Dan went to serve a customer. "Just be you, Airlie."

"Is that enough?"

Dan handed change to the customer and returned to the table. "You're a good-looking girl. You make Rachel laugh, and you're genuine and loyal and have weird taste in just about everything." He smiled. "You're too busy beating yourself up to notice the good bits."

For the remainder of the afternoon, they chatted and drank Dan's amazing coffee. She had only intended to stay for a while, but they were discussing things she wanted to know, or had been too scared to talk about. For the first time in her life, Airlie was having a *real* conversation about being gay. It wasn't like the confessional she'd endured with Olivia. She wasn't upset, and she wasn't telling Dan anything he didn't already know. They were sharing experiences, and Dan tactfully slipped in the odd piece of advice here and there.

"It's a revelation," she said. "But it's daunting at the same time."

"Baby steps." His smile was reassuring. "Our experiences shape our perception. Your relationship experience was with Sam where nothing felt right, so I'm guessing that even though you went through the motions with him, doing exactly what all your friends were doing with their boyfriends, you never felt completely content."

She'd waited for a feeling of completeness that never came.

"You have a quirky and unique perspective on everything but

yourself. Rachel sees glimpses of that and she likes it. She likes you for who you are. You don't have to pretend anymore." He looked at his watch. "Don't you have to be ready by five? It's already four."

She hadn't realized it was so late. "How come you know so much about my night out?"

"I know everything about your *date*, darling, and don't even bother trying to get me to tell. My lips are sealed."

"Can I at least pay for the coffees?"

"No, you most certainly cannot." He ushered her out the door.

"Thanks for the chat. I really appreciate it."

"Don't mention it." They hugged and kissed good-bye before he pushed her onto the footpath. "Have a good night, Airhead."

Worried she might be running late, Airlie caught a cab back to the flat, a ball of excitement swelling in her stomach in anticipation of her night out with Rachel.

## CHAPTER TWENTY-ONE

From the front door, Airlie heard the shower running so she bounded upstairs, two steps at a time. She stole a look at Rachel's bed for any indication of appropriate dress, but nothing had been laid out. She waited for the shower by standing in front of her open wardrobe hoping for a bolt of inspiration.

"Jeans will do."

She turned. Rachel stood in the doorway, hair dripping wet, a towel around her. "And a nice top, maybe."

"Okay. So where are—"

"Don't even bother. It's a surprise. Bathroom's free though." She closed her bedroom door.

Airlie picked her favorite jeans and an insanely expensive top she had bought in Galway a few weeks back with Olivia. Casual but a bit special. It would have to do. Her thoughts wandered to Olivia. She had her own life, and a husband that came first in all she did. Airlie must pave her own way in the world and learn to understand and accept that they would only ever be friends.

All set for her mysterious evening, she took one last glance in the mirror. Her hair was out, the designer layers more prominent after a quick go with the straightener. She'd used makeup, not a lot, and she wore her favorite bronze shade of lip gloss, which she put in her pocket, on hand, to apply throughout the evening. With a deep breath and a final once-over, Airlie conceded that she looked okay, good in fact.

A strong waft of expensive perfume met her on the stairs. In the kitchen, Rachel and Hannah were busy filling three champagne flutes. From a discreet peek, Airlie observed that Rachel looked stunning. Her hair was down, and the tight expensive jeans enhanced her slim figure. A revealing black top accentuated her neckline and cleavage and looked a million dollars under a suede jacket that Airlie had never seen before.

"What's with the champagne?" Airlie attempted to slow her racing pulse.

"Well." Rachel handed her a glass. "First, I'm trying to get you as drunk as possible so I can have my wicked way with you, and second, Hannah and Liam are moving in together."

Airlie hadn't seen that coming. "My God, you're an actual grownup now." She drew Hannah close. "Congratulations. That's excellent news."

"Which bit?" asked Hannah. "Rachel plying you with alcohol or me moving out?"

"Obviously Rachel's underhand tactics are fantastic, but you and Liam moving in together is wonderful." They clinked their glasses in a toast. "When did this all happen?"

"Just last night. He brought it up, not me, and I figure, what the hell."

"You're leaving me," Airlie said sadly.

"You left me ages ago." Hannah pulled her close again. "Plus, you know you'll never really get rid of me."

Airlie pushed her away. "As much as I try."

"As long as you're happy." Rachel refilled her glass. "An extra bit for you, my dear."

With the aid of the champagne, Airlie felt the tension in her shoulders dissolve and her anxiety subside as they discussed when Hannah would be moving out—possibly in the next week or two if all went to plan and Liam continued to behave himself. When the bottle was empty, Rachel threw her car keys at Hannah.

"Hannah's going to drop us off."

"So, can you tell me where we're going yet?"

"Patience, my dear." Rachel took Airlie by the shoulders and led her out.

Airlie allowed herself to be swept away in the moment. She felt flushed by the alcohol, and some of her apprehension was replaced with a warm tingle of excitement. She'd never been on a date quite like this one. She'd never been on a date with a woman before. She felt like the inner workings of a clock. Somehow, all the cogs had shifted into place.

Hannah insisted Airlie and Rachel ride in the back, and before pulling out, took a little peak cap from the glove box and set it on her head. "Do I look like a real chauffeur?" She didn't wait for an answer and turned on the radio.

After cautiously negotiating narrow streets and lane ways that Airlie never knew existed, Hannah parked in a small, secluded alley about three blocks from the fringe of Temple Bar. She glanced around. There didn't appear to be a pub or a restaurant in sight. She observed other cars scattered along the alley, but besides the numerous rubbish bins, the area appeared deserted.

"We're here."

"We are?"

Rachel held the door open. "Thanks for dropping us off, Hannah."

Hannah beeped the horn and weaved carefully out of sight. Airlie and Rachel stood in the middle of what appeared to be a dirty, lifeless alleyway.

Rachel looked Airlie squarely in the eye. "Today's lesson is on appearances. Things aren't always as they seem. The outside doesn't always reflect the inside, and most of the time, it's the inside that counts, right?"

"Okay," Airlie said.

"Shall we?" Rachel held out her hand. "Come on, I won't bite."

Airlie hesitated, but not for long. She wanted to touch Rachel, even though the thought made her childishly nervous. Undeterred by her clammy palms, she took a deep breath and surrendered. As their skin made contact, Airlie was surprised how wonderfully soft and warm Rachel's hand was. It seemed bigger than hers, although it probably wasn't, and Rachel gripped her confidently. Airlie felt like she could follow her anywhere in the world.

They walked deeper into the alley until they came upon an enormous navy blue wooden gate. As they stepped through, Airlie felt her jaw drop. In front of her was a wall of glass about twenty meters in length. Beyond the glass was a glowing room filled with people and art. "Is this where we're going?" It looked incredible.

"Sure is." Rachel took her hand again, this time without asking. "It's the Liquid Art Gallery. Tonight is the opening of three exhibitions in photography, painting, and sculpture." She smiled at Airlie. "The theme is love."

Airlie was impressed. "Do you come to these things often?"

"Sometimes. Although in fairness, I was only invited to this because my cousin is one of the artists. She should be here somewhere."

"Amazing." Airlie skipped toward the entrance, pulling Rachel with her. The gallery was wonderful, the people were remarkable, and Airlie felt deliciously comfortable in the stimulating atmosphere. Rachel seemed to know quite a few people, and she introduced Airlie to everyone she spoke to.

Airlie met some of the talented artists, including Rachel's cousin, and spoke at length with many of them, discussing mediums, inspirations, and endless views on what love really was. Airlie turned as a gentle hand rested on her lower back.

"You having a good time?" asked Rachel.

Airlie pointed at a piece depicting religion, sexuality, and science. "I love this one. It's just one contradiction after another."

"Some people are like that."

"Maybe they're confused."

"Or scared?"

Airlie smiled. "Or they were scared, but not so much anymore."

Rachel scooped two glasses from a waiter and handed one to Airlie. "Do you want to stay round for the official bit?"

Airlie hesitated. She couldn't bear it if the night ended now, and she couldn't remember the last time she desperately wanted the night to continue. She hedged her bets, relying on Rachel having something else planned. "Not if you don't. I'm okay to leave when you're ready."

"Excellent. Let's go. We have a dinner reservation at eight."

"We do?"

"Yes, and I'm starving. Drink up." They snuck away, Rachel's arm remaining lightly on the small of Airlie's back.

Airlie was abuzz with a pleasure she hadn't experienced in a long time. If she were being honest, her ego was also enjoying the attention. Flattery, it seemed, was her weakness. She could feel herself being drawn to Rachel. The sensation excited her.

In the sharp autumn evening, surrounded again by bins in the alley, they walked in the direction of the Liffey River. Unable to gather the courage to take Rachel's hand, Airlie took hers from the safety of her pocket, hoping to encourage Rachel to initiate contact again. When at last she did, her touch sent heat through her. Longing for the inevitable next step, Airlie was ready. She stole a glance at Rachel's glossy lips and nearly lost her footing on the uneven pavement. Rachel gripped her hand tighter and smiled, continuing an easy conversation about art.

Within minutes, they turned left and then right again and found themselves in the bustling Temple Bar, swept along with hordes of people, enjoying the thriving Dublin restaurant scene.

Airlie stiffened amongst the crowd. This was the first time she'd been openly gay in public. This was the first time anybody looking at her would know, for certain, she was a lesbian. Her senses were heightened, and she was convinced people were staring. She fought the urge to wrench her hand from Rachel's and jam it safely in her pocket.

"You okay?" Rachel could read her like a book. Or maybe she was just easy to read. "People might look, but chances are they don't care."

Airlie sucked in the chilled air. Rachel was right. Her panic subsided.

Before long, a young group of boys yelled from a first-floor window. "Can we watch?"

Rachel laughed. "See, you're a celebrity."

"Why do I feel like they're about to throw rotten eggs at me, then?"

"They've just spent the last cash they had buying weed, as if they have a rotten egg to spare."

Airlie laughed despite herself.

"We can stop holding hands if you'd prefer?"

"No way." Airlie felt a brave burst of defiance. "I wouldn't give them the satisfaction."

"Is that the only reason?"

"No." Airlie stopped to look Rachel in the eye. "I don't want you to stop holding my hand. I don't want you to stop doing anything you want to do."

They walked another block in silence, dodging throngs of people jostling to read menus posted in restaurant windows. Without warning, Rachel directed Airlie into a secluded doorway.

"What do *you* want me to do?"

"Pardon?"

"You said you don't want me to stop doing anything I want to do, and I fully understand I'll be making the moves here. But what do *you* want me to do?"

"Right now, I want you to kiss me." Her eyes met Rachel's. She was trembling.

Rachel stepped close and softly touched her cheek. The scrutiny was embarrassing. Airlie broke eye contact and lowered her head. Rachel leaned in and brushed Airlie's lips with hers. So soft was the contact, that if it wasn't for Rachel's warm breath, Airlie might never have known it happened. She closed her eyes, and Rachel kissed her again, firmly this time, her arm slipping around Airlie's waist, holding her tightly.

This kiss was nothing like Edinburgh. Christ, if Airlie had reacted this way in Edinburgh, she'd have probably been naked within seconds. Her entire body responded as if awakening from a deep sleep. Airlie had never felt this way kissing anybody. Ever. Losing herself, she returned the embrace. Rachel's tongue entered her mouth. Airlie caressed the curves of Rachel's back and her tight bottom. This amazing kiss lingered for a long time.

When Rachel struggled to pull away, she explained to Airlie there was plenty of time for that whenever she liked, but for now they had dinner reservations and it was rude to be late.

The kiss was, by far, the single sexiest experience Airlie had had in her life. She reminded herself that the night was young.

The restaurant Rachel had chosen was Italian—Airlie's favorite—and like the gallery, it was nestled in an obscure location amongst old brick buildings in another alleyway and up a flight of stairs. The meal was delicious, and they sat at a cozy corner table, surrounded by expensive and well-kept plants. The dimly lit, charming dining room was decorated with rich red, brown, and green tones. The walls were scattered with hundreds of small framed pictures. Plied with fabulously authentic Italian dishes, they drank and talked for what felt like hours, before Rachel declared it was time to leave.

"We're going home?"

"We most certainly are not." Rachel frowned. "Unless you want an early night?"

Airlie was beginning to wonder if Rachel wasn't deliberately trying to make her cheeks flush. She had a wave of courage pass through her and wanted to say, "Yes, please take me home and take me to bed," but her bravery disappeared as quickly as it arrived. Instead, she giggled and allowed Rachel to take her hand and lead her to the next mystery venue. *Smooth, Porter. Real smooth.*

Feeling like a teenager in love, or perhaps lust, for the first time, Airlie was consumed with the thought of kissing Rachel, and although Rachel had leisurely taken her hand, courage eluded her, and the moment passed as they turned onto a busy street again. Within ten minutes, Rachel stopped at the door of the bar Airlie had seen months before. It was the Dungeon. A gay bar.

"You ready to dance your socks off?" asked Rachel.

"Sure, let's do it."

The club was enormous, with people everywhere. Men with men, women with women, women with men. It was nothing like Airlie expected. For some misguided reason, she'd expected it to be sleazy and dirty. She was wrong again.

"Drink?" Rachel yelled over the music.

Airlie nodded. The diversity in ages amazed her. Some people barely looked old enough to drink, while others appeared to be her mum and dad's age. At the bar, Rachel sat and pulled another stool close for her.

"You've never been to a gay bar before, have you?"

"Am I that obvious?"

"No, but you look like a kid let loose in a chocolate factory."

"I'm quite selective when it comes to chocolate."

"I see. You don't just go stuffing your face with any old cheap rubbish then?"

"It's not really my style, plus I don't think you have to eat *all* the chocolates to know what they taste like."

Rachel slipped her hand onto Airlie's knee, moving to kiss her. To suggest Airlie was aroused was an understatement. The slightest touch from Rachel left her tingling and desperate for more. They talked, drank, and kissed until Rachel suggested a dance.

The dance floor was a crowded, heaving mass of people, enthusiastically appearing to participate in a standing, fully clothed orgy. This was no time to be precious about personal space, and as a song came on that was obviously one of Rachel's favorites, she hauled Airlie into the middle of the sweaty dance pit where there was no room, just body heat and the smell of active deodorant.

Rachel pulled her close. They danced for a long time, becoming entranced with the music and each other. Their kisses became longer and deeper. Rachel's hands began to explore Airlie's body, just as her tongue had explored her mouth. Rachel's hand slid beneath Airlie's top and caressed her back. Skin on skin sent her legs to jelly. Airlie sank deeper into the embrace, and in response, Rachel's hand moved inside the back of her jeans.

Airlie was aroused with a painful ache in her crotch, so when Rachel pulled her to the rear of the room and pushed her against the wall, breathlessly whispering that she wanted to take her home, Airlie eagerly kissed her.

"I don't think you understand. I *really* want to take you home." Rachel paused. "To my bed."

Airlie at last found some courage. "I understand perfectly. Take me."

## CHAPTER TWENTY-TWO

The taxi ride home was a blur. Beyond all the kissing, breathlessness, and fondling, Airlie was terrified. It all seemed so simple in the club—two adults sharing a need the other could fulfill. She berated herself for simplifying the issue, then again for complicating it. She remembered what Dan had said, that it could be as easy or as difficult as she made it. She relinquished control and let Rachel push her tongue deep in her mouth. They continued to kiss while the driver glanced in the rearview mirror more often than necessary for safe driving.

Airlie remembered what Rachel had said in Edinburgh. That she didn't want to be her first. The words filled her mind. Was this a test? She had to come clean, before it went too far.

Hannah and Liam were home, his car on the street outside, and it proved impossible to enter the house quietly, no matter how hard they tried. First, the door slammed, then Airlie stumbled knee-first into the hallstand, knocking the telephone clean off, sending it crashing to the floor. Hannah's door opened.

"Is that you two?" Liam's deep voice croaked.

"Hi, Liam, yes, it's us. Sorry about that. No harm done. Sorry." Rachel attempted a convincing sober tone.

Rachel's room was dark until she fumbled on her dresser to light a candle before closing the curtains. Airlie looked on, nervously alive with sensations she had only ever dreamed about. She could fake many things, but this wasn't one of them. Rachel crossed the room to her, and before she could take her in outstretched arms, Airlie blurted out her semi-rehearsed speech. "You'll be my first."

"What?"

"I'm sorry. I should have told you. I know what you said in Edinburgh. I know I've misled you, but I want this, I really do. Why do you have to put me through this with someone else? Why can't it be with you?"

The desperation in her voice scared her. She was ready. The next step was here, in front of her, and she was ready to take it. "Please, Rachel?"

Rachel lifted a finger to Airlie's lips. "Hush." She took her in her arms.

Airlie began to cry. The thought of the night ending now was unfathomable. She couldn't get this close and not go through with it. She wanted to be with Rachel, and although tears streamed over her cheeks, it wasn't sadness she was experiencing.

"Forget what I said in Edinburgh. It was stupid, and it was because of something that happened in my past. You're not my past. I want this to happen tonight, between us. Is that what you want?"

"It's what I want. I'm certain." She lowered her eyes, hoping the truth would set her free. "But I'm terrified. Maybe I should have more to drink."

"I promise you, you don't need any more to drink."

"Just one?"

"Just nothing."

Rachel didn't kiss her immediately, but touched her, running her hands slowly over her back, caressing her bottom. Eventually, her hand slid under Airlie's top, and she skillfully released her bra clasp.

Airlie felt lightheaded, and it wasn't from lack of oxygen; she was breathing deeper by the second.

Rachel's hand glided over Airlie's skin, maneuvering beneath her bra, gently touching her breast. Airlie flinched. At last, a woman was touching her in ways she'd only ever imagined. It was exquisite, it was sensual, and no fantasy could have prepared her for how she was feeling, how she knew she was reacting, and how wet and ready she was.

At last, Rachel kissed her and Airlie thought she'd died and gone to heaven.

"Look at me," Rachel said. "Airlie, look at me."

Airlie focused on Rachel's intense brown eyes. She thought how beautiful they were, how rich in color. Without breaking eye contact,

Rachel lifted Airlie's top over her head and removed her bra. Airlie let her. She hoped her submission and the desire in her eyes reassured Rachel she wanted to go all the way. The intense stare remained while Rachel unbuttoned Airlie's jeans.

Playfully, Rachel pushed her onto the bed, straddling her while removing her own top and bra. She exposed perfect pale breasts, and they were the most beautiful thing Airlie had ever seen. Rachel's soft lips kissed down Airlie's body, to her neck, her chest, and she took a nipple in her mouth. Airlie's back arched, and the yearning between her legs sent her body writhing.

Airlie released all inhibitions. She pulled Rachel to her and caressed her breasts; they felt so perfect, so appropriate in her hands. Timidly, she lifted one into her mouth. Rachel moaned as the nipple hardened.

Rachel slid her hand between Airlie's legs. Even through her jeans, the touch was exhilarating. Airlie reached a heightened state of desire that escalated when the hand slid inside her jeans, gently massaging through her underpants. At last, Rachel's hand found flesh, and her fingers plunged deep inside.

Within seconds, Airlie experienced her first explosion of absolute satisfaction.

## CHAPTER TWENTY-THREE

The morning after was never a time or place Airlie particularly enjoyed. Quite often, Sam would have woken with an erection, along with the fanciful hope of starting the morning as the night had ended. By that stage, however, Airlie was stone cold sober and not interested.

The morning after with Rachel was different. First, she woke alone in the bed, and second, she was completely naked. Airlie never slept naked, but Rachel had explored every inch of her body, so this morning there shouldn't have been any need to feel insecure.

There was no clock, so Airlie leaned over the edge of the bed to find her jacket and check the time on her phone. It was 10:23 a.m., and she had received a text message. Her initial instincts told her it would be from Rachel.

She was wrong. The satisfying aftermath of the previous night disappeared. She read the words over and over again. "Wish you were here." The sentence was finished with a small cartoon picture of the Eiffel Tower.

Olivia was on her second honeymoon. She had no right to wish Airlie was anywhere near her. Exactly which part did she wish Airlie was there for? Why was she even thinking about Airlie? She threw the phone back to the floor.

Airlie studied Rachel's room. Suddenly, it all felt wrong. She fled across the hall, pulled on her nightshirt, and crawled into her cold, unwelcoming bed. Rachel had left without a word, and it felt inappropriate to remain where she obviously wasn't wanted. Airlie snuggled deep and pulled the covers to her chin. It had been too good to be true. Rachel hadn't wanted to be there when she woke. The harsh reality gripped the seed of self-doubt in her stomach and twisted it violently. She tried to think about what she'd done wrong. Of course, the sex was going to be lousy, it was her first time with a woman, but she'd tried to be attentive, tried to give as good as Rachel had given her. If this was the outcome of sleeping with a woman, it wasn't any better than a man. Caring for someone inevitably hurt. Airlie hurt.

Sleep hadn't been a priority last night, and within minutes of sobbing into her pillow, Airlie drifted into a deep slumber.

The first thing she registered upon rousing was her throbbing head. This was new. She didn't remember feeling unwell before. The second thing she registered was someone saying her name.

"Airlie, what are you doing in here?"

It was Rachel. The morning came flooding back. Reluctantly, she opened her eyes.

Rachel stroked the hair from her forehead. "Good morning."

She blinked before focusing. "Good morning, yourself."

"Do you know where you are?"

"I thought you'd left."

"Left?"

"Gone out or something." Airlie pushed thoughts of Olivia's message from her mind.

"Gone out where?"

"I don't know." She felt stupid. "I guess I didn't know what to think."

"Let's get one thing straight," Rachel's tone was serious, "I wouldn't, and will never, go out and just leave you in my bed, without at the very least kissing you good-bye."

"Forgive me?"

"I cooked you breakfast, if you're hungry?"

"Is that where you were? Making breakfast?"

Rachel nodded, but her expression conveyed disappointment.

"I'm so sorry. I'm not very good at all this."

"You're very good at some of the bits. And you're forgiven."

Airlie knew she was blushing.

"You just have to learn to trust me. Why didn't you at least come and look for me?"

It was a good question. Why didn't she? "Because I'm an idiot."

Olivia's message echoed in her mind. She hated that it could affect her this way. "I guess I convinced myself that you didn't want to see me. That leaving was what I was supposed to do." She inhaled deeply. "I panicked. I'm sorry. I honestly don't know what I'm supposed to do."

"Right, well, you're *supposed* to trust me, but I understand that might take some time." She smiled. "I'll earn your trust. I promise."

"Maybe I need to trust myself."

"Start with me." Rachel kissed her forehead. "I'm a sure bet." She stood and stretched, her T-shirt rising to reveal just enough to cause a tingling sensation between Airlie's legs.

"Hungry?"

Airlie nodded.

"I'm afraid breakfast can only be served in my bed, and to be granted admission, you have to lose the nightshirt."

"It's a small price to pay."

"Oh, it's not the price. You can pay after you've eaten."

Airlie raised her eyebrows before bursting into laughter.

"Too much?" asked Rachel. "A bit porn star-ish?" Airlie nodded. "Yeah, I thought so." She grabbed Airlie by the hand and dragged her back to the adjacent room where breakfast waited on a tray by the bed.

As Airlie stuffed the last of the toast in her mouth, she sensed the closeness of Rachel's naked body, and it invoked memories from last night, the gallery, dinner, the club, and then the remainder of the evening in bed. In a flourish of confidence, she snuggled down as Rachel held her close and began slowly stroking her breast. There was little chance of anything but a repeat of last night's enchantment, and by mid-afternoon, they were spent and sound asleep in each other's arms.

That evening, as the streets became silent, and with the lingering taste of Rachel still dancing on Airlie's tongue, she lay reading on her bed, relaxed and content, when Hannah poked her head in.

"I thought you might be asleep?"

"No, just taking some time out. Come in," said Airlie.

Hannah struggled to suppress her grin. She stood with the door closed behind her. "So, how was last night?"

"Please, God, never take up professional poker."

"What? Why?"

"Could you be more obvious? Your face is a dead giveaway."

Acknowledgment of her sole purpose for being in Airlie's room was evidently all she needed before rushing to the bed excitedly. "Tell me everything."

"Everything?"

"Okay, well maybe not everything. I reckon I can fill in the blanks. So, how was it?"

"Good. Great, really."

"And...how was Rachel?"

"She was good."

"And by good you mean?"

"We had a nice time."

Hannah's eyes flicked toward the bed. "But how was she? I mean really. How was she?"

"You're disgusting."

"I bet she's hot naked. You can just tell."

"This is our friend you're talking about. Show a little respect."

Hannah flopped on the bed. "Just give me something. Anything?"

Airlie let out a long whistle. "She was fucking unbelievable."

"I knew it!"

"It just feels so right. It's hard to explain. It was *nothing* like with Sam. It turns out I don't hate sex after all. I was just doing it with the wrong person."

"Oh my God, you did it? The whole shebang?"

"Shoosh. She'll hear you."

"I thought you might have just fooled around, kissed a bit?"

"There's only a few centimeters between fooling and fucking, you know?"

Hannah flung her hands over her ears. "Okay. That's enough."

"Don't you want to hear how many times she made me come?"

Hannah rushed to the door. "Leaving now."

"What about what she tastes like?" Airlie heard Hannah thump down the stairs humming loudly.

"What who tastes like?" Rachel appeared.

"Jelly Babies," Airlie blurted. She shrugged. It was plausible.

"Really?"

"No."

"Do I need to remind you what I taste like?"

Airlie choked on her own saliva.

"I'm going to shower. I suggest you find your way to my bed. Naked. I'll be there in five." Rachel disappeared from sight.

As soon as Airlie remembered to breathe again, she discarded her pajamas and dashed through to Rachel's room. She didn't need to be told twice.

## CHAPTER TWENTY-FOUR

Rachel was unlike anyone Airlie had ever experienced. She had the ability to seduce and make love to Airlie, setting her free night after night. Never in her life had Airlie actually desired anyone intimately. Finally experiencing these feelings was something of a revelation. At last, women were sexy, Rachel was sexy, and emotionally, Airlie had stepped up to a wonderful new level.

The feelings she harbored for Olivia began to dissolve, and the reality of their situation was no longer a bitter pill to swallow. Olivia was a married woman who more than likely experienced a romantic and nostalgic second honeymoon. She was relieved; Olivia was a friend, a dear friend, but Rachel was her lover, and that seemed the natural way of things. Without the need for verbal confirmation, Airlie and Rachel slipped comfortably into a serious relationship.

On the eve of their six-week anniversary, life was good. Airlie was cooking dinner while Rachel poured wine and talked enthusiastically about her day. Then the doorbell rang.

"You need to tell Hannah to just use her damn key," Rachel said.

"She's worried she might interrupt something if she just barges in."

"She can barge in loudly. Hell, she used to when she lived here. What's changed?" Rachel ambled toward the door.

Airlie smiled. Everything had changed.

"Babe, your friend Olivia is here," called Rachel.

*Olivia?*

Since Olivia had returned from Paris, contact had been minimal. So minimal, in fact, Airlie had avoided telling her about Rachel. Of course it never popped up in conversation. She'd never even hinted to Olivia that she was actively looking for a girlfriend, and Airlie had been too yellow-bellied to come straight out and tell her.

Now Olivia was at the door and Rachel had called her babe.

*Shit. Shit. Shit.*

Rachel ushered Olivia through to the kitchen saying how lovely it was to finally meet her. One look and Airlie knew Olivia didn't share the sentiment. Olivia was caught off guard. Airlie embraced her, but the return hug was feeble and brief.

She looked at the chili simmering on the stove. "I'd have made more of an effort if I knew you were coming."

"I'm not staying. I just called in."

"You drove four hours just to call in?"

"I've been at a work thing. A conference." Olivia avoided eye contact. "I just thought I'd call in on the way home."

Airlie looked her up and down. She was wearing jeans and a jumper—hardly conference attire. It was possible she changed for the journey home, but she wasn't convinced. "Where did you stay?"

"What?"

"The hotel? Which one?"

Olivia hesitated.

Airlie waited.

"The Westbury."

Rachel seemed oblivious to the awkward exchange and was busy pouring an extra glass of wine. "I hear they renovated there recently," she said.

Olivia gulped the wine. "Yes. I think they have."

Airlie stared. She had no proof, nor did she intend to seek any, but something told her Olivia was lying. She'd have wagered her left arm that there had been no conference and that Olivia had driven to Dublin that afternoon.

"So, how long have you two been together?" Olivia's tone was sharp. Rachel carried on, but Airlie didn't miss it.

She wanted to ask her why it mattered. Why it was any of her business? Why did she send that message when she was in Paris? Why, since returning from Paris, had Olivia happily been playing husband and wife with Gavin, when it clearly hadn't interested her while Airlie was around? Airlie felt like Olivia was avoiding her, but then, maybe she was guilty of that, too. After all, she'd made no real effort to tell Olivia about Rachel. "Will you excuse me?" She thrust the wooden spoon toward Rachel, leaving her to answer the question. Airlie escaped to the bathroom and locked the door. She leaned heavily against the cool timber.

The truth would probably never surface, but she felt sure Olivia's visit was meant to be a surprise. Hell, anyone driving four hours to see you was a big effort. Six weeks ago, Airlie would have burst with excitement. She could only imagine the look on Olivia's face when Rachel called her *babe*. The thought troubled her, but she knew it shouldn't matter. She was with Rachel now, and she *was* Rachel's babe. Whatever was going on with Olivia would either be revealed over dinner or remain a mystery.

She splashed cold water on her face. The chilly liquid snapped her out of her self-absorbed state. What if there was something wrong? What if Olivia was in some sort of trouble? She stared at her reflection and wondered how she managed to have an entire thought process that centered around *her* feelings before she even considered Olivia's. If there was one thing she was learning to accept, it was that not everything revolved around her sexuality. One of the countless pitfalls of living in denial for so long was the self-centered, insular thinking that absorbs you when only you know a secret. It wasn't until Rachel pointed it out that Airlie realized it was happening.

Not everyone had an opinion on her sexuality, not everyone stared at her and thought she was gay, not everyone was homophobic and repulsed by her, and certainly not everyone cared who she slept with behind closed doors. Olivia's appearance might be nothing to do with her at all.

She pulled herself together and returned to the kitchen. "We have a spare bed if you'd like to stay the night," she said.

Olivia shook her head. "No, thanks. As I said, I'm just passing through." She glanced at her watch.

Airlie got the impression that dinner couldn't come and go quickly enough. She tasted the rice. It was nearly cooked. "Are you sure you're okay?" She smiled warmly and genuinely. "It seems like we haven't seen each other in ages."

Olivia's shoulders dropped slightly. She briefly returned the smile. "I'm fine, honestly. It's just been a busy week. Can you excuse me for a moment while I call Gav and let him know my movements?" She escaped to the hallway.

Airlie frowned. Olivia had never bothered to call Gavin in the past. As far as she knew, they shared an understanding that the only time a call was expected was when neither of them was returning home to sleep. Olivia had made it clear she wasn't staying, so why did Gav need to know her movements? Perhaps it was something that had rekindled after the second honeymoon. Perhaps it wasn't. Curiosity won out, and while Rachel busied herself with cutlery and crockery, Airlie slipped into the hallway.

"—sorry, I'm going to have to cancel my reservation for tonight. Eight o'clock." Olivia was whispering. She sounded impatient. "Yes, for two people. Swanson is the name."

Airlie swallowed hard. Olivia had arranged a night out, and although she knew it was necessary from Olivia's point of view to save face, the fact remained, she was lying to her, and none of it was making sense. Had she not have known better, a surprise visit and dinner reservations could certainly be construed as romantic, but why would Olivia need to be romantic with her? She dismissed the notion. Why would Olivia *want* to be romantic?

Airlie returned to the kitchen, grabbing a candle from the hallstand on her way. The pretense of searching for a candle was the best cover-up she could manage under the circumstances. "I knew it was there somewhere." She held the candle aloft. "My favorite candle."

"It is?" Rachel was dishing up.

"Yeah. I told you how much I like," she read the label on the bottom, "mandarin and vanilla." She hated vanilla.

"You did?"

Olivia walked in and glanced over her shoulder. "So that's definitely not your candle then. You always say vanilla reminds you of public toilets."

Rachel paused and stared.

"What did I say?" asked Olivia.

"That's her favorite candle."

Olivia shrugged. "Well, it must be the mandarin because she can't stand vanilla, can you?"

Airlie stumbled on her words.

Olivia continued. "I had to change perfumes because she hates vanilla so much. Do you remember that?" Olivia seemed amused. She was the only one. "You said if we were going to spend so much time together, I'd have to stop stinking like an ice cream van."

Airlie remembered. Of course she remembered.

"And we shopped in Galway that afternoon for my new perfume. Do you remember? You made me buy your favorite except it was men's perfume, or whatever they call the stuff men wear to smell nice."

"I thought Pride and Joy was your favorite perfume?" asked Rachel.

Pride and Joy was Airlie's second favorite perfume. In fact, she only liked those two perfumes. All the rest smelled too sickly or too flowery. She liked spicy, and she liked those two in particular. She'd bought Pride and Joy for Rachel, and she'd talked Olivia into purchasing the other. Two sets of expectant eyes stared at her.

"What can I say? I like what I like." It was a politician's answer.

"But which one is your favorite?" Olivia asked. "When did you get yours, Rachel?"

Olivia was turning the issue into a competition. A competition she knew she would win.

"We can stand here all night and discuss the scents I most enjoy or we can eat dinner and relax. Which is it to be?" asked Airlie.

Rachel lowered her eyes and turned away.

Olivia smiled, but it wasn't a warm smile. It was a sign that she'd just won the pissing competition. Airlie had to let it go. Rachel's body language had changed. She was suddenly stiff and swift in her movements, and it wasn't fair to pursue a discussion out of principle when the outcome would only hurt her.

Airlie bit her lip and counted to ten. "Shall we go through to the dining room?"

There was no meaningful conversation over dinner, just empty small talk that everyone knew was ignorant but necessary. Within barely a polite time frame after they cleared the dishes, Olivia made her excuses and left. Rachel said it had been nice to meet her, but even a deaf person would have known she didn't mean it.

"Why is a married woman jealous of me because I'm with you?" asked Rachel.

Airlie had hoped once Olivia left they could enjoy a lazy Friday evening together. She was wrong.

"I don't think she's jealous. She has nothing to be jealous about. I just think she was a little put out because I'd not told her we were together."

"And why is that?"

Why indeed? Airlie wasn't sure she knew the reason. It just seemed too difficult, too complicated, and too much hassle that she could do without. She hated confrontation, so while it was no surprise she'd not told Olivia, it was understandably a surprise to Rachel. "We haven't spoken all that much lately." That wasn't a lie. She felt it was a good start.

"Do you like her?"

"No." That was a lie. *Shit.* "I did. Well, I think I did." There were many things Airlie hated herself for, but she'd never been a liar.

"She's married."

"I know. Which is exactly why I realized it was stupid for me to become more infatuated than I already was. She's happily married. Gav's a nice bloke. I think I was just getting carried away with accepting I was gay. She was hugely supportive at the time. I kind of latched on to that, and it went a bit weird for me for a while. It's not weird now though." She kissed Rachel tenderly. "There was something there once, but it's not there now. I promise. Olivia and I are just friends. That's all we'll ever be."

"Have you ever kissed her or anything?"

"Whoa, no, seriously, she's a happily married woman. I swear, whatever went on was only in my head, not hers and it certainly wasn't anything I acted upon."

Rachel seemed satisfied, and Airlie relaxed in the relief that the truth was out. There was no longer anything between them. It felt good. She sighed. Almost the truth.

Rachel ran a firm hand the length Airlie's neck and over her breasts. "Early night?"

Airlie nodded. Under the circumstances, it was the least she could do.

## Chapter Twenty-five

Months flew by, and Christmas was suddenly around the corner. The silly season had certainly begun. Airlie remained in her job, and her boss had worked tirelessly to eventually gain her permanency in a supervisory role. He'd persuaded management to sponsor Airlie, and the process of pushing the application through the system was commenced in time for her visa renewal the following February.

In December, there were more functions to attend than there were days available, and they decided to spend Christmas evening at their place with Hannah, Liam, Dan, and Sean.

The dynamic between Olivia and Airlie had naturally shifted. It wasn't appropriate for Airlie to travel to see her anymore, and regardless, she wanted to spend her weekends with Rachel. She missed Olivia, they were good friends, but life carried on.

Because her visits had all but ceased, she made a point of phoning Olivia at least once a week. She reclined on the couch, her feet in Rachel's lap, and dialed Olivia's number.

"I'm glad you called."

Airlie didn't even have a chance to say hello.

"I know it's late notice, but what are you doing for Christmas Day? You and Rachel, I mean."

Airlie had contemplated raising the subject with Rachel and discuss inviting Olivia and Gavin over for Christmas, after all, they knew Hannah as well, but she kept putting it off. In the end, she justified her lack of enthusiasm by convincing herself that if Olivia wanted to spend Christmas Day together, she would have asked. With less than a week to go, it was too little too late.

"Sorry, but we've arranged to have Christmas evening at ours."

Rachel's head snapped in her direction.

Airlie shrugged, and with her eyes, tried to ask Rachel if she could extend the invitation to Olivia and Gavin.

Rachel understood and finally nodded before returning her attention to the television. Her nod of approval contradicted her look of disappointment.

"Sorry. I thought it might be too late. We've only just decided what we're doing," Olivia said.

"You're welcome to come to ours. It won't be lavish or anything, just a roast dinner and plenty of wine."

"I'll check with Gavin."

Airlie heard a rustling in her ear. Olivia was holding the phone's microphone to her chest. She wished she could hear the conversation.

"We appreciate the offer, but it's a long drive. He seems keen to stay at home. Maybe next year."

Airlie experienced relief and disappointment simultaneously. "Maybe Easter? Keep up with the religious theme of the occasion." It was meant to be a joke, but Olivia didn't seem to get it. Perhaps it was a Catholic thing.

"Well, I hope I see you before Easter," Olivia said. "It's been too long as it is."

Airlie wondered if Olivia genuinely thought that. The last time had been awkward at best. Maybe next time would be better.

"Have you made any plans for New Year's Eve yet?" said Airlie.

This time Rachel glared at her. "What are you doing? We haven't discussed the new year."

Airlie shrugged. She wondered how often she could shrug before Rachel became tired of the apologetic gesture.

"Nothing solid planned. Probably just the usual. I'll go out and Gav will stay in. Why?"

"Come to Dublin. It'll be fun. You and Gav, of course. Have a night on the lash in the big smoke."

"I'll run it by him. I think it would be great. We'd get to know Rachel better, too."

Rachel, who was still eyeing her, looked anything but pleased.

When Airlie ended the call, she knew she was in trouble. She had no excuse, so didn't bother making one up. "Sorry. I know I should have spoken to you first. It kind of just came out. I guess I wasn't thinking."

Rachel's eyes softened. "I don't mind having to spend time with them. Until I came along, Olivia was a big part of your life. But in the future, can we discuss those things before you go inviting all and sundry to something we haven't even yet organized ourselves?"

Airlie nodded. She grinned. "Can we play some Christmas carols?"

"You're such a child."

"We can play your favorite album if you like." Airlie snuggled close.

"I do not have a favorite Christmas album."

"Yes, you do. You just can't admit it yet." Airlie kissed her. "Repeat after me, I love the old crooners."

Rachel pinned her to the sofa. "How about you repeat after me, Rachel darling, take me to bed and fuck me."

Who was Airlie to argue with that.

❖

Tired of Airlie's incessant complaints about always being cold, Rachel surprised her with an early Christmas present, a warm woolen jumper and two thermal tops. Unfortunately, there was only the slightest chance of a white Christmas, but it was absolutely freezing and both Airlie and Hannah felt chilled to the bone, never remembering ever being so cold. With no idea what to buy Rachel at all, let alone for an early gift, Airlie left work one lunchtime and snuck home to decorate the house. She left the tree until last, wanting to share that with Rachel, but the rest of the flat looked stunning. To create atmosphere, she bought fairy lights, although during installation, she had to rush to the corner store on three separate occasions for supplies—tacks, electrical tape, and candles to complete the effect. When Rachel arrived home, Airlie met her at the door with a piece of cheap plastic mistletoe and a drink. That evening they decorated the tree, switched on the fairy lights, and played Christmas carols as they snuggled by the fire.

❖

Christmas evening was a hoot. After Airlie and Rachel's quiet day, spent mostly in bed, the gang joined them for the evening. They took turns showing off their gifts and exchanging even more.

Rachel said buying for Airlie was easy, and first thing that morning, excited beyond what should be normal for a thirty-one-year-old, she presented Airlie with a small framed painting, one of Airlie's favorites from the opening night at the gallery. Airlie thought it was possibly the most thoughtful gift she'd ever received.

Airlie had struggled to even think of one idea for Rachel, and it was actually Olivia who'd suggested a spa voucher; Rachel was constantly bemoaning her aching bones and had been intending to book a day of pampering for some time. Airlie was a lousy masseuse, so it was the perfect gift. For something a little more personal, Airlie downloaded some of her favorite songs and made a CD for her. They were mostly love songs, and Rachel thought it was cute. Instead of lunch, they made love listening to the CD.

The following day, St. Stephen's Day, was a complete write-off. Their guests left early, opting to relax and enjoy their gifts in their own space, and Rachel and Airlie rugged up, and despite the bitter cold and relentless drizzle, took a long walk, hand in hand, around Dublin. Nothing was open of course, but it seemed others had the same idea, and Airlie found the cold air invigorating after their Christmas hibernation.

Cold and wet, they trudged through the front door, ready to run a bath when Rachel's phone rang. Airlie's ears pricked up when she detected anxiousness in her tone.

Hand on hip, Rachel frowned. "When? Okay, right. Well, it's a bit late for that now. No, I didn't know. How would I know that?"

Airlie rushed to her and mouthed words of concern. Rachel rolled her eyes and shook her head before continuing. "Not today. I'll come in the morning. As if one more day will make a difference at this stage. Okay, bye."

"Is everything all right? It didn't sound good. Who was it?"

"That was my dad."

"Your dad?"

"Yep, my caring and sharing dad." She sighed. "My mother's in hospital. She's had some sort of stroke. I'm sorry, but I'm going to have to go down there tomorrow."

"Oh my God, is she bad? Well, of course you have to go. I'll come with you."

"That's not a good idea."

"Why? I want to come with you."

"The reason my parents don't speak to me is because I'm gay. I have no intention of letting them anywhere near you."

"Sorry. I forgot." She hugged Rachel. "I'm sure she'll be fine. Will you be okay about seeing them again?"

"He didn't have to call, I suppose."

"No, I guess not. Will they at least be civil to you?" Airlie was yet to tell her parents she was a lesbian. They'd be shocked, but she hoped they wouldn't disown her. Rachel had probably thought her parents would come around eventually, but look how that had turned out.

"Trust me, we've exhausted all the shit conversations that surrounded me coming out. The only thing they know now is how to avoid the topic and be civil. I'll be fine."

Airlie knew Rachel hated being the stereotypical Catholic Irish girl whose folks couldn't cope with her sexuality. The situation did little to hasten her own coming out.

## CHAPTER TWENTY-SIX

On December thirtieth—the day Rachel was to return from Waterford—her ailing mother suffered another minor stroke, and as a result was not discharged from hospital as expected. If it hadn't been for the fact that her mother had offered an olive branch, Rachel would surely have left Waterford and returned home in time to enjoy New Year's Eve.

"Will Olivia and Gavin still come down?" asked Rachel. "I don't want to ruin New Year's."

Apparently, Gavin had taken some convincing, but Olivia had persuaded him to travel to Dublin for the New Year celebrations.

"I'll call her to discuss it. It's the least of your worries. Don't give it a second thought."

"I really wanted to see the New Year in with you. Honestly, Air Bear, I'm not convinced my family possess the right, after all these years, to instigate any form of treaty."

Airlie wasn't convinced either, given the appalling treatment Rachel had received in the past. It was her elder sister who'd orchestrated the reconciliation, and although they'd remained in contact over the years, it was strained. Her sister had lived and worked in Waterford all her life, never traveling farther abroad than London on just one occasion, and while she apparently sympathized with Rachel's predicament, she'd remained close to her parents despite their archaic beliefs. Airlie thought she was an idiot.

"I think you should reconsider allowing me to come down." Airlie gave it one last push. "I'll stay in a B&B nearby or something. Just tell them I'm your friend. Just tell them anything. I'm worried about you, and I want to be with you."

"I know you do, and I'm sorry this has taken longer than expected, but I want to stay. I have to do this on my own."

"I'm really worried about you."

"I'm fine, honestly. Until now, I had nothing from my parents, so if it goes balls up, I'll be no worse off." She laughed, but it lacked conviction. "I've not been sleeping well, so I'll probably see in the New Year wearing my pajamas drinking hot chocolate."

Airlie sighed. "So, how's your mum doing?"

"The second stroke was only minor, but it was still a stroke. It's probably delayed her homecoming by a day or two. She's tough. She keeps making sure I'm not leaving yet. I think it's a good sign. Maybe she got to the pearly gates and was sent back, I don't know, but I've got nothing to lose hanging around to find out."

"You do what you need to do."

"Why don't you see if you can go to the west for New Year's instead of Olivia and Gavin coming down here?"

The thought of doing anything without Rachel left her feeling deflated. "I'll see what she says. Is there no chance you'll get back in time?"

"If this reconciliation is successful, I don't want to rush off with things left unsaid, and trust me, I have a lot to say."

"I really don't want to go on my own. Please, can't I come to you instead?"

"Airhead, go and have fun. You haven't seen Olivia in ages. She's probably feeling rejected. It will be no joy here, and to be honest, I'd rather know you were off having a good time. The last thing I need is the pressure of feeling guilty about ruining your celebrations. I don't want you around my family. Not yet."

That was the end of the discussion. "There's no pressure. You take your time. I'll talk to Olivia. You won't need to worry about a thing."

It surprised Airlie how comfortable she felt returning to Olivia and Gav's warm and welcoming little world. The only difference being that the spare room she had previously occupied was now made up for Olivia, who had taken to sleeping solo on occasion when Gav's snoring became unbearable. In the end, it had been easier for Airlie to pack a bag and jump on the train. Olivia hadn't minded where she spent New Year's, but Gav had apparently been delighted not to have to drive four hours with the dog.

New Year's Eve had begun dreadfully early, and it was midday when she arrived at Westport train station. Olivia greeted her with a coffee and muffin and they drove straight home to preserve their energy for the evening's celebrations in Finbeigh.

When eight o'clock struck, Airlie was surprised to discover Gav in his track pants and slippers. "Aren't you coming?" She and Olivia had spent the last half hour trying on outfits, applying makeup, and giggling with anticipation, so much so, Airlie hadn't even noticed Gav wasn't dressing to accompany them.

"You girls go out and have fun. I'll just cramp your style."

"Don't be ridiculous. You won't cramp anything, except maybe your leg with all the dancing. We'll wait. Get dressed, we've plenty of time."

Gavin smiled, but it lacked conviction. He held his can of Guinness aloft. "No thanks. You go ahead. I've got all the fun I need here."

Airlie found Olivia in the bedroom. "You didn't tell me Gavin was staying home."

"I didn't know. Is he not coming? He mentioned he wasn't all that interested."

Airlie was a little stunned by Olivia's reaction.

"Oh, come on, Aerobar. You know Gav. He'd rather just stay home. He's happy. Leave him be." Olivia rolled her eyes and pushed Airlie out the door and into the crisp night air before carefully negotiating the pitch-black valleys along the windy road to Finbeigh.

They hardly recognized the pub when they walked in. Ross had completely transformed it with colorful decorations that only a man who was also possibly color blind would employ, and Airlie had never seen so many people squashed into Bridge End. Ross announced he'd miraculously lined up the Popues from Doolin—a brilliant cover band of the famous Pogues.

Airlie snuck outside to phone Rachel, but there was no answer. It was after visiting hours at the hospital so she would surely have been home by now. After another three attempts during the subsequent thirty minutes, she was beginning to feel worried. Pacing on the uneven cobblestones, she retrieved Rachel's parents' telephone number and pressed the call button before she could change her mind.

"Hello."

The male voice sounded annoyed. Airlie glanced at her watch. It was nine thirty, possibly too late to call, especially if your wife was ill in hospital. She could have kicked herself. "Is Rachel there, please?"

"No, you've just missed her, love." The man's tone softened. "If you head down to the Metropolitan, they should be there soon. At least I think that's where they're headed first."

Because she didn't know what else to do, Airlie played along. "Great, thanks. That's all I needed to know."

"No worries, love. Have a good night and tell her not to drink too much." He laughed before hanging up.

Airlie leaned against the cold stone wall. Rachel had gone out to celebrate New Year's Eve. Without her. Disappointment slapped her in the face. Was it betrayal, deceit, or just plain selfishness on Rachel's behalf? It was certainly possible Rachel's night had been organized at the last minute, but why not call? Airlie would have been pleased she wasn't stuck at home.

Who was she kidding? Airlie was anything but pleased. She was hurt because her girlfriend had decided to go out in her hometown with her old friends, probably school friends, and although Airlie had already made last-minute plans, she would have at least liked the option of spending the evening with Rachel.

Rachel had had a taste of what life was like without her, what it was like to be accepted by her family and fit in with all the friends she had back in school. It hurt to think there wasn't room for her in all of that. It hurt more to think that Rachel had deliberately excluded her. It simply fucking hurt, and she hated it.

The Popues took the stage at ten o'clock. The merry crowd heaved and cheered, and the building pulsed in time to the bass as they began to play. Airlie searched for Olivia, who mouthed, "Are you all right?" to which Airlie simply nodded. She wanted to go back to Roaring Bay, but it wasn't fair to Olivia to have her celebration ruined. She checked her phone one last time. Nothing from Rachel. If she left it on, she knew it would just distract her, so she switched it off, shoved it deep in her pocket, and did her best to forget about it and the reason why it hadn't rung.

For a cover band, the Popues were convincing, and the more cider Airlie consumed, the more enthusiastic she became. The atmosphere was electric and addictive with barely a person sitting until the band finished their first set. Olivia and the choir were vocal in the corner, encouraging some poor young man to take off his shirt and flex his muscles during the break. Airlie escaped to the bar before they encouraged her "to cop a feel of his pecs." She wasn't averse to touching a man's chest; she just wasn't in the mood to pretend she was straight. It was going to be a long night.

It felt like the actual stroke of midnight lasted for an hour. By the time Airlie reached Olivia, after hugging and kissing dozens of people, it all seemed redundant. She missed Rachel.

"Saved the most important till last, eh?" Olivia pulled her close.

They simultaneously moved to kiss each other's cheeks. Instead, the corners of their mouths connected. Airlie pulled away. If it wasn't bad enough that she'd not heard from her girlfriend all evening, the last thing she needed was a misunderstanding with Olivia.

"I don't have germs, you know." Olivia looked hurt.

"I know. Of course you don't. Sorry, I just didn't want any awkwardness."

"Between us?"

Airlie recalled the night Mikey died when they shared a bed at Grace's. It seemed so long ago now. She felt a warmth for Olivia she couldn't explain, and a loyalty to Rachel she could. She knew it was human nature to find comfort in the things you understood. Sometimes the simplest road was the easiest to follow.

"I didn't mean it like that. I guess friends don't kiss each other on the lips, and I'm gay, so I didn't know if you'd find that awkward. Not that I wouldn't, or necessarily would, for that matter." She was rambling.

"Oh, Airlie, shut up and come dance with me." Olivia dragged her to a tiny space where Grace was dancing and singing to an old eighties classic.

❖

When Airlie heard the key in the lock, she rushed to greet Rachel. They'd spoken briefly since New Year's Eve, when Rachel had forgotten to charge her phone, and consequently hadn't called her. Airlie couldn't stay mad for long. It was an easy mistake and Rachel had been apologetic when they'd finally spoken.

Airlie hauled Rachel and her bag over the threshold. "God, it's good to see you."

Rachel's return embrace was feeble. "I have something to tell you."

"Is your mum okay?" Airlie felt panic spread through her chest. Rachel looked awful, like she hadn't slept for days.

"Yes. It's nothing like that." She closed the door. "I've done something terrible."

"What is it? What have you done? You're scaring me."

Rachel held her hands in a praying gesture. "Please forgive me. You have to."

Airlie stepped back. "Rachel, I mean it. What's going on?"

"I let someone else touch me." Rachel began to cry.

When she realized exactly what Rachel was saying, she cried, too. It was odd, being told you'd been cheated on. In one moment, you wanted to know everything. In the next, you were terrified to hear it.

"Touch you how?" asked Airlie.

"In the wrong way."

"In a sexual way?"

Rachel nodded. She sobbed.

"Inside you?"

Rachel began to shake. She nodded.

"Who was she?" Airlie asked.

"It doesn't matter who it was. It meant nothing. I know everybody says that, but I was drunk, too drunk, and I barely remember it. I'm so sorry, Airbear."

"It matters to me who fucks my girlfriend, so tell me."

"Her name was Sophie. That's all I know. It was New Year's Eve, and it meant nothing, I promise."

"No, that's a lie. If you could do this to me, then *I* mean nothing. Did you touch her?"

"I kissed her."

"And?"

"That's all, I swear."

Airlie laughed. "And you expect me to believe that? You let someone screw you and in return they got nothing."

"It's the truth. Please believe me. I didn't touch her. I realized what I'd let her do. I didn't want her to touch me. It just happened."

"So she raped you?"

Rachel cried. "It all happened so fast, and I know this means little to you, but it meant nothing. If I could take it back, I would. If I could not hurt you, I would. If I could go back in time and never meet her, I would."

"But you did meet her. You did more than just meet her." Airlie paced, angry now. "And there I was, worried about a little misunderstanding with Olivia on New Year's Eve. We went to kiss each other's cheek and accidently brushed the corners of our mouths and I felt weird. But you, you go and let some woman fuck you. Jesus Christ."

Rachel straightened. "It didn't take long for her to come into the conversation."

"Leave her out of it. And an awkward kiss isn't a fucking patch on what you did."

"Were you even that bothered that I wasn't there?"

"Yes. I fucking was. Although you clearly aren't bothered about me." Airlie had heard enough. All she could think about was moving her stuff into Hannah's old room. She needed to be alone. She needed to cry.

"I'm so sorry," Rachel called after her. "I don't know what else to say. I promise it won't happen again."

Airlie stalled at the top of the stairs. "How can you be sure? How can I trust you again?"

"Please try. I can't stand feeling like this. I can't bear that I've hurt you. I would never put you, or anyone else, through this again."

No. She wouldn't put Airlie through it again because she wouldn't let her. There were many things Airlie could forgive, but she wasn't sure infidelity was one of them.

## CHAPTER TWENTY-SEVEN

Airlie and Rachel remained friends, and although distant and at times strained, their separation continued amicably. At first, continuing to share a home was strange, but they both worked long hours, providing a distraction and a legitimate excuse to stay away from each other.

"I'm sorry it didn't work out with Rachel," Olivia said.

Airlie sobbed.

"It's difficult for any relationship, let alone a vulnerable one, to survive infidelity."

"What do you mean by vulnerable?" Airlie sniffed loudly.

"Outside your circle of friends, who knew you were together?"

"I talked about Rachel all the time at work."

"As your partner, or did people just know you shared a place together?"

"I'm a private person. You know that. I don't have to stand on a mountaintop and announce my homosexuality. I don't recall anyone at the office introducing themselves to me and saying, 'Oh by the way, I'm heterosexual.' Why should I say I'm gay?"

"You never once had the opportunity to drop into a conversation that you were in a relationship with Rachel?"

There had been plenty of opportunities. Airlie had been too chicken to take them. She saw the point Olivia was trying to make.

"I know most people don't go announcing it on their first day, and there are people who never mention it due to the nature of their job, as sad as that is, but whatever you had with Rachel seemed so insular and so private you couldn't share it. You never even told me you were with her."

She realized that beyond the safety of the flat and her small circle of friends, being Rachel's partner wasn't as important to her as she'd wanted it to be. Convenient, yes. Significant, not so much.

❖

Less than a month later, Airlie had accrued so much overtime, her boss insisted she take a day off. She leapt out of bed with unexpected enthusiasm. The sun was shining, and it seemed that a bright day was all she required to lift her spirits. Sun filled the lounge room. Of course, it was freezing outside, it hadn't reached double figures for some time now, but she welcomed the beams of light, although they were completely void of warmth. With the house to herself, she stood in the middle of the lounge, the radio blaring, pondering what to do first. She dashed back upstairs, threw on some clothes, and strode to the corner shop to collect a copy of *The Times*. She would cook pancakes and leisurely read the newspaper. The thought of doing something so normal was exciting.

Olivia's famous pancake recipe was scribbled on a tattered piece of paper stuffed inside her only recipe book. It was only famous between the two of them, and only after Olivia confused that recipe with another and tripled the mixture. They had more pancakes than they knew what to do with.

Airlie sent Olivia a message. *Sitting in beautiful warm sun (not), reading The Times with hot coffee and pancakes, not too many tho! How's work? Xx*

Her mobile rang.

"Great pancakes, absolutely delicious."

"Good morning to you, too," said Olivia.

"No really, they're amazing. I've made them just how you like them."

"I wouldn't know about that. You've never cooked them for me."

"Of course I have."

"I always make them for *you*."

Airlie strained her memory. "Surely I've made them at least once?"

"When?"

"I can't think of an exact time right now, and even if I haven't, you can rest assured, if I ever do, they'll be good." Airlie made a slurping noise, followed by a moan of gratification.

"You're mean, Airlie Porter."

"You love it."

"Maybe." Olivia paused. "So, what are you up to for the rest of your day off?"

"I'm not sure. I think I'll visit some places I've never been before."

"Great idea."

"Have you got time to complete *The Times*' personality quiz?" asked Airlie, flicking through the newspaper.

"Okay. Five minutes."

"Excellent. After this enlightening questionnaire, we'll know your celebrity shag, and precisely what personality trait such information suggests is your finest quality."

"Sounds thoroughly scientific, although I'm pretty sure I don't even have a celebrity shag."

"Of course you do. Everyone does."

"Nope. Not me."

"Now come on, there must be some celebrity, *someone* you'd do it with?"

"I just said I can't think of anyone. Now, will you get on with the questionnaire?"

Airlie pushed. "Not one person in the entire world you can think of?"

"Just leave it alone."

"Not one?"

"No, not one."

"Not a movie star or a singer?"

"No, I've no idea."

"Everyone has a celebrity shag."

"Well, I don't."

"You mean to tell me, that if you could have sex with absolutely anybody in the whole entire world, male or female, there is no one, not one person, who takes your fancy?"

"Yes, Airlie, that's exactly what I mean. Is that so hard to understand?"

"Frankly, yes. You're not asexual, so there must be *one* person you'd want to screw?"

"For Christ's sake, Airlie, what do you want me to say?"

"I want you to tell me one person who you'd have sex with. It's not that difficult."

"One person?" Her raised voice suggested her agitation was escalating.

"Yes. One fucking person."

"You!"

The word was snapped out almost accusingly, and the silence that followed was deafening.

Airlie jumped up. *Fuck.* The heavy sound of Olivia's breathing filled her head.

"I didn't mean that, Airlie. I'm sorry. I have to go now." Olivia's voice was deeper. It sounded foreign.

"No, wait, hang on. Did you just say *me*?"

The breathing was replaced by beeping.

"Liv? Olivia, are you there?" Airlie phoned back, but predictably, the call went to message bank. She continued to redial, but there was no answer, just Olivia's carefree voice requesting the caller to leave a message. Airlie couldn't leave a message. What would she say?

Her last hope was Olivia's office number, but that glimmer was quashed when a man advised her Olivia had gone home for the day. He wouldn't tell her why. She dialed Olivia's mobile again. No ringing this time, just message bank. She paced the lounge room for fifteen minutes before calling her at home. No answer. This time it was Gav's monotone voice asking her to leave a message. She cursed. Airlie showered on autopilot, her relaxing day a distant memory.

For the next two hours, she attempted to reach Olivia. Just before lunch, she gave up. The most ridiculous thoughts raced through her mind. Underpinning them all was a sense of excitement and an optimism that came with the possibility that somewhere deep inside Olivia, there was an attraction. All this time, she had felt a connection, stronger than anything she'd ever experienced, and now perhaps there was a possibility it could be more than just good friends.

The tiresome lounge room walls began to close in, and she resisted the urge to throw her phone into the fireplace. When even an inanimate object continually rejected you, the frustration was tormenting. Her phone was the only connection to Olivia. She had to do something to provide distraction. She snapped out of her trance, grabbed her coat, and stepped into the sunshine. It truly was a glorious day. The refreshing air was invigorating, awakening a sudden urge to visit the sea.

Hannah had mentioned a place called Howth, and she knew it was north, but getting there was a bit sketchy. She didn't mind. She walked with a lightness in her step to the nearest DART station and hopped on the first train that arrived. The graffiti stained board inside the carriage indicated she was on the correct train and the trip took thirty minutes. It could have taken all day; she didn't care. Time was suddenly insignificant. Her mind wandered from one thought to another, her stomach fluttering every time she recounted Olivia saying, "You."

There were many empty seats on the carriage, and most people were silent, except for the tourists who pointed with excited gestures. The sun gently warmed the side of her cheek. For what seemed the millionth time, she checked her phone. Olivia hadn't called. Reestablishing a connection was at the forefront of her mind. She contemplated sending a text message, but there was no guarantee of a reply. This situation was delicate. She needed to be smart. Pushing Olivia away was the last thing she wanted to do.

Howth boasted a colorful Viking history, but today Airlie was only interested in negotiating the steep streets, past cheerfully bright colored houses, toward the water. As she stepped off West Pier onto a gravelly beach, she experienced a peculiar sense of elation. She stood tall and filled her lungs with the salty air, staring beyond the boats toward the dark blue Irish Sea. She removed her shoes and socks, ignoring the freezing sensation of exposed feet, and as she did, a thought crossed her mind, solid and powerful; she was in with a chance.

Although the pebbles were smooth from years of punishment, she hobbled over to where the water lapped the shore. Her entire body shivered as the icy sea, dusted with sandy sediment, seeped between her toes before splashing around her ankles. The feeling excited her. She felt alive. Alive with an opportunity that she had previously accepted to be a dreamy fantasy.

She wasn't sure what Olivia would do in this situation. Would she call? Come and see her? Talk about it, or perhaps simply pretend it never happened?

Airlie procrastinated. Calling Olivia had been hopeless, but in hindsight, this might have been a good thing. But would a confrontation work? Should she just appear on her doorstep unannounced? And even if she did, would Olivia want to talk about it? She thought carefully about writing her thoughts and sending them to her, but the possibility that Olivia might not reply wasn't a chance she was willing to take.

She reminded herself that she must practice patience and restraint. There was no guarantee anything she attempted would be successful. Olivia might choose never to speak to her again, but if what she had said was simply an honest slip of the tongue, why did she react in such an extraordinary manner? It was certainly plausible that Olivia had made a mistake, spoken out of turn, and might genuinely have no feelings for her at all, but she had to find out for sure. There might never be another chance with Olivia.

*Don't fuck this up.*

## CHAPTER TWENTY-EIGHT

At exactly 4:06 a.m. the following morning, Airlie formulated a plan. It certainly wasn't foolproof, but it was the best she could come up with *and* have the courage to execute.

She would give Olivia until the end of the weekend to make contact. Failing any contact by Sunday evening, she would take the initiative and make the call. If Olivia spoke to her—and this was where her plan could easily fail—she resolved not to mention the conversation that had been playing over in her mind all day and now half the night. Once back on speaking terms, she would rebuild their friendship, and although Airlie was hesitant not to pressure Olivia, in exactly three weekends she would go to her and explain her feelings.

It was the best she could do.

Sunday morning arrived, and Olivia had not contacted Airlie. It wasn't surprising. At six that evening, she prepared to make the call. It was easier said than done. She'd rehearsed the conversation, but now that the time had arrived, her heart raced and her hands became sweaty, shaking, useless limbs.

*Get a grip.*

She picked up the phone, scrolled through her contacts list, selected Olivia's home number, and pressed the green call button.

The phone rang at least four times.

"Hello."

The relief that Olivia had answered was soon replaced with fear. This moment could possibly be the most important in Airlie's life. She didn't want to fuck it up.

"Hi, Olivia, it's me." She crackled the words out.

"Hi, me, how are you?"

No hint of animosity. "I'm good, thanks. How are you?" She crossed her fingers.

"I've been mad busy these last few days."

"Yeah." Airlie sighed heavily for effect. "I've been pretty busy, too."

Until this was resolved, the situation would remain difficult. While she was pleased that Olivia was talking to her, a nagging voice told her to be insulted and annoyed. Olivia had shut her out for days. She'd said one word that felt life-changing and then she took it back. Olivia disappeared from the radar, and now she'd returned, continuing as if nothing happened.

Airlie chewed her lip, determined to stick to the script. "How's the choir?"

Olivia enthusiastically relayed an amusing story from choir practice, perhaps *overly* enthusiastically, but within minutes, they were laughing and joking as if nothing as profound as a possible sexual desire had ever been mentioned.

Nearly an hour later, Olivia had to dash. She was yet to make a start on dinner, and although Gav was going to be late, she still wanted to cook him something substantial. Airlie flinched at the mention of Gav, but hearing his name was inevitable. She'd have to accept that reality for the time being. The phone call ended with the situation as normal as could be expected. Airlie's plan was under way.

Monday was a no contact day, as per her schedule, meaning she wouldn't initiate contact with Olivia, but would respond if Olivia contacted her. Concentrating was difficult. She caught herself staring aimlessly at her monitor on more than one occasion, but she worked solidly. Her phone never beeped to signal the delivery of a message, even though she checked it with desperate regularity. Regardless of the outcome, there was much at stake. There was a real possibility that she could destroy their friendship. What she really wanted to do was take the next train to the west.

It was nearly midnight, and Airlie was fighting sleep. She needed to sleep, but any time unconscious was time she couldn't think of Olivia, and thinking of Olivia was her favorite thing to do. As her thoughts began to jumble, just moments before she would have to give in, the phone vibrated beside her pillow. She rushed to open the message: *Bell*

*X1 on the TV. Don't know if you're watching, might be too late. I'm recording it for you. Xx*

Bell X1 was Airlie's favorite band. She'd known weeks ago about the concert, but it had slipped her mind with everything going on. The message caused her heart to race. Olivia had been thinking of her, and *she* had made contact. This reinforced her commitment to the plan. She couldn't appear too keen, so to give the impression that she'd been asleep, she'd text a return message first thing in the morning. It took all her willpower to force herself to sleep without responding.

During the subsequent week, Airlie counted the days until her planned visit to Olivia's.

Early the following Sunday morning, there was a loud knock at the door. Airlie was snug in bed and reluctant to move, so she waited for Rachel to answer it, but when the knock became more insistent, and there was no movement in the house, she begrudgingly climbed out of bed and answered the door, wrapped in a blanket.

Hannah stood beaming on the stairs, balancing coffee in one hand and pastries in the other. "Hey, sleepyhead." Airlie frowned. Hannah's unusual early morning enthusiasm was disturbing. "I know it's early, but I don't care. Can I come in?"

Airlie stepped aside. "What time is it?"

"Just after eight. Rachel not home?"

"Um, I don't know. I don't think so."

"That's okay." Hannah offloaded the goodies. "All the more for us."

"Let me get some clothes on." Airlie ran her fingers through her hair, struggling to wake up.

"We're celebrating," yelled Hannah from the lounge room.

Airlie was on her way back through the kitchen, grabbing plates and cutlery. "Pardon?"

"I said we're celebrating."

"Okay, good." Hannah's smile nearly broke her face. "Hang on, what are we celebrating?"

Hannah thrust out her left hand. Airlie was slow, but eventually caught on. "Is that an engagement ring?"

"Sure is. Do you like it?"

"You're engaged?"

Hannah nodded.

"You're getting married?"

"Oh keep up, Airlie. Yes. I'm bloody well getting married."

The news was fantastic, and in no time, they settled into a long, delicious breakfast while Hannah recounted how Liam had secretly whisked her away to Prague and proposed on Charles Bridge. They had only returned last night.

"I can't believe it. We're sitting here talking about weddings and honeymoons. Don't tell me you've already set a date?"

"Yep. End of autumn."

"I'm guessing that's autumn here, not home?"

"We want to get married here. I know Mum and Dad will make the trip over. It will finally give them a good excuse to come and visit." Hannah took another Danish. "Actually, I have a favor to ask. Do you fancy being my bridesmaid?"

Airlie gulped and swallowed. "Absolutely. Of course. I'd love to." They hugged. "I'm honored."

"There's just one thing. I'd like to ask Rachel to be a bridesmaid, too. Is that okay with you?"

"Of course it is. We'll be the best bridesmaids you'll ever have."

"I hope I only need one set of bridesmaids."

What was left of the morning, they spent drinking more coffee and chatting excitedly about the endless arrangements that cropped up when planning a wedding.

That evening in bed, Airlie pondered what it would be like to get married. She imagined the excitement and the thrill and contentment in finding the person she wanted to spend the rest of her life with. The only person Airlie could imagine herself with forever was Olivia. She had no idea if any of her feelings would be reciprocated.

She allowed herself to fantasize a future with Olivia. They would live in an old house with dark polished floorboards, antique furniture, walls adorned with beautiful art, and Norman Lindsay's *The Sphinx* hanging proudly above the open fireplace. All their friends and family would be delighted that they had found each other. "The happiest couple in the world" is what their friends would say. Olivia would love her unconditionally and overwhelm her with affection.

Airlie's last thought before sleep was of Olivia, beckoning her toward their bedroom.

She'd decided to wait until the last minute to let Olivia know she was visiting. It was exactly as she planned. The anticipation, not to mention apprehension, played on her mind.

On Wednesday evening, she fidgeted on the edge of her bed, wiped sweaty palms the length of her thighs, and made the call. Butterflies lurched in her stomach. A nervous heat swept over her, but she swallowed hard and dialed the number.

A soft male voice answered. "Hello."

Airlie hadn't expected this. "Gav, it's Airlie." *Shit.* She had no idea what to say. "How are you?" She hadn't thought about Gav in this at all. She felt wretched for not considering him. Backing out would be the honorable thing to do, but the thought of missing this chance overwhelmed her. She had to go on.

"G'day, Airlie. I'm not so bad, and yourself?"

"I'm good, thanks." She stumbled over her words. "A…A…Any news?"

"Not one bit of news here, I'm afraid. I hear Hannah is getting married?"

"Liam proposed in Prague. The wedding should be in autumn, and the ring is beautiful. Hannah is over the moon." She rolled her eyes. *What are you doing? Get on with it.* "Is Olivia about?"

"Yes, my beautiful wife is here somewhere. I'll get her for you."

Airlie stood and then sat again. She could hear the television volume increase followed by a loud crackling noise as Gav passed the phone.

"Hi, honey." The smooth, tender voice caused Airlie's heart to skip.

"Hey, Liv, how's it going?" She battled to sound casual and normal.

"What's up?"

Olivia was no fool.

"Nothing's up." She was losing her nerve. "I just thought I'd call, have a chat, and see what you were doing this weekend." There was no turning back. She pushed on before Olivia had an opportunity to interrupt. "I thought I might come over for a couple of days. You know, get out of the city and away from all this wedding talk for a while."

The long pause left Airlie's heart sinking.

At last, Olivia softly spoke. "Is it getting to you?"

"Is what getting to me?"

"All this talk of marriage and weddings."

"Oh, that?" Her relief was almost tangible. "Yes, actually, it is a bit much sometimes. It's just not me with all the dress talk and hen night stuff."

"You should definitely come over this weekend. You know this is where you can come to get away from it all. Plus, I haven't seen you in ages."

*Happy days!*

Airlie began to wonder if Olivia had completely erased their strange phone call from her memory, but she knew that wasn't important right now. What was important was the invitation.

"I certainly wouldn't mind a break. I might see if I can get the afternoon off and catch the lunchtime train."

"Great plan. Hang about in Westport until I finish work, and I'll collect you on the way through."

Airlie finally relaxed.

They chatted for a while before cutting their conversation short. After all, they would be seeing each other on the weekend and could talk at length then.

Airlie pumped her fist then flopped on the bed. Her racing heart slowed to normal. The final stages of her plan were under way, and she welcomed the thought of finally relieving herself from the burden of her feelings.

Speaking of her feelings was scary, but speaking of them to Olivia in person was downright terrifying. Airlie understood that her revelation could end their friendship. She could have it all, or she could be left with nothing. She realized she'd probably been in love with Olivia for some time. The denial she endured surrounding her sexuality had clouded her feelings. She recognized that in the process of becoming who she was, the floodgates opened and allowed her to be herself and feel what was in her heart.

She wished Gav hadn't answered the phone. Guilt rushed through her like a plague of rats. What would happen to Gav? What if Olivia *did* have feelings for her? Would she act on them? Would she ignore them? Would she lie to Airlie and live the rest of her life in her spurious bliss? It took her breath away, and she could barely think about it. What if Olivia saw their relationship as nothing but a strong friendship, a genuine and purely platonic, special relationship?

Endless scenarios flooded her already congested mind. She loved Olivia. It was the only certain truth. She also knew that she couldn't live the rest of her life wondering if she'd squandered her only chance. If she lost Olivia, she would attempt to accept that she wasn't hers to have in the first place. She had no idea how she would move forward if Olivia didn't want her; she just knew she needed to try.

## CHAPTER TWENTY-NINE

Not one thing concerning the train ride to Westport was enjoyable, other than it was going to Westport. The scheduled departure time was delayed for no apparent reason, locating a vacant seat took forever, and Airlie was in a foul, apprehensive mood.

Everything unsettled her; she was positive the train was slowing prematurely on its approach to every station, and she was convinced it crawled away again much slower than necessary. The glossy magazine she'd purchased held her interest for little more than five minutes, and she wished she'd remembered her iPod.

She was gazing out the rain-splattered window to a gloomy day when her phone rang. It was Olivia, and for a split second, Airlie couldn't decide whether to answer it or not. "Hi, Liv."

"You on the train?"

"Sure am, although the bloody thing's running about half an hour behind."

"Shame, but it will work out well because I'm finishing early, so we'll probably arrive at the station around the same time."

Airlie thought Olivia sounded a little distracted, which was a good thing. Hopefully, she wouldn't detect the nervousness in her voice.

Olivia continued. "How do you feel about dinner at the Lounge tonight, my treat?"

This was perfect. And although she wondered how she would get through dinner, Airlie agreed. The Lounge was her favorite restaurant, after all. "Italian sounds divine."

Airlie's butterflies refused to settle. The farther west she traveled, the clearer the day became. She pulled off her jumper. She was sweating, but glancing around, realized she was the only one looking uncomfortable. She attempted to admire the countryside again and lapse back to her daydreaming. It was hopeless.

After an excruciating crawl toward Westport station, the train stopped and Airlie jumped off, dumping her bag on the closest seat. She sprayed perfume and stuffed five mints in her mouth.

She was psyching herself up for possibly the biggest night of her life, when a hand softly slid round her waist and a familiar voice whispered, "Hey, you." Olivia's sweet, soft lips gently kissed her cheek.

Airlie jumped. Not out of shock, but nervousness. "Hey, yourself." She attempted a casual tone, trying to ignore the warm arm around her and the tingling sensation left on her cheek. She returned the kiss, her eyes lingering on Olivia's plunging neckline. A pale blue striped shirt revealed her cleavage, and the fleeting glance caused Airlie's heart to race.

Olivia stepped back and held her at arm's length. "You look tired. Are you all right?"

"Of course." Airlie managed a half smile. "I'm fine." Olivia raised her brow. "Honestly, Liv, I'm okay."

"Good. Give us an old hug then." Airlie's chest rapidly became the most sensitive part of her body. She could feel Olivia's breasts pressing against hers as they hugged long and close. "I feel like I haven't seen you ages," Olivia said.

Airlie dismissed any doubts. She wanted this embrace to be hers. She wanted to be able to feel Olivia's chest firmly against hers whenever she liked. This embrace deserved a life of its own, to develop into a kiss, a casual fondle, or an explosion of passion. Airlie wanted Olivia in every sense, and she was surer than ever that she must disclose her feelings and discover if Olivia felt the same way. She would risk everything, but it had to be that way. If Olivia truly didn't want any part of this madness, then she could move on and eventually stop the outrageous thoughts that consumed her. As things stood, she was trapped, unable to break free from her own desires and her deep love for this woman.

*Let me be yours, or just let me go.*

From the moment Airlie sat in the car, time seemed to slow as if someone had taken their foot completely off the accelerator, allowing the car, and the night, to coast along.

Dinner was perfect. After a warm greeting from Anton, they settled in with a bottle of red. Airlie surprised herself by devouring everything served to her.

Olivia chatted about her week and choir practice antics, but Airlie drifted off, unable to concentrate. She studied Olivia's beautiful brown eyes that, in the daylight, often appeared a warm caramel color. Tonight, they were rich, dark brown. She imagined herself rising from the chair and leaning over to kiss her full on the mouth. Olivia's lips were perfect, her straight white teeth and warm smile entrancing.

❖

They had reached Murrisk, about halfway home, before Airlie roused a smidgen of courage. "Can we talk?"

"Of course we can. What's up?"

"Can we stop at the beach? The one below Ballycrest and talk there?" Ballycrest was a secluded stretch of coast nestled below small cliffs. It was only a slight detour.

"Sure we can, although you're scaring me a little." Olivia glanced toward her. "You sure you're okay?"

"I'd just like to talk to you, that's all."

Olivia nodded and clicked on the indicator to enter the hedged gravel lane that terminated in a barely adequate car park. Airlie suppressed the urge to either run away or vomit. She'd come this far. There was no turning back. She breathed deeply and focused. This was her moment.

Olivia cut the engine as she pulled into the deserted parking area, facing the moonlit beach. She unbuckled her seat belt and waited.

"Can I please have the keys?" Airlie extended her hand.

"Pardon?"

"Do you trust me?"

"Of course I do."

"Then can I please have the keys?"

Olivia frowned but removed the keys from the ignition, surrendering them in silence. Adrenaline pumped through Airlie's veins. She unlatched her seat belt and turned to Olivia, stuffing the keys in her coat pocket. Her rehearsed speech had disappeared from memory. She swallowed hard to find her voice.

"There's no easy way to say this."

"You're sick, aren't you?"

"What? No, I'm not sick. I'm okay, honestly."

"Well, you're scaring the hell out of me, Airlie. Just spit it out, please?"

"I'm not with Rachel anymore. You know that, don't you?"

Olivia nodded. "Has something happened between you two? Is she kicking you out? You know you can come back here anytime you like, but what about your job?"

"Liv?"

"Bit rough that you have to move out though."

"Liv, it's nothing like that." She had to get it out before Olivia drained her of courage. "I'm not with Rachel anymore and it's okay because I figured out that I'm in love with someone else."

Silence.

"I've tried to shut this out."

"Who is it?" Olivia's voice was barely audible.

"I've tried to rationalize it as something other than it is, but it's no use."

"Who is it, Airlie?"

The moment arrived.

"It's you." Airlie stared at her fidgeting hands. "I'm in love with you."

From the corner of her eye, she could see that Olivia's gaze was fixed directly beyond the windscreen and into the night. Overcome by a sheer sense of relief, Airlie began to cry. She looked up, willing Olivia to hold her and tell her that no matter what, it was going to be all right. The last time she had confessed a secret, Olivia had held her tight and made it better. Tonight, there was nothing, just cold, empty silence. Olivia left her crying and alone.

Airlie sobbed. "I'm sorry. I've ruined everything, haven't I?"

"No," muttered Olivia before rushing from the car. Airlie knew she was unable to bear her one moment longer.

"Fuck!" Airlie slammed her fist on the dash. She watched Olivia stride to the water's edge, a silhouette in the moonlight.

Airlie leapt from the car, pursuing as fast as she could. "Liv, just wait." Olivia didn't alter her gait. "After what you said, I had to tell you how I feel. Please, just wait a second. I'm sorry."

Olivia spun to face her, tears glistening in the moonlight. "What are you sorry for?" She barked. "Really, Airlie, what are you sorry for? I thought we were friends. What I said on the phone was crap. It meant nothing. What the fuck am I supposed to do with this? I'm thirteen fucking years older than you. Why the fuck would you be in love with me?"

Airlie trembled, not from the cold, but because she had known all along that this reaction was a possibility, more likely a probability, but now that her secret was out, she was falling apart. How was she ever going to deal with the consequences?

Olivia stormed toward her. "I'm a fucking married woman, Airlie. Christ almighty, what do you think I can do about this?" She paced back and forth.

"I can't help it. You must know how you make me feel?"

"I didn't know I made you *feel* anything. What the fuck did you think I was going to be able to do about it?" Olivia stormed off again.

Airlie turned her face to the sky, hoping the right thing to say would miraculously dawn upon her.

"Olivia, please stop!" Airlie yelled so loud her voice echoed off the cliffs. "I've fallen in love with a married woman. I'm not proud of myself, I can assure you. And you don't have to do a damn thing about this. What you do with what I just told you is your choice. You don't have to do a fucking thing."

"I don't have to do a thing? Really, Airlie? Do you think we can just go on now as friends after this?"

"I told you all this knowing I could lose you, so you choose what you do with it. What do you feel? What do you want?"

Olivia offered nothing.

"Well? What do you want?"

Airlie walked forward until they were standing no more than a meter apart. More than anything, she wanted to take Olivia in her arms and wrap her in love.

"This is the moment, Liv." Airlie spoke gently. "What do you want?" She took the plunge. "If you don't love me, just say."

The longer Olivia took to answer, the greater the distance grew between them. The answer Airlie so anxiously hoped for wasn't forthcoming. Olivia didn't love her. Why would she? Why would she love a twenty-eight-year-old messed up idiot? Why on earth would she feel the slightest hint of anything except pity for her? All this time she had simply read the situation wrong. They were friends, nothing more and nothing less, although now they were completely nothing. Her head dropped. She had nothing left to give, and there was nothing left to take. She moved to pass Olivia and walk home. It didn't matter what happened now. She would make her own way back to the house and leave first thing in the morning. She had hoped they could still be friends, but that wasn't to be, not tonight anyway, maybe in time.

As she passed, Olivia's hand grabbed hers, tightly.

"Wait."

"It's okay. You don't have to say it. I know." Without meeting her gaze, Airlie pulled away from Olivia's grasp, took the keys from her pocket, tossing them on the sand. She pushed past her, walking away.

Her eyes had adjusted completely now, and if it were not the worst night of her life, she might have enjoyed the calm, mild evening and the beautiful light of the moon as it reflected over the shallow water. She didn't look back. The sight of Olivia traipsing toward the car would have been unbearable, and even though she knew this scenario was likely, now that it had transpired, the pain was excruciating, and the loss was worse than any before in her life. The tears continued flowing, and her mind filled with white noise. Even the melodic drone of the waves lapping on the shore was distant. Airlie knew the numbness would come, as it had before, and she intended to wait for it to overwhelm her. Airlie cursed for expecting a different outcome, although it wasn't so much that she had expected it, more that she had hoped with all her heart that Olivia would give her a chance for a future together. She hadn't anticipated a confession of love; that would have been a dream, but something, anything besides this cold, lifeless ending was preferable.

At least now she could move on and eventually recover from the peculiar love she harbored, although it seemed impossible to imagine feelings so deep for anyone else. She longed for the numbness to take her.

Somewhere in the distance, she thought she heard her name being called, but she didn't turn. It was her mind playing tricks. She marched on.

Olivia. Words to express her love, her adoration, failed. Being completely consumed by the thought of someone was an entirely foreign sensation. Never had she longed just to be in someone's company. Being together was all she desired, alone or with others, it didn't matter, as long as they were close. Their conversations and the time they chose to share with each other were amazing. Airlie's heart ached with the pain of it being over.

"Airlie, wait!"

A hand grabbed her shoulder. She jumped. She had no idea how long she'd been walking, but Olivia was puffed, and the end of the beach loomed, cliffs towering above them. Olivia stepped in front of her, walking backward as Airlie continued walking forward.

"Airlie, will you please stop for a second?"

"No." Airlie felt no need to expand. She felt no need to talk anymore at all.

"Can you *please* just stop to hear me out?"

"I don't want to hear anything." Airlie looked through Olivia and stepped around her, lengthening her stride.

"You don't want to hear that I'm in love with you, too?"

Airlie froze. She turned. Olivia was only meters away, yet she wasn't convinced. "What did you say?"

Olivia took a step forward, and instinctively, Airlie retreated. "I said that I love you, too. Well, no, actually, I said that I'm *in* love with you, too."

"You love me, too?"

"Yes, Aerobar, I do."

"Why?"

"Why?" Olivia frowned. "I guess for the same reasons you love me."

"Oh." Airlie's ability to speak remained elusive.

"Can I walk toward you now without you stepping away from me?"

Airlie nodded. Olivia stepped closer.

"I've been calling you for ages. Why didn't you stop?"

Airlie stared for a long moment, her mouth seemingly disconnected from her brain. "I didn't hear you."

Olivia took another step closer. She was crying again. "I'm sorry about just now. My mind went mental. Christ, it's still going mental. I'm just so fucking confused."

"I know the feeling."

"I guess you do. How long have you felt this way? It can't just have been since that phone call?"

Airlie became fixated on making a pattern in the sand with the toe of her right shoe. "A long time, I think. Probably since we first stayed with you." She lifted her eyes to gauge Olivia's reaction. There was no shock or surprise, so she continued. "I've tried to stop. I know you're married. But when I think of things, I think of you."

"What sort of things?"

"I think of you when a love song comes on the radio. I think of sharing things with you, like traveling, books, galleries, just experiences, I suppose." She worked her foot to increase the size of the groove it had impressed. "Life. I think you complete my life."

"I'm much older than you."

Airlie eyed her. "I don't care how old you are."

"You don't now, but will you in twenty years' time?"

"Will you be with me in twenty years' time?"

"I don't know, Airlie, will *you*?"

"I know I want to spend the rest of my life with you, and I know I can say that without a shadow of doubt."

"How about we just work this out now." Talking of the future seemed to add to Olivia's confusion.

"I think about you all the time. I know what I want and I know that's you."

"I think about you all the time, too." She reached for Airlie's hand. "What do we do about this now?" Her smile did little to conceal her fear.

For the long term, Airlie had no idea what they would do. As early as tomorrow morning, she still had no idea what they would do, but here, now, tonight, she knew exactly what they should do.

Airlie stepped into Olivia. She took her hand and gently kissed her palm before placing it on her cheek. A burst of electrifying passion passed through her, and she knew Olivia felt it, too. It was as if they'd unleashed a torrent of suppressed desire. Airlie cupped Olivia's moist face and kissed her for a long time, slowly and tenderly. At first, Olivia allowed her to gently part her lips and explore her mouth. Olivia's mouth and tongue became hungry. Their kiss was explosive.

When the kiss ended, Airlie held her tightly. She squeezed hard as if her life depended on that moment of togetherness. Olivia snuggled into Airlie's neck, and her body heaved under the weight of tears. Airlie let her cry. She didn't know what else to do. There was no script for what was happening. The emotions they both felt were new, never experienced before, and most likely never to be repeated.

At last, Olivia spoke, her face remaining concealed. "I don't know what this means."

"I guess I don't really, either." Airlie couldn't pretend she was in control. "I just know I want you."

"Take me somewhere," said Olivia. Their eyes met. "Please?"

## Chapter Thirty

Airlie led Olivia to the car, holding her hand tightly. She must have been walking for a long time before Olivia caught up with her. The car seemed miles away. She softly asked for the keys, and within minutes, they were returning to Westport. Airlie knew the Windy Point Hotel, the largest in town, had a twenty-four-hour reception; she just hoped to God they had a vacant room. The drive seemed endless. Olivia placed her hand affectionately on Airlie's leg, and she was grateful for the contact. It seemed to keep the connection alive, but she had difficulty concentrating on the deserted road.

Upon arrival, Airlie stopped the engine and turned off the lights. "Is this okay?"

Olivia nodded.

Airlie kissed her again. She'd thought of nothing else during the drive, and now that they were just minutes away from the inevitable, a sense of urgency crept through her. Airlie moved her hand to Olivia's knee, up her inner thigh, over her stomach, before urgently caressing her breasts.

Olivia moaned. "I want you."

Airlie broke the embrace and asked Olivia to hold tight until she had a room sorted.

Within minutes, she returned. "Madam." She offered her hand.

"Why, thank you, my darling."

While they weren't in Roaring Bay, Westport was only twenty minutes away, and two Australian women walking into a hotel at midnight was conspicuous. Airlie had booked the room under the pretense of it being a surprise for her friend whose husband was arriving later. The receptionist thought it was a lovely thing to do and wistfully wished she had friends like that.

On the approach to the entrance, they broke from all affection and walked directly through the doors and into the lift. There was no luggage to haul, but no one took any notice; in fact, the front desk was unattended.

Airlie struggled to open the door to room 121. The key continually slipped in the dimly lit corridor. Making the task more difficult was Olivia sliding her hand from Airlie's shoulder to the small of her back and then into her jeans pocket.

Her mind warmed with the sensation of a rush of blood.

Olivia breathed heavily on her neck. "You okay with that key?" Her hand moved to Airlie's breasts.

She let out a sigh and a frustrated moan as Olivia fondled her through her top. "I'm having a bit of trouble, and that isn't helping."

"What's not helping?" Olivia groped her harder and bit her ear.

At last, the door swung open and they stumbled over the threshold, finally isolated from the rest of the world.

Airlie had briefly considered what would happen once they reached the seclusion of the hotel room. She'd wondered if Olivia would reconsider, and if so, at what stage would that occur.

"I can't explain how I feel," said Olivia, her eyes wide and so brilliantly alive.

Airlie kissed her and finished the job of tugging the shirt from her trousers. "It's a good feeling though, right?"

"It's the best feeling. I feel like I'm high." She brought their foreheads together. "Take me higher. Please."

Something told Airlie that Olivia wouldn't back out now. The window for second thoughts had come and gone, and all she could focus on was Olivia's first orgasm. She pushed her toward the sideboard and lifted Olivia to sit on the edge. Regardless of what she wanted to do to Olivia, the next few minutes couldn't be slowed or altered. Something bigger was forcing them together. Airlie unbuttoned Olivia's trousers and pushed them down until they scrunched around her ankles. Her knickers followed. She knew that moment before penetration. She loved that moment, and she wanted Olivia to love it, too.

She knelt between her legs.

"Oh, Jesus."

Airlie danced her tongue on the edge of Olivia's opening before finding her clit. She knew she'd found the sweet spot when Olivia's hand shot to the back of her head, holding her down.

"You're driving me mad."

Airlie replaced her tongue with her fingers. "I've only just started."

"Amen to that."

They kissed deeply as Airlie slid her fingers through the moisture. She pulled back to watch Olivia's expression and knew it was the most monumental moment of her life. Olivia closed her eyes and rested her head against the wall as she found rhythm riding Airlie's hand.

The sideboard rocked against the wall as Airlie increased in speed and force.

She knew what Olivia wanted, and Olivia seemed to trust her enough to deliver. Another change in pace and she knew Olivia would be all hers. She moved steadily inside her until a sharp intake of breath signaled she was close. Airlie pumped faster as a heavy moan escaped Olivia. She clasped her arms tightly around Airlie's neck and came, fast and spirited. She enjoyed aftershocks for many minutes.

The hours before dawn were exquisite. After recovering from her first ever orgasm, Olivia tenderly undressed Airlie, but it wasn't long before her slow, seductive pace increased to frantic and desperate. With Olivia inside her, Airlie experienced a connection she'd never imagined. A connection where two people truly became one. If she'd have said as much, it would have sounded as corny as the movies, but it was true, their togetherness was deeper and more intense than a simple physical connection. Yes, it was quick and at times clumsy, but the passion left Airlie craving more.

In the early hours, before sleep took them both, Airlie rolled onto her elbow to look at Olivia. "Are you okay?"

"I'm very good, thanks." Olivia smiled but with tears in her eyes.

"You did want this, didn't you?"

"I did. Of course I did. I have so many emotions, I don't know what to do with them all."

"But you're okay?"

"I'm more than okay, I promise."

"You're so beautiful."

Olivia laughed nervously. "In moonlight, just about everything is beautiful."

"You're awful sexy, too." Airlie traced a circle of eight around Olivia's breasts.

"Stop it, you." She pushed Airlie back and moved on top of her.

"You're beautiful, sex—"

"Shoosh, will you."

"Hot, smart, very smart."

"Airlie, shut it."

"And above all, do you know what you are?"

"Go on. What am I, above all?"

"You're in bed with me."

Olivia knelt between Airlie's legs and sighed, admiring her. "Yes, my love, I'm in bed with you." Their fingers entwined. "And you make me feel amazing."

Airlie sat up and buried her face in Olivia's chest, wrapping her arms around her and holding tight until her hand slowly parted Olivia's legs, causing her to flinch.

"Oh God, Airlie."

They made love one last time before sleeping. Airlie fell asleep in Olivia's embrace knowing that the only thing that mattered was their love for each other and their shared desire to please each other. Nothing outside of the hotel room was important. The rest of the world did not exist.

## Chapter Thirty-one

As the sun crept higher and the shadows grew shorter, Airlie squinted, irritated by the brightness. Then, remembering the sight of Olivia's body in the moonlight, her mood softened. Last night had been incredible. She wanted to scream to the world that Olivia loved her, that she had *made* love to her. Her elation was indescribable, and the moisture between her legs at the memory of Olivia inside her was indication enough that she was so remarkably in love. She shivered at the thought.

Olivia stirred and backed into her arms. Airlie gently slid her hand lower until Olivia was wide-awake, her body writhing in pleasure.

"I can see myself becoming a morning person," Olivia said.

Airlie kissed the back of her neck.

"What time is it?" Olivia's breathing increased, keeping pace with Airlie's pulsing fingers.

"Time for this." Airlie rolled Olivia onto her back and began gently nibbling her ear before she kissed her way southward.

"Yep. Now is certainly a good time for this."

It was ten past nine on Saturday morning, and although they were oblivious to the rest of the world, life for most continued as normal. So normal, in fact, that Airlie failed to consider the fact that right at that moment, someone might be missing Olivia.

Airlie's seduction was long and sensual, and just as Olivia reached climax, her mobile rang. Airlie hated that the world dared to interrupt them. The phone lit up and vibrated on the bedside table, oblivious to her contempt. There had been only silence and the sound of two people making love; now the digital, synthetic ring was an intrusion and a reminder that they weren't the only people in the world. The real world stung like a slap in the face.

Olivia pushed her away. "It's Gavin," she said. Airlie detected a hint of panic and sadness in her voice.

"Just leave it." Airlie was desperate to steal back the moment. "Please, just leave it for a while, yeah?"

"I'll let it go to message bank."

Airlie silently claimed victory and resumed her seduction, gently kissing Olivia's inner thigh, convinced she could make them both forget the call.

She was wrong.

"We have to think of what we're going to say." Olivia broke the spell and covered herself with the sheet. "We have to get our story straight before I call him back."

This was inevitable, Airlie knew, but she'd relegated the unfathomable problem to the back of her mind. There was a lot to consider. Lying to Gavin would be difficult for them both, but supporting Olivia in this whole mess was imperative. Being together would have many repercussions. Gavin was probably at the forefront of Olivia's mind, and Airlie understood why. She knew Olivia couldn't live a lie, not for long, but choosing the exact time to confess was up to her. Airlie imagined it wouldn't be today, but she would make damn sure she was there for her when it happened. They were in this together, and she would be patient.

"When are you going to tell him?"

"Tell him what?"

"About us."

"Are you insane?" The words rang in Airlie's ear like a burst balloon. "I can never tell him about us." Olivia glared. "I'm sorry, Airlie. I don't know what you thought last night meant, but I can't tell Gav any of this. It would break his heart."

The Olivia that had been in bed with her only moments before was gone. This Olivia, the one rigid with apprehension, was like an alien. Airlie wanted the confident, loving, and affectionate Olivia back. This frightened, confused little sparrow had stolen her lover.

The plume of pure love previously floating in the room solidified and crashed in a shattered heap. Airlie collected her thoughts. *What about me? What about my heart?* She tried to think of something profound to say, but the most honest question passed her lips. "I thought you said you loved me?"

"I do love you, honey." Olivia sighed and moved to touch her on the cheek, but she pulled away. "Airlie, I do love you, but we can't be together. How can we? This is Catholic Ireland, you're a lesbian. I don't know what I am, but I have a life here, and it's with Gavin."

Airlie's brain flicked between what Olivia was saying and the love they made last night.

"So, why did you do this?" Airlie's eyes were moist, but the growing disappointment held her tears at bay. "Why did you let last night happen?"

"I don't know. I don't know what I'm doing. To be honest, I didn't think you were asking me to leave Gavin and be with you."

"I love you. I'm *in* love with you. Doesn't that mean anything?"

"Nothing I said to you last night was a lie, but in the cold light of day, I don't see how we could make it work. I thought you understood that this is all we could ever have. It doesn't have to end now, like this. I can come to Dublin and you can come here to me. This doesn't have to end, but I can't tell Gav. I won't tell Gav."

"So you just want to have sex with me every now and again?"

"No, that's not what I'm saying. I love you, but I love Gavin, too. I'm a married woman."

"So were you faking it last night?"

"Which bit?"

"*It.* Did you orgasm or not?"

Olivia sighed. "I did. You know I did."

"Do you ever want to have sex with me again?"

"Airlie, please don't do this. Don't spoil what we shared. You know I want you. You make me feel amazing."

"So, let me recap. I can make you come, unlike your husband, you actually *want* to have sex with me, again, unlike your husband, and I make you feel amazing? Notice the pattern here?" Airlie shot out of bed and threw her arms in the air. "I like Gav, I really do, and this is crap for him, but in case you hadn't noticed, you just spent the night fucking me."

This was her worst nightmare. Olivia was confused, she knew that, but her feelings of anger and disappointment were too strong for sympathy, and she couldn't look at her any longer.

"I'm taking a shower," Airlie said. "You call Gavin and make up the lie. Tell me what I have to say. I'll be going straight to bed to catch up on sleep when we get back, and then I'd like for you to take me to the train station to catch the evening train back to Dublin." She stood in the bathroom doorway, staring at the hinges. "Please."

"You don't have to go." Olivia moved toward Airlie.

"I don't want to stay." Airlie slammed the bathroom door and locked it. She let the tears engulf her. Her feeling of elation had disappeared, and everything began crumbling away.

Olivia's lie was simple. They had run into a friend of a friend from Olivia's work, no one Gavin knew, and they had become embroiled in a raucous session of music and drinking and decided to stay the night. She'd fallen asleep before she'd called him. Airlie was in no mood for talking so there was little chance of putting her foot in it if Gavin probed. As soon as they returned home, she excused herself and went to bed.

She was tired, exhausted in fact, but sleep eluded her for a long time. That feeling of contentment that filled her waking in Olivia's arms had disappeared, extinguished in one conversation and a disastrous aftermath. She longed for nothing other than for Olivia to be by her side, in bed, blissfully recovering from their amazing night together.

When she woke and dressed for the train, a headache loomed heavy, like a hangover, but perhaps it was her heart feeling the pain. The house was quiet, and as she walked to the kitchen, she passed Olivia and Gav's bedroom. Olivia was in bed asleep; Gav was next to her on top of the covers, reading.

He interrupted Airlie gulping her second pint of water. "Liv said you have to get back tonight." His mood was casual. "I'm supposed to wake her so she can take you to the station, but I think I'll let her sleep. She was dead tired."

*Damn.* She had wanted to talk to Olivia alone. It was her intention to convince her to think about a future together, to consider other options, and to reassure her that any path forward would be taken together. Airlie wanted to touch her and kiss her good-bye, stir undeniable arousal again, and leave her with a lingering sensation to ponder. She wanted to ask her, as she caressed between her legs, if Gavin could make her feel what she could make her feel? Above all, she wanted to ask if she would be happy living a lie for the rest of her life.

Before panic overwhelmed her completely, Airlie inhaled, slowing her racing pulse. She realized that particular conversation would have to wait. She refocused and agreed with Gav that Olivia should sleep. It had certainly been a late night.

"You two must have really tied one on? Pity neither of you bothered to call me." He grabbed his coat and car keys. "Did you sleep at all?"

"A little." Airlie was in no mood for small talk. "I'll nod off on the train."

Within minutes, they were driving along the same road she had driven with Olivia's hand on her leg the previous night.

Airlie was broken. Not her heart—that was being held together by the slightest of threads, the knowledge that Olivia loved her. She felt broken because she was running away from the one person she wanted to be with. Nothing had been decided. There was no conclusion to their predicament. She was sure this wasn't the end of whatever they had begun. What they had experienced was unlike anything either of them had even come close to in the past. Olivia wouldn't be able to forget it; she knew she would want more. Airlie was forced to bide her time.

## CHAPTER THIRTY-TWO

The half-empty train hurtled along, swaying back and forth as it sped across the countryside. Airlie dozed but was desperate for her own bed. She was surprised by how quickly the stations came and went, a vast contrast to the opposite journey. When her phone chimed like a doorbell, she knew it was a text message, and her instincts told her it was Olivia. The dread of learning Olivia might never want to see her again loomed, but she only hesitated briefly. *Sorry. I told Gavin to wake me. I'm sorry about this morning. We need to talk, in person. Do you agree?*

There was no kiss to end the message. Why was the letter X such a profound and significant way to end a message? She looked again. No X.

Her carriage was quiet, almost empty. Most people had better things to do on a Saturday night. She sighed and sent a return message agreeing that they should talk. She added two kisses before sending. The conversation would, in all probability, not be one she'd want to hear, but it was a chance she was willing to take. Her spirits lifted slightly when she considered they would meet and talk in person. She was already planning a seduction—making love to Olivia was all she could think of.

The next message from Olivia was, upon reflection, predictable. Airlie's own lack of insight was disappointing, for she had not seen it coming. *I can't look at him. I can't believe I've done this to him. I'm everything I despise. As soon as your fingers went inside me, I thought of him. I'm going to hell.*

Airlie slumped, exhausted and deflated. She was nearly home, and it had been a long day. There was nothing she could do about Olivia's guilt. She knew this because she felt little of it, even to console her would be difficult; Airlie was the reason for the guilt in the first place.

She endeavored to pin down a time when they would talk, but Olivia was noncommittal. She had her own issues to wade through. Airlie tried calling but hung up just as message bank clicked on. It was a gamble, but Airlie's last text, just before the train slowed into Heuston Station, said she was there for her no matter what, and she ended it with *I Love You.*

For the next week, she received no response and it nearly killed her.

When you sleep with one of your best friends and it all goes horribly wrong, it becomes strikingly obvious that you've lost a confidant, someone you turn to when you want to talk problems through and a shoulder to cry on. Airlie had lost the one person who always said the right thing and made her feel better.

A small part of her refused to feel bad. That part was the jubilant, lovestruck corner of her brain that recalled, with alarming frequency, that she had made love to the most amazing woman in the world. The fear of losing Olivia counterbalanced that joy. Things were so uncertain that it was best to keep this problem to herself, and for the most part, she maintained a convincing façade. *Patience*, she reminded herself daily. *Patience.*

Airlie remained busy, working long hours and spending time with Hannah and Liam, chatting about the wedding and the engagement party. Throughout the day and night, she checked her phone for messages or missed calls. Nothing. Well into the next week, Olivia remained elusive, and it occurred to her that perhaps she had blown it entirely. The urge to call, make some sort of contact, nagged her incessantly, but she was fearful of placing pressure on the situation. Time and space were required, and even though she was exhausted from restless nights, she persevered with keeping her distance, convinced she was slowly going insane.

Ten days had passed and still no word from Olivia. Airlie was becoming frantic and irritable. Rachel was out most of the time. She rarely mentioned where, but kept herself to herself. Airlie had taken to drinking almost a bottle of wine a night and flaking out on the couch because she was so tired.

It was an extraordinarily cold Thursday evening, and she'd left work at a reasonable hour, not so much because of her headache from lack of sleep, but because she needed to detour to the local supermarket for dinner supplies. She craved a cigarette and bought a packet.

Satisfied with the nicotine hit, she strolled homeward, ignoring the cold and savoring every contaminated inhalation. As her house came into view, she recognized a familiar red car parked outside. It looked like Olivia's, but she knew it couldn't be. From behind, the car certainly appeared to have someone inside, but walking closer, almost parallel, she realized the possible figure was only a coat hanging over the driver's seat.

She pulled another cigarette from the packet and thought only of cooking dinner and relaxing with a drink before she showered and settled in front of the TV.

She flicked the temperamental lighter impatiently. Finally, ignition. Airlie held it to the tip of her cigarette, poised to draw back, when a familiar voice spoke from the top of the stairs.

"Are you doing that all the time now?"

Airlie jumped. She held her hand on her heart, as if to hold it in. "What are you doing here?"

Olivia patted the concrete step next to her. "Sit. Tell me about your day?"

"It's freezing out here." Airlie was both delighted and baffled. "Don't you want to go inside?"

"Don't you want to have your smoke?"

"Not really. Not now."

"Just sit. Watch the world go by with me."

Airlie glanced the length of the street, observing how peculiarly empty it appeared for this time of evening, but she sat nevertheless.

"So, how was your day?" Olivia asked.

"Okay, I guess."

"And work, is that going okay?"

"Work is fine, it's just work. Look, are you okay? I really think we should go inside." Airlie moved to stand, but Olivia's hand, firm on her knee, forced her down.

"Don't go in, not yet."

"You're not staying, are you?"

For the first time, Olivia looked at her, not fleetingly, but really took her in. "What makes you say that?"

"You're here unannounced, and you don't want to come in. I'm not stupid."

"I know. I never said you were."

Airlie stood. "So, say what you have to say and leave."

"What do you think I'm here to say?"

"Just say it." The quicker Olivia confessed, the quicker she would go home and Airlie could pick up the pieces. Again. "Why did you bother driving all the way down here for this?" Then the final insulting penny dropped. "You're not here to see me, are you? You have some work thing on and just thought you'd kill two birds with one stone?" She kicked a crushed cider can onto the road.

"Please, Airlie, just sit down for a minute." Airlie glared and Olivia glared back. "Sit."

She returned to the step but retrieved her smoke and lit it in protest. Olivia smiled.

"Do you think this is funny?"

"No, not at all."

Airlie hugged her knees.

"The city is so noisy, isn't it? I mean, compared to the country," Olivia said.

"Yes, Olivia, the city is noisy." Airlie had exhausted all her patience reserves. "Why are you here?"

"I wanted to see you. I needed to see you."

"Why?"

"Because I've missed you."

"And?"

"Isn't that enough?"

Maybe it was enough. Airlie didn't know anymore. "You could have called, or sent a message."

"I only decided to come the moment I left work this afternoon. Plus, I wanted to surprise you."

"So, are you here for work?"

"No, I told you. I wanted to see you."

"So, now that you've seen me are you just going to get back in your car and drive home again?"

"I don't think that was my intention."

"But you won't come in?"

"I never said I wasn't going to come in."

The conversation was becoming more ridiculous by the second. "So, can we go in now?" Whatever game Olivia was playing was insensitive and its purpose bewildering.

Airlie had reached her limit. Olivia could stay outside for all she cared. She began to retreat indoors when Olivia spoke at last. "I want to sit outside for a while, because behind that door," she tilted her head toward the house, "we'll be alone."

Airlie knew there was more. She waited.

"Behind that door, the world out here won't exist. So, if we stay here and talk for a while, it will mean that I haven't driven four hours to simply walk through that door and rip your clothes off, like I would very much like to do. It will mean that I've come to visit you because I miss you and want to talk to you, but eventually, after we have talked for a while, I'll want you more than you could possibly imagine. To be honest, I'm hoping you'll want me, too."

"Oh."

"So, I'll ask you again, how was your day?"

"My day was good, thank you." It took all her composure not to rush and describe everything in thirty seconds so she could get Olivia inside. "I've missed you, too."

Olivia reached around Airlie's shoulders and drew her close, kissing the top of her head. The chilled air seemed insignificant, and as if it were now safe to do so, the street once again came to life with cars and pedestrians, returning home from a long day.

"You hungry?" Airlie asked.

"I am, actually. Are you going to cook me dinner?"

"If you're game." Airlie stood and offered her hand.

It was impossible not to pretend that all she wanted was to kiss Olivia the instant the front door shut behind them, but she resisted the urge. The house was warm from the central heating, and Airlie suggested Olivia select some music while she lit candles.

Within a few minutes, the place was glowing beautifully in

candlelight, Pavarotti's greatest hits were softly playing, and they stood in the middle of the lounge facing each other, red wine in hands.

"To us," Airlie offered.

"To us." They clinked glasses and drank.

Airlie glanced between her wine glass and Olivia, whose eyes refused to stray. The distance between them was short, less than a meter. Olivia spoke. "Come here." She held Airlie's gaze. Airlie smiled. "Come here, please."

Arousal threatened to render her incapable of movement. She stepped in.

"Closer."

The candlelight danced on every surface, the flames fueled by invisible drafts, and Airlie was filled with thoughts of how Olivia's skin glowed in the light. Imagining her naked, she stepped in so close that their noses were only centimeters apart.

"I really have missed you," said Olivia.

"I've missed you, too."

Olivia traced a line down Airlie's face, from her forehead to her chin, her finger lingering on her lips.

"You're always in my thoughts."

"I'd be disappointed if someone else was in your thoughts right now."

"I'm trying to be romantic here. I'm trying to tell you how I feel."

Airlie laughed and kissed her, quickly but affectionately. "I know, and you're gorgeous, but right now, I need to cook you some dinner, so you're welcome to come into the kitchen and keep me company, or you can stay here and relax."

"Considering you're *actually* cooking, I think this is something I need to witness firsthand. Plus, I want to make sure you do cook something and don't sneak out for takeaway."

Within an hour, a Thai green curry was simmering in the wok and they were finishing the wine. There was no talk of the future or the barriers they might encounter if this was indeed a lasting relationship. Airlie was simply happy to be near Olivia again.

Dinner was delicious and as "Nessun Dorma" played, Airlie's favorite, Olivia rose, formally requesting a dance. Airlie accepted her outstretched hand, until a thought came to mind. "Actually, can you pause for a moment?"

"Pardon?"

"Can you just wait one second? Please stay where you are. I promise I'll be back in a jiffy."

"Are you deliberately sabotaging my every attempt to seduce you?"

"Liv, rest assured, you don't need to try very hard." Airlie rushed to the bathroom and within two minutes, returned, restarted the music, and swept Olivia from the couch. "Right, let's dance."

It was awkward at first, both having only ever slow danced with men before, but they quickly found the best place for arms and hands and became lost in the drama of the music, the movement, and each other.

"I love this song. But it's so sad," Olivia said.

"It is?"

"It's from *Turandot*. The Prince, Calef, has solved the riddles that will allow him to marry Princess Turandot, but she is mean and balks at the thought of marrying him. Calef, madly in love with her, gives her one last chance by giving her until dawn to guess his name. If she does, she can execute him. If she doesn't, they must marry. The selfish princess then announces none of her subjects shall sleep until they have discovered his name. If they fail she will kill them all."

"My God, that's terrible. I never knew that."

"There is a line though, that is rather romantic. 'And my kiss will dissolve the silence that makes you mine.'"

Airlie smiled and nestled in.

"Why did you rush off before? Did you leave the stove on or something?"

"No, nothing like that. I'm running a bath for us." She crossed her fingers hoping it wasn't too presumptuous.

"Really?"

"With bubbles and all." She waited for a reaction that didn't come. "You don't mind, do you?"

"Mind? Not at all, but what's your water pressure like?"

"Shit!" Airlie raced from the room.

The bath resembled a giant snow cone, mountains of bubbles threatening to take over, but thankfully, the water wasn't overflowing.

"Jesus, that was lucky. I could've ruined the night."

In no time, they stood nervously facing each other by the light of a solitary candle. Airlie took a deep breath and began to undress.

"No, wait. Can I do it?" Olivia stepped forward.

To the sound of Pavarotti and the crackling bubbles in the bath, they undressed each other. The sweet scent of apple bubble bath filled the air, and they stepped naked into the bubbles, entwined in each other, sinking through the foam and under the water.

# CHAPTER THIRTY-THREE

Their destructive love affair developed into a world of deception and self-indulgent behavior. For Airlie especially, it was a most thrilling time.

"What time's he leaving?" Airlie whispered across the lounge room. She was watching the clock. It had been almost thirty minutes since Gavin had begun preparations for his monthly card night with work buddies, and she was becoming incorrigible.

Olivia shrugged.

The anticipation of what was to come left Airlie agitated.

"In here or in my room?"

"Your room." Olivia's eyes never left the TV.

Five minutes passed before Airlie whispered again. "Can we shower together first?"

Olivia nodded.

"God, how long does it take him to get ready?"

"Be quiet."

Another agonizing ten minutes passed while Airlie bit her fingernails. "I don't think I can wait for the shower."

Olivia continued to stare at the TV.

"Have you got a bra on?"

Olivia shook her head.

"Have you got *any* underwear on?"

She shook her head.

Airlie flopped back. Olivia ignored her.

Finally, Gavin waltzed in, dressed in tan trousers and a navy blue shirt. He looked like most other middle-aged men, and a strong waft of aftershave sucked through the door after him.

"Hey there, hot stuff." Dealing with Gavin was the one thing Airlie hated, besides the fact that he was married to Olivia. There was evidence to suggest that the chemical produced in your brain while having an affair was like a drug. Addictive. What they were doing behind Gavin's back was wrong, but she couldn't stop, and it appeared neither could Olivia. "You sure you're only going to play cards with the boys?"

Gav flushed red but ignored her and turned to Olivia. "Bye, love, I won't be late." He kissed her. "What are you two planning for the evening?"

Airlie shrugged, pretending to be engrossed in the news.

"We might just watch a movie. Maybe play Scrabble or something. Nothing as exciting as your evening, I'm sure."

"You should have organized a night out yourselves. It's not too late. I can drop you off on the way if you like?"

Airlie knew Olivia wasn't expecting this. An awkward pause ensued; no one seemed to know what to say. Finally, Olivia gathered herself. "To be honest, we thought about it." A blatant lie. "But we simply can't be bothered. Plus, Airlie is a bit strapped for cash right now." Another lie. "So I think it best to just stay in and open a bottle of red. Our lounge room is as good as any pub sometimes."

Gavin gazed curiously between them. "Okay, as I said, I won't be late. You'll probably be up when I get back."

"Take your time. You don't go out often, you should live it up when you do."

Olivia tenderly squeezed his backside. Airlie didn't care. She knew what was coming, and his arrival home, early or not, was unimportant.

After what felt like days, Airlie heard the front door slam. Olivia switched the TV to mute. Within ten seconds, a car door shut and the engine sparked into action. It was usual practice for Gavin to let the car warm up for at least thirty seconds before driving off. Airlie and Olivia waited in silence. Finally, they heard the crunching of the gravel driveway and listened for the sound slowly fading as he negotiated the gate and took off down the long driveway.

Airlie rose from her chair.

Olivia signaled for her to stay put.

The desire building inside was unbearable.

Olivia remained alert, listening for any sound out of the ordinary. Airlie knew she had to be sure Gavin had driven far enough away to avoid returning for anything he might have forgotten. He'd at least remembered his wallet; she'd watched Olivia feel for it in his back pocket.

She observed Olivia's expression in silent anticipation. Turning from the window and switching off the TV, Olivia smiled, nodding subtle permission. Airlie unbuttoned her jeans, yearning for satisfaction. So intense was her desire, she had barely removed her pants from one leg before straddling Olivia and demanding instant gratification.

It was customary for them to make love as soon as possible after meeting at the train station, usually in the car, somewhere secluded. This evening, however, Gavin had been with Olivia on account of her car being at the mechanic's. He'd driven her to work and had driven them both home. Olivia had sent word of the altered arrangements, so it was no surprise, but it was unusual to be in each other's company for nearly three hours, barely able to touch. The desire Airlie experienced was addictive. The horny teenager inside her relished the prolonged abstinence, and subsequent passion it would induce.

By the time Gavin left, Airlie was convinced she was as aroused as humanly possible in a situation void of physical contact. It was as if foreplay had begun hours ago. When they were cooking dinner, as Gav threw the ball for Ash in the yard directly outside the window, they had flirted and groped each other below the height of the benches. The tension had been almost tangible, and for hours, Airlie had waited with indescribable lust on her mind.

Tonight's unusual circumstances led to passionate and experimental lovemaking. After initially satisfying Airlie in the lounge, Olivia led her to the spare room, undressed her, and tied her to the bed—something they'd never tried before. She produced a box of sex toys, ordered on the Internet, and they spent the next two hours experimenting and exploring each other's bodies, desires, and fantasies.

❖

Airlie wondered what Gavin would do upon his return to the house. As he turned the key in the lock, would the house appear unusually quiet? Would he know they weren't yet in bed, and as he hooked his coat in the hall, would he hear something unusual and be suspicious? Would he even stop to listen?

Airlie and Olivia had had sex many times, showered, and were now waiting for him to return. The ropes had left no marks on her ankles and wrists, and the light spanking she'd received had left her backside tingling for more. They had fucked each other, made use of nearly all the toys, and then made love.

Airlie was on the floor in her pajamas cuddling Ash when Gavin returned.

"Nice evening?" asked Olivia. She flicked the channel on the TV.

"Yes, fine." He stared around the room for a long moment.

"How was cards? Did you wipe the floor with them?" asked Airlie.

"I won a few hands, played quite well actually. I think I'm improving."

"Great, good for you."

"Honey, why don't you join us?" said Olivia.

"Thank you anyway, but I think I'll go to bed. Can I expect you along soon?"

The invitation sparked jealousy in Airlie.

"We're hanging out for the late movie. It doesn't start until midnight, so I won't be in for a while yet, sorry," said Olivia.

He looked disappointed. "Okay, but try not to be too long."

At midnight, the late movie began. They had both seen it before so would be able to answer any questions, should they be quizzed the following morning. The volume was low enough not to disturb Gavin but loud enough to be heard clearly. The head of the sofa bed was set against the wall, shielded directly behind the door, should Gavin return.

In the dim TV light, Airlie silently rolled on top of Olivia. Having savored every minute of her naked earlier that evening, she accepted the need to remain clothed; it was too risky to undress now. She slipped her hand inside Olivia's pajama pants, edging her open enough to fit her hand comfortably between her legs. After playing with her opening and gently teasing Olivia's most sensitive spot, Airlie pushed three fingers inside deeply and slowly. She would explore further with her mouth in good time, but for now, she brought Olivia to climax with one hand in her pants and the other firmly placed over her mouth.

## CHAPTER THIRTY-FOUR

Is everything okay?" Hannah asked. She was visiting one Friday evening, and Airlie knew she was angling for a dinner invitation. Sneaking around with Olivia was becoming complicated.

"How do you mean?"

"Just in general, I guess. I suppose more specifically between you and Rachel. Are you two still getting on?"

Airlie was relieved. Hannah's concern was regarding the wedding.

"Of course. That stuff between us is all old news. She's seeing a girl called Celia."

Hannah nodded. "The masseuse she met when using your Christmas voucher."

"Ironic really. But I hope she's happy."

"She and I were talking and we figured *you* must be seeing someone."

"Me?" Airlie laughed and glanced at the clock. "And what brings you both to that conclusion?"

"You seem rather content these days, and you're constantly on the train to Westport. I just thought there might be someone special over there?"

Airlie tensed. She knew this conversation was coming. She inhaled before answering. "You've got Liam now, and hanging around Dublin every weekend isn't all that much fun. Besides, it's just a train ride; I'd only be sitting at home watching TV or reading a book. I might as well read and go somewhere at the same time."

Hannah shrugged, but Airlie couldn't read her.

"So, have you been staying with Olivia?" asked Hannah.

"Of course."

"And she comes down here quite often, also?"

Airlie realized this was now an interrogation, not just friendly interest. "Sure. Actually, she's on her way now."

"Here to stay?"

"Well, I'm hardly going to make her sleep on the street."

"Incidentally, where does she sleep?"

"Hannah! Give it up. She sleeps in my old room."

"And everything's okay?"

"Of course. Everything's fine. What's the big deal?"

"There's no big deal, I guess, but it does seem a little odd that a married woman spends so much time with you and not her husband."

"What's your point, Han?" It was a gamble, but Airlie needed Hannah to get this out of her system before Olivia arrived. If she had something to say, Airlie wanted to hear it sooner rather than later.

"No point. I'm just wondering if everything is okay between Olivia and Gavin."

"As far as I know, everything's fine. Couldn't be better, I'm sure. You can ask her yourself when she arrives."

"So, you're inviting me for dinner then?"

There was no way Airlie could avoid inviting Hannah without raising further suspicion. The enjoyable romantic dinner was now something she'd have to endure as a threesome. "Of course. I'm surprised you were waiting for an invite. Rachel's out, but there's more than enough for three."

Hannah looked pleased. Airlie put her to work setting the table and putting out the rubbish. She became nervous, unsure of Olivia's reaction to having a guest. They had lived so tightly in their own world lately, it felt odd sharing it with someone else under circumstances that would be a lie.

By the time Olivia arrived at eight thirty, Airlie was on her second wine. She'd messaged to warn her about Hannah but received no reply. The lack of response wasn't because Olivia was driving, it was because she was annoyed. Airlie could read her like a book. Sneaking around was thrilling for them both, but in some circumstances, it left Olivia cold and bitter. Guilt could do strange things to people, and it was Airlie who bore the brunt of Olivia's shame.

"So, you've been visiting quite a bit lately?" Hannah asked Olivia. Her intense stare made it clear she expected an answer.

"I guess I have. It's lovely having a friend to visit. There's so much to do in Dublin. I suppose I'm rather rude taking advantage of Airlie and her offer of accommodation so frequently."

"Funny you should mention that, because Airlie was just after saying how boring Dublin is."

Airlie and Olivia exchanged looks.

"And how's Gavin these days? Fending for himself quite a bit, I gather?"

A frown creased Olivia's brow. "He's a big boy. I'm sure he's fine."

Airlie shot Hannah a warning look. She was dangerously close to overstepping the line.

"What do you two get up to over there then?"

"We just hang out," Airlie said.

"That's a long way to go to just hang out."

Airlie's heart quickened and her knife slipped in her sweaty palm. "What do you and Liam get up to all weekend? Just hang out, I suppose?"

"We're getting married, Airlie, so yes, that's exactly what we do."

Olivia continued to eat, eyes fixed firmly on her plate. Airlie had nothing to say. Silence was her only friend now. She hoped Hannah would drop it.

"Is that your *Westport Weekly* in the bin outside with Westport jobs and flats circled, Air Bear?"

Airlie nearly choked.

"If you'll excuse me, I need the bathroom." Olivia's eyes never left Airlie's until she was out of sight. Airlie wanted the ground to crack open and swallow her.

Hannah knew.

Even without confirmation, she knew. Hannah was smart, and Airlie knew how her mind worked.

"I should go," said Hannah.

"It's not what it looks like, Han."

"What isn't? The thing that's *not* going on between you and Olivia isn't what it looks like?"

"There's nothing going on."

Hannah collected her coat. "You're a shit liar, Airlie. I don't know what you're playing at. I just hope you know what you're doing."

Airlie flopped in the chair as Hannah left and Olivia returned. If the scene had been animated, Olivia would have had steam pouring from her ears and her eyes would be staring daggers at Airlie.

"Christ, Airlie! Maybe we should get each other's names tattooed on our foreheads. That might be a little less obvious than that conversation."

"Sorry, I didn't know—"

"And what the *fuck* are you thinking? You can't move to Westport. If Hannah knows what's going on, Christ knows who else does. This is great, just fucking great. Well done, Airlie."

"Hannah doesn't know anything for sure. I kept my promise to you. I've not told a soul."

"A fat lot of good that's done. She fucking well knows."

This conversation was bound to occur sooner or later, and Airlie refused to let the opportunity pass. "So what if she does know? Does it really matter? She won't tell Gavin. She wouldn't even tell Liam if I asked her not to." Something told Airlie that Hannah had probably already discussed it with Liam and probably even Rachel. "What does it matter? She knows I'm gay. She just wants me to be happy, and if you make me happy, then she'll be fine with it."

"Are you listening to yourself? Are you? *No one* can know about us. This has to stay hidden, damn it. I have a husband. Do you understand, Airlie, or should I get back in my car and drive home now?"

"No."

"I beg your pardon?"

"No, please stay."

"Do you want me to leave?"

"I said no."

"Then, I asked you a question. Do you fucking well understand me?"

"Don't leave." She began to clear the table. "I understand perfectly."

Arlie was now ready to be herself, to be gay, and to be with the love of her life. Olivia was this love, she was sure of that, but there was nothing to indicate this relationship would grow into anything more than it currently was. Indeed, their argument substantiated this.

Olivia was the polar opposite, nowhere near ready to leave her husband, and no closer to making changes in her life.

It had been a testing evening that predictably ended with sex. Rough, angry sex at first that left Airlie feeling used, but as the hours passed, Olivia's rage faded, and they tenderly made love. Hands behind her head, Olivia stretched back on the pillows. "If I hadn't experienced this for myself, I wouldn't have thought it was possible for me to like— no, make that crave—sex with you so much."

"So, it's okay then?"

"Are you kidding? It's amazing." She looked Airlie in the eye. "Honestly, I never thought I could feel this way." She kissed her cheek softly. "I love you so much. But we need to be much more careful in the future."

Airlie went to speak, but stopped herself. It was a decisive moment, but she ignored it, especially given the events of the evening. There was a conversation that needed to occur, but this wasn't the right time. There was never going to be a right time. So instead of asking Olivia where she thought their relationship would go, or perhaps end, she smiled and replied that she loved her, too.

Feigning a yawn, Airlie snuggled down, facing away from Olivia so she could hide the tears dampening her pillow. Her heart was breaking. She couldn't believe how much she was in love with this woman, this woman who snuggled behind her. She couldn't believe how fortunate she was, how blessed to find her one true love. Perhaps this sort of love was more common than she thought, and although the circumstances weren't in her favor, she couldn't help but feel lucky.

Speaking with Olivia about their future would put an end to their relationship, or whatever it was. Therefore, to *not* speak of their future would prolong the fantasy they were living. It was Airlie's belief that any form of relationship was better than nothing. What she really wanted was for Olivia to leave Gavin, and for them to move toward a committed, monogamous relationship. Airlie wouldn't hesitate to marry Olivia. The question of spending the rest of her life with her was never in doubt.

Olivia's grip on Airlie loosened. She was sound asleep, and the alarm clock showed four a.m. Airlie slowly wiped her eyes, careful not to make any sudden movement. It was difficult to believe she could be so lucky, yet so unlucky at the same time. It was true, she had taken years and a great deal of soul searching to be comfortable in her own skin, and she recognized that she should afford Olivia some time to come to terms with the situation and the reality that her future may not involve Gavin.

Airlie's plan was to bide her time and wait.

## CHAPTER THIRTY-FIVE

Since that Friday evening when Hannah had caused a great row, she'd been walking on eggshells, too scared of losing Olivia again to even mention the issue that drove them apart in the first place.

Silently making love in the lounge room while Gavin slept soundly at the other end of the house became common practice.

It was three in the morning. "You have to go back to Gavin now." Airlie hated this moment, not only because Olivia was leaving her to be with her husband, but because of what they had just done. Gavin didn't deserve to have his wife cheat on him, especially with Airlie. The guilt was becoming ingrained. Airlie wondered how long she could continue the façade.

"I'm sorry it has to be this way," Olivia said.

Airlie wanted to ask her why it had to continue, why she refused to do nothing about it, but she just shrugged and nodded instead.

"Perhaps we should get away for a few days next time. I don't think this situation is healthy for either of us."

Airlie went to bed in the spare room wondering why she was helping to conceal their affair when it only served to hurt her. Why was she allowing the love of her life to return to bed with her husband? She began to wonder why she remained with someone who didn't love her enough to end her marriage.

When she returned to Dublin, this list of "why" questions grew daily. Airlie was jealous and disillusioned. She despised the last message she would receive of an evening. *Night, honey, I'm off to bed now, sleep well and sweet dreams. I love you. XX.*

But how could Olivia love her? She was unfaithful to a man she slept with nightly. She lied to him, deceived him, and said she loved Airlie. She reread the message and found no solace in Olivia's words. She found anger and pain, and to compound the situation, jealousy was leaving her feeling dangerously irrational. Her first thought every morning was of Olivia, having sex with *him* the previous night. It consumed her. She imagined him kissing her good-bye each morning, shaving in the bathroom while she showered, ogling her naked body. It wasn't his to ogle. It was hers. How long would Olivia let this go on? Airlie's failing sanity was pushing her to the point where her only option was to find out.

It was the midst of summer, Friday evening, and Airlie was on her way to meet Olivia in Athlone. It was the weekend of the Birr Castle Fair, a popular country event. Olivia had always intended to visit, and it seemed that yet another weekend away together was enough incentive to make the trip.

The late afternoon train coasted along, nearing Athlone, and Airlie headed to the bathroom to freshen up. She flushed the toilet as the train jerked from side to side. To steady herself, she gripped the edge of the sink. Her reflection was frightening. She was a mess. The dark circles beneath her eyes were prominent. She calculated the amount of sleep she'd had in the last week. Fifteen hours, give or take. That was about fifteen hours of thinking when she should have been sleeping. She pulled her top down and traced a line over the bones in her neck and upper chest. She'd never had prominent bones in that area before; her weight had dropped dramatically, especially in the last few weeks. Olivia had noticed of course, especially when she lay on top of her, but Airlie lied and said she was eating loads, but was on a fitness regime. The ease of the lie shocked her, but she realized her whole life was a lie, so what could one more hurt? *Here a lie, there a lie, everywhere a lie, lie.*

The usual sense of anticipation danced in her belly, but even that feeling was becoming tired. Her time with Olivia always began that way, but it rarely ended on a high note. She'd grown bored of having a weekend relationship, although they had been unable to see each other last weekend due to one of Gavin's work dinners. She'd remained disappointed and dejected all week. The annoyed, jealous, and utterly disrespectful feelings she experienced when Olivia broke the news to her hadn't subsided. If she were to be honest, she was holding on to them like a bag full of millions.

A few passengers disembarked at Athlone, more than Airlie expected, and her eyes narrowed as the sun shone brightly. She wasn't in the best frame of mind for a romantic weekend, but the choice was hers to make. She could either ignore her anger and jealousy and have a great time, or she could start an argument. She was compromising her integrity, and it had ultimately caught up with her. She was a liar, and it was all for the love of a married woman.

Olivia was late, and Airlie waited outside the train station for twenty minutes before the red BMW raced around the corner. There were certain rules Olivia insisted upon that governed displays of affection in public. Rule number one was no public displays whatsoever within a one-hundred-mile radius of Roaring Bay, Galway, Co Mayo, or, so it seemed, the entire Republic of Ireland. Rule number two was only a quick kiss as a greeting in public anywhere else. Airlie was allowed to rest her hand on Olivia's knee if she was driving, and often they held hands in the car, but if a bus or truck pulled alongside, Olivia would push her away. Perhaps the passenger had nothing better to do than gawk at the filthy lesbians. Besides all that, behind closed doors, there were no rules, and usually no clothes, but plenty of sex.

Airlie threw her bag into the back.

"Hey there," said Olivia. Her smile was stunning. "How's my girl?"

Forcing a smile, Airlie leaned over for the quick peck she knew was allowed. "I'm fine, thanks. How are you?"

"Much better for seeing you." Olivia took off, her left hand reaching to massage Airlie's crotch. "Yep, much better for seeing you."

Airlie allowed Olivia to grope her. They hadn't seen each other for two weeks, and Olivia was evidently looking to make up for lost time. When she was like this, it usually meant they would have sex most of the weekend. In the beginning, she loved it when Olivia wanted her all the time. Sometimes, while out shopping, they would have sex in change rooms, and often, while driving back to Airlie's place in Dublin from a night out, Olivia would detour to an isolated park, pull the car over, and order Airlie into the backseat. Airlie thrived on the excitement, and the throb it provoked between her legs.

"Undo your pants for me?" said Olivia. The inflection in her voice gave the misleading impression it was a question, an option. Airlie knew it was neither.

"Don't be ridiculous," she said.

"Undo them."

"We'll be there in five minutes."

"Airlie, do as you're told. Undo your pants."

"How about you just concentrate on driving."

"How about you undo your pants? I want to touch you."

"You'll have an accident."

Olivia laughed. "I will not. Just let me get my hand in there." She'd already managed to undo the top buttons.

"Stop it. You'll just have to wait." Airlie pushed her away.

"Spoilsport." Olivia sulked and focused on the road. "You look tired," she said finally. "Are you okay?"

"I'm fine. I am a bit tired, but I'm good."

"You're not sleeping well?"

"Not really," Airlie admitted. "Maybe I could do with some more iron in my diet or something."

Olivia grinned. "Sorry, but I think I'm about to tire you out even more. I reckon you'll sleep well tonight." She winked. "If I let you."

Airlie laughed, but it lacked conviction. She wished they could just go out for a nice meal or snuggle in front of a movie, but she accepted she probably had more chance of flying to the moon. She turned to gaze out the window. She was weary from all the lying, and the constant state of jealousy left her agitated. It was exhausting. In spite of the strength of these feelings, she knew her own weakness. She would conveniently set aside any reservations long enough to enjoy Olivia's seduction and subsequent lovemaking.

With Olivia in her current mood, Airlie understood she would be submissive tonight. Within thirty seconds of the door shutting behind them, Olivia would, at the least, strip her naked. Shortly after that, they both would have climaxed at least once, before most likely taking a bath and beginning a long night of lovemaking. What Olivia wanted, she received, and as often as she liked. Airlie was addicted to the way Olivia made her feel, and like all addicts, she needed her fix at any cost. Airlie was placing increasingly less value in herself.

Her deteriorating self-esteem was becoming progressively difficult to ignore. Every time they made love and Olivia went home to her husband, she felt just a little bit more worthless inside.

## CHAPTER THIRTY-SIX

The Birr Castle Fair was surprisingly interesting. The midday sun labored to compensate for the chilly morning, but it beamed upon them, alone in a cloudless sky. The familiar smell of barbecues and food stalls wafted through the grounds. It was invigorating. The love they made last night had been unbelievable, and Airlie again pushed her demons aside when this morning she woke to feel Olivia's hand edging up her thigh.

The journey to the castle had been pleasant. They chatted effortlessly, not about anything in particular, but a general catch-up with each other's lives. Airlie basked in the relaxing confines of the car, which soon became a warm, cozy cocoon. They drove through small country towns and past green fields separated by dry stone walls and bedraggled hedges. It was Airlie's hand this time, high on Olivia's leg. Every now and then Olivia would take a hand off the wheel and reach down to stroke her.

With the windows lowered, the soft breeze filled the car as they crawled along, one of many cars trapped in the ridiculously long parking queue. The slow progress wasn't enough to dampen their high spirits, and for a while, they seemed perfectly happy to pretend there was nothing wrong with the picture they were painting.

There was much to see and do at the fair. Stalls with handmade crafts, jewelry, and clothing lined the little avenues weaving through the castle grounds. It was the amazingly gigantic telescope, however, situated in the middle of the grounds, that demanded Airlie's attention. Olivia wandered off to find the toilet while Airlie stared at it for a long time, in awe of the massive construction. Its sheer enormity captured her imagination. She thought back to the time in history when they built the telescope. Back even further to when the idea was conceived. She imagined what sort of person would have had such a vision, a vision to see the stars, and dare to attempt to build something so complex. No one Airlie knew now, or ever had the pleasure of knowing, could possibly have imagined such a futuristic concept.

Suddenly, the world appeared to be saturated with too many people, far too many people to distinguish those who imagined bigger, dreamed beyond what was normal, and backed themselves to see their dream through. The world was full of people who couldn't see past their own nose. The world was full of people like her and Olivia. Airlie wondered where all the imaginative, visionary people disappeared to and why didn't she know just one person with vision? Why didn't *she* have any vision?

Airlie imagined the excitement of working on the telescope, not knowing if it would be successful and fulfill its purpose. She tilted her head to the sky. Someone believed in an idea so vehemently, they built a massive contraption at great expense. Someone, years ago, actually decided to build a telescope that everyone else probably thought would never work. Someone believed. Shockingly, Airlie realized she didn't believe in herself or in the choices she was making.

"A penny for your thoughts, sweetheart." Olivia rested a hand momentarily on Airlie's lower back.

Airlie ignored her, her gaze lingering on the telescope for one last second. "We need to talk." She turned. "We need to talk, now, but not here. Can we go?"

"Go?"

"Yes, I want to go."

"Is everything okay?"

"Someone had the balls to build this telescope. Christ, they had the balls to just think of it. You and I have no courage at all, no courage to face anything, no drive to change anything. You and I are nothing."

Olivia became aware people were beginning to stare. "What the hell has gotten into you?" She took Airlie sharply by the elbow and led her to a more discreet location. "What do you mean we're nothing?"

"I mean just that, Liv. Exactly fucking that. We. Are. Nothing."

"Will you keep your bloody voice down?"

Airlie threw her head to the bright blue sky. "That's my point.

Don't you see? We can't even have a fight in public. Heaven forbid someone might see us. I can't touch you or kiss you. Sometimes I just smile at you and you give me your look of disapproval. We sneak around, and behind closed doors you're amazing, but away from all that, you're just a scared, middle-aged woman who wants to use me so she can get fucked now and then."

Olivia leaned in. Airlie could tell she was furious. "We are not having this conversation here." She turned and walked toward the entrance.

Airlie followed in silence, rushing after her. They were clear of the gate before she responded. "Of course we can't talk about it here. *Someone* might see us."

Olivia seized Airlie by the shoulders. "Will you just fucking shut up? What in God's name is wrong with you? Why are you doing this to me?"

"Why am I doing this to *you*? Why are you doing this to *me*?" Her body went limp and her voice failed as tears came.

They stood in a long alleyway, lined on one side by a thick green hedge and on the other by a high, solid, stone wall. Moss grew on the uneven ground—the pavement starved of sunlight.

There was no turning back. "I love you more than I imagined I would ever love anyone, and I can honestly say, without a doubt in my mind, that I want to spend the rest of my life with you—"

"Airlie."

"I haven't finished. Please, let me finish." She shrugged from Olivia's grasp. "I want the world to know I've found you and that I want you and no one else. I want us to start a life together and stay together forever. I can honestly say this without hesitation. I know you love me, and I know that if you weren't married, this wouldn't be an issue. But what I don't understand is how you can love me so deeply, then leave me and go home to your husband? You make love to me, not him. You spend every spare minute with me and not him, but I'm the one you want to hide, the one you're ashamed of. I'm the one you only want to have when it suits you.

"I don't care if you think you're a fucking lesbian or not, it makes no difference to me, but make no mistake, what we do and how we make each other feel, isn't exactly hetero." She drew a much-needed breath. "This situation is tearing me apart. I love you so much, but the jealousy is killing me. I was prepared to do whatever it took to have you, in any capacity, but this is doing my head in. I lie awake at night and wonder if you and *him* are doing it—"

"We don't have sex anymore, Airlie. I told you that."

"It doesn't matter. You're *there*, next to him and not me. You choose to be with him, not me, and that hurts. I want to be yours, give myself to you, but you don't appear to feel the same. Until now, I've been too scared to ask how you feel, or what you want, for fear of it not being me, but you have to tell me the truth now, Liv, what do you want?"

"I want you, I do, but I just can't see how we can be together."

The answer seemed outrageously simple. "You leave your husband, Liv, that's what you do. That's how we can be together."

"I don't know if I can. I don't think I can do that to him."

"But you can do *this* to him? You can cheat, lie, and love someone else, but not leave him?"

"Maybe this is just a phase."

Airlie laughed. "A fucking phase? Jesus, I've heard it all now. You fucking my brains out last night is just a phase, is it? You inside me, making me come, is just a fucking phase, is it? You're unreal, you really are, and you know what, Liv? I reckon we're done here. I can end your pathetic little *phase* right here and now. If he's the one you truly love, then stay with him, be with him. Is that what you really want?"

"No."

"Jesus Christ! Then what do you want?"

"I want you both."

"Really? You want me to be miserable and jealous and at call for you to have whenever you feel like it?"

"No, I didn't say that."

"Then tell me how you want this to work?"

Olivia turned and pressed both palms against the wall, her forehead resting on a large square stone. She remained silent for a long time. "I won't leave Gavin. I can't do that to him." She faced Airlie. "My marriage is important to me, and I have already lied to him for too long. I feel you are pushing me to make a choice between you and him. I can see you don't want things to continue as they are, so I have no option but to walk away from this."

This wasn't the response Airlie had hoped for, but it was the response she should have expected. She refused to beg Olivia to rethink. "Can you please take me back to the B&B?"

The return drive was a long, somber affair. Neither uttered a word, and Airlie stared calmly over the countryside. The tears would come like a torrent, but for now, she held them back. She refused to fall apart and have Olivia bear witness.

She packed in silence while Olivia watched. In less than three minutes, Airlie left, bag slung over her shoulder. She possessed neither the energy nor the inclination to consider catching the train back to Dublin, and although she had every intention of drinking herself into oblivion, she desired no audience and wandered past at least four bars. For half an hour, she walked to put distance between them. She eventually stopped to buy vodka and cigarettes. The first B&B she stumbled upon had a vacancy. The landlady was kind enough to allocate her a small room with a tiny balcony on which she drank until sunset, when she passed out.

## CHAPTER THIRTY-SEVEN

A string of bitterly cold days ensured summer became a distant memory. Autumn and its dreary demeanor left Dublin gray and lifeless. The harder Airlie tried to make the days pass quickly, or the nights be filled with restful sleep, the more forlorn she became. Returning home to Australia was an option, but besides the Olivia affair, her time in Ireland had been a remarkable, life-changing experience, and she simply wasn't ready to leave.

The wedding was almost upon them. Hannah and Liam were smart enough to arrange cellar parties, pre-wedding parties, and the traditional bucks' and hens' nights well before the big day.

At the hens' night, the group of about twenty women drank themselves into a pickled stupor from lunchtime to midnight. The obligatory stripper was the highlight of the evening, taking a particular liking to Airlie. Rachel kissed her full on the lips as a joke to deter him, but he wasn't fooled.

"Hi, I'm Nate."

He wiped perspiration from his brow.

"Short for Nathan?"

"No, Ignatius. My mother hated me."

He smiled, and Airlie realized it was a joke. His accent was South African.

"I'm sure being a stripper has made her proud and she loves you now."

"You think so?"

Jet-black hair flopped shoulder length, and strands fell across his eyes no matter how many times he pushed them back. His tailored stubble and appealing dark eyes were intriguing. Fully dressed in his designer jeans and pale pink polo shirt, he was handsome.

"Has your girlfriend gone off with some other woman?" He ordered a lemon squash and pulled a stool close.

"Oh no, she's not my girlfriend, although she was once." She nodded toward Rachel and Celia kissing on the dance floor. "They're together. She was just messing around." Airlie wondered if her words were slurring. "I think she was messing more with you than me."

"I think you're right, and to be honest, if you're going to get the message a girl is a lesbian, then to see her kiss another girl right in front of you is okay."

Airlie liked his accent. She especially liked how well-to-do he sounded as he enunciated all the important letters. She also realized that practically every other person, including herself, was rather drunk, barely capable of stringing a sensible sentence together, so naturally he was bound to sound interesting and sweet.

"So, you used to go out with her, and now she kisses you in front of her new girlfriend? She is a very brave woman."

"We kiss all the time," Airlie joked.

"Like that?" He sounded unconvinced as they both stared at Rachel and Celia.

"I think there's only one person in the world who could kiss me and make me feel anything right now."

"They sound like the words of someone with a broken heart?"

She snapped out of her indulgent self-pity and gulped the last of her cider. "Maybe, but it sure is good for a girl's ego to have a fine looking thing like yourself chat her up."

"So it wasn't her who broke your heart?" He cocked his head toward Rachel.

"Rachel? No, she's beautiful, but we weren't destined to be together."

"You say that like you missed the boat or something?"

"What do you do when you think there is only one person who can complete you, make you not wonder what else is out there, one person to put your heart at rest? What on earth do you do when you find that person and they go away?"

Nate ordered a whiskey, and Airlie wished she'd kept her mouth shut. Why would he want to hear about her pathetic life?

"Did she die?"

She laughed before she could hold it in. "No, she's not dead, but you'd think she was, the way I'm carrying on."

"Does she know you love her? I mean does she know that she's the one for you? That if you could choose anyone on this earth to be with, it's her?"

Airlie smiled. "Yes, she knows all that."

"Oh dear."

"That's one way of putting it."

"So, is your love unrequited?"

"Oh, she loves me. She says more than anything else in the world, she loves me."

"Really? Jesus, what's her problem then?"

"She's married. To a man."

Nate whistled. "Kids?"

"No, she can't have children."

"Did you sleep with her?" He blushed. "Sorry, you don't have to answer that. It's a bit personal. I'm guessing you did sleep with her, or how else would you know you love her so completely. Stupid question really."

"I knew I loved her before I slept with her."

"So, not so much a stupid question, but you've answered it. She cheated on her husband then. Perhaps she can't deal with the guilt?"

"It's too late for that though, she's already cheated. She can't erase that. Staying with him won't undo it. She's running away."

"Has she left Ireland because of your affair?"

"No." Airlie laughed. "Although I wouldn't put it past her. No, she's running away from me because if she wants to be with me, she has to leave her husband. If she's with me, she's not married anymore, and even though her marriage is crap, her choice is to stay and be an unhappily married gay woman."

"Maybe she just needs time?"

"Maybe. And maybe we've talked enough about me." Airlie smiled. "What's your story? What led you into the glamorous life of stripping? My guess is law or engineering, perhaps?"

"You really are a lesbian."

Airlie frowned.

He smiled. "Only a lesbian would think I actually have a brain and don't do this as a career choice. And trust *me* to be attracted to a smart girl who's attracted to other girls."

"So, what are you studying?"

"I'm in my final year of economics."

"Wow, you really must be smart."

"And you'll think of me as an even bigger dork when I tell you I love it."

"Actually, I think of you as an even bigger dork because you just used the word *dork*."

They both laughed, Airlie a bit louder and longer than necessary.

"See," he said. "I'm not so cool after all. No wonder I can't get a girl."

"You're not helping yourself by sitting at the bar talking to a lesbian when you're surrounded by all these attractive women."

"No, you're right, but you're all pretty drunk and that would be taking advantage." He smiled, handsome and polished. "And why would I want to take advantage of these women, when I can chat to a broken-hearted lesbian?"

"Is this where you tell me a good seeing to by a sexy South African called Nate will cure me of my ghastly anguish?"

Before he could refute the accusation, or perhaps confirm it, Airlie's phone vibrated. She glanced at the caller display, saw it was Olivia, and answered. "Hello." She threw a quick glance of apology in Nate's direction before making her way into the hallway.

There was a pause before Olivia spoke. "Shit, you answered. I didn't think you would be up. I was just going to leave you a message."

The sound of Olivia's voice sent her heart racing, and she knew answering was a mistake. Olivia's voice was so wonderful to hear; she missed it incredibly.

"It's Hennah's hans' night," Airlie blurted. "I mean, it's Hannah's hens' night. The wedding is soon."

"Oh, okay, well then, I'm sorry to interrupt."

"That's okay. I was only chatting to the stripper who was trying to pick me up until Rachel kissed me." She cringed. She had no idea why she even mentioned that. Her mouth was working independently of her brain.

"So, you and Rachel are back on then?"

"No, I didn't mean it like that."

"You don't have to explain yourself to me. What you do is your business."

"Liv, let me explain. It was just a sequence of events, that's all. There was—"

"I just called to say I was thinking of you and missing you," she interrupted. "But clearly you don't feel the same and have moved on, so I'll let you get back to your hens' night and your girlfriend."

The tight grasp constricting Airlie's heart loosened. "Go fuck yourself, Olivia." Her body straightened. "You've got no right to get shitty with me." She raised her head, pacing the narrow space. "For your fucking information, Rachel kissed me as a joke. She's seeing a great girl called Celia, and they're very much in love. And just because you don't have the balls to want me doesn't give you the right to wish a lifetime of loneliness and misery upon me. Perhaps you'd prefer it if I just stayed single and pined for you, while you sit over there with your poor, downtrodden husband who shares a bed with his cheating wife. Would that make you happy?"

"I'm sorry. I shouldn't have called. I'll let you get back to your friends." Olivia's voice was soft again.

"Thanks for that. Thanks a fucking bunch for ringing to tell me you were thinking of me and missing me. I feel so much better knowing that. I feel so much better knowing you feel the same way I do and *still* have no intention of doing anything about it. Thanks for letting me know how you feel and setting me back weeks on my way to getting over you. Thanks—"

There was more to say, much more, but she could hear beeping in her ear, and when she checked, Olivia had hung up.

## CHAPTER THIRTY-EIGHT

Airlie woke the following morning and embraced the remarkably satisfying sensation of drinking water, gulping mouthful upon mouthful, convincing herself that the act itself should have a word all of its own. Nothing on earth was like the feeling of being hungover and desperate for water. Even though she could feel her head pounding in some far off corner, the instant relief was heavenly. She rolled over to sleep it off again.

She dreamed of Olivia. Sexy, lustful, pornographic dreams that jumped from one scene to another. She ran after Olivia, on high windy cliffs, a huge black dog by her side. She heard her name being called. Deep in the throes of the dream, she worried as Olivia walked purposefully and dangerously close to the edge. Rain teemed down, and Olivia appeared to move faster than her legs were walking, and Airlie soon realized, as the voice calling her continued, that it wasn't coming from Olivia, the sky was calling her.

"Airlie, wake up."

Frightened, Airlie ran as fast as she could, but no matter how hard she fought, she gained nothing on the distance between them. The big black dog ran off toward Olivia, and Airlie fell to her knees in despair.

"Airlie, you're dreaming. Wake up."

The dog was now respectfully walking by Olivia's side. The last thing she saw before the dream disappeared was Olivia reaching down to stroke the dog behind the ear.

"Airlie, it's all right. It's just a dream. Please wake up."

The voice was real. She welcomed the awareness that she was warm and dry, but her head was in excruciating pain. Relieved that the wintry cliffs were not real, she reluctantly opened one eye to reveal Rachel standing over the bed.

"Bloody hell, thank God you woke me. I was having the weirdest dream."

"I've been trying to wake you for ages."

"Is everything okay?" she asked, digesting Rachel's concern.

"I've got some bad news. The phone just rang. You obviously didn't hear it—"

"Rach, what is it? Just tell me." Panic pulsed through her, and she sat rigid and upright, her armpits sweating.

"It's Olivia."

"Oh, Jesus, no." Airlie threw back the covers and swung her legs over the edge. "Please tell me she's all right?"

Rachel rested a hand on Airlie's shoulder. "I don't know, Aerobar. Grace said she's had a pretty bad car accident, the Galway side of Maam Cross. They've rushed her to hospital."

"So she'll be okay then, right?" She could feel herself shivering.

"I honestly don't know. Grace didn't know a great deal herself."

"But she's alive?"

"From what I could tell, it's touch and go, but yes."

Airlie thrust her head in her hands. "When did it happen?"

"This morning. In the early hours. Apparently, she was in Galway, was supposed to stay the night, but decided to drive home at the last minute."

"Please, God, this can't be happening." Tears flowed as Rachel drew her close.

"Shh, honey, we'll get you showered, and I'll drive you over to her straight away."

The tears turned to hysterics. Airlie pushed Rachel away and jumped up. "This is my fault," she blubbered. "Oh my God, I did this to her. It's my fault."

"You need to calm down." Rachel tried to placate her, to gently sooth her and reassure her it was an accident, but Airlie would have none of it.

"You don't get it! She rang me last night, after Nate arrived at the party."

"Who?"

"Nate. The fucking stripper. I was talking to him, the phone rang, and it was her."

"What did she want?"

Airlie paced the room in her knickers and relayed the conversation before flopping back on the bed, shaking and cold with her head again buried in her hands. She ignored Rachel's attempts to convince her that accidents happen and harsh words are only really ever said in the heat of the moment. Even Airlie could hear the worry in Rachel's voice.

Airlie looked up. "What I said to her, our conversation, it made her drive home."

"You don't know that."

"Yes, I do. I know her better than anyone, and I know I did this to her." She rushed to the shower.

Within thirty minutes, Rachel and Airlie were weaving through the streets of Dublin before cruising on the N4 toward Galway. Nausea threatened to turn Airlie inside out. Her mouth was dry, and her throat felt constricted as if one more millimeter might render her breathless. She prayed, to whatever God would listen, to keep Olivia alive, and to make her better. She imagined Olivia lying in a hospital bed, a crisp white sheet stretched over her, tucked in too tightly. *They always tuck you in too tightly.* The image triggered memories of a most beautiful scene when Airlie had reclined on a windowsill looking out over Dingle Bay. Olivia slept peacefully while a brilliant stream of sunlight shone diagonally across her. It was one of the most exquisite sights she'd ever seen, the soft white sheet draped across Olivia's beautiful body.

Airlie waited patiently for the painkillers to numb her throbbing head. She looked to Rachel, who was driving to the speed limit and concentrating on the road. She unscrewed the cap from a water bottle and handed it to her. Rachel gulped half the bottle and handed it back.

Airlie resumed staring through the passenger window. Her imagination filled with surgery, blood, panic, and Olivia. The bile rose dangerously close, and she had to ask Rachel to pull over so she could open the passenger door and throw up.

Airlie phoned Grace. Her worst fears were realized. Olivia had arrested four times on the way to hospital and once during surgery. The thought of Olivia's body, naked and exposed on an operating table—convulsing as the defibrillator sent charges through her—was horrendous. Grace informed her Olivia would be relocated to intensive care when she became stable. At least she was alive. It was unclear precisely what her injuries were—Gavin was still waiting to talk to the surgeon—and the police were working to try to establish the cause of the accident.

She was alive. It was all that mattered.

She resumed her stare out the window.

Only the humming of the engine was audible before Rachel spoke. "Aerobar?"

Airlie faced Rachel.

"Was it an affair? Hannah thinks it was."

"Yes."

"Is it over?"

"Yes."

"Can I ask why it ended?"

"She won't leave Gavin. She loves me more, but she won't leave him. Perhaps she doesn't love me at all."

"And you've shouldered this all that time and never mentioned it?"

"I promised her I wouldn't tell anyone. Until now, I've kept that promise."

"You still love her, of course. How on earth have you been coping?"

"I guess I've been waiting for her to come round. I've also been trying to move on. I'm doing okay."

Rachel reached over and squeezed Airlie's hand.

As the minutes continued to pass in silence, Airlie repeated over and over in her mind, "Please don't die, please don't die." Looking beyond the road toward light green fields, cottages, cattle, and sheep—a landscape she cherished—she saw nothing but Olivia. Her thoughts flooded with everything they had shared and everything she wanted to tell her when she eventually woke up. Her heart raced. *This can't be happening. Please, God, don't let her die.* She desperately wanted to say sorry. Sorry for the way she spoke last night, sorry for relaying the ridiculous story about Rachel and the kiss. Ultimately, she was sorry for her lack of patience. Airlie had spent years in denial, but she was slowly coming to terms with her sexuality. Only now, confronted with the possibility of losing Olivia, she understood that she had needed every single second of that time. Pushing Olivia to leave Gavin was wrong. Olivia needed to come to that conclusion herself, in her own time. She wished with every cell of her being that last night she had been in Galway with her. She wished that their relationship was still young and fresh, and for Olivia's sake, still a secret. If they were still together, if she hadn't pushed Olivia to be someone she wasn't yet ready to become, they would have stayed in Galway, in a cozy hotel, and made love until dawn. There would have been no need for Olivia to drive anywhere. This was all Airlie's fault, this whole damn mess they were in, and the possible fatal mess Olivia was in, was her fault, too.

# CHAPTER THIRTY-NINE

The approach to Galway Hospital was fraught with mixed emotions. She desperately wanted to see Olivia, but the feeling that this might be the last time she would see her alive dominated her thoughts. As the car came to a halt, Rachel tenderly placed her hand on Airlie's.

"You need to try to be strong, for Olivia's sake."

"I know. I'll try." She took a deep breath.

"And I'm here for you, no matter what, okay?"

"Thanks." Airlie appreciated the sentiment, but she also understood the underlying message; no one else knew about her and Olivia, and this wasn't the time or place to change that. With Rachel's hand firmly gripping hers, they stepped through the sliding glass doors and into the sterile, orderly world of the hospital. A kind young man at reception located Olivia on the system and directed them to a waiting area.

Rows of connected pale blue chairs lined the room. An extended family, all in a jovial mood, occupied an entire corner. They seemed to be either waiting for a new arrival or perhaps they'd already received good news. *Lucky them.* Airlie hesitated as her attention turned to Gavin and Grace. They looked forlorn, sitting on opposite sides of a vending machine, not looking at each other or speaking. It was a peculiar sight, to see two people, there for a common cause, but not really sharing the burden. They both rose as Airlie held her breath and entered. Gavin reached her first and took her in his arms.

"Any news?" Airlie asked. She wrapped her arms around him, noticing the broadness of his back and how solid he felt compared to Olivia's smaller, delicate, frame.

He released his hold, but held her forearms. "She's still in recovery.

I saw a nurse just now. You name an organ and it was damaged, but she's holding on. She's strong, you know. She'll pull through."

He was trying to convince himself more than anyone else. She heard Rachel and Grace in the background, introducing themselves. Airlie's eyes met Grace's, and an awkward moment passed between them, as if Grace hadn't recognized her at first. Perhaps it was her hesitation, or the slight narrowing of her brow, but in that second, Airlie realized that she knew. She knew her secret. She knew everything. And it was true, Grace didn't recognize her, not this particular Airlie. Grace was looking at the person who slept with her best friend. This was the first time she'd seen Airlie as Olivia's lover. She was meeting Airlie for the first time all over again, and Airlie had no idea how to read her expression.

The pounding in her head became a noise, and her stomach heaved as if the bottom had dropped out. How on earth had she thought she could cope with this? She didn't have the strength to defend her actions, and the guilt she entertained in every cell of her aching body wouldn't have allowed her a defense in any case.

Airlie concentrated on replenishing her fluids with coffee, the thought of food was still beyond her, and while her hangover slowly abated, nothing could stop the slow, insistent pounding in her head. Rachel, in contrast, was eating crisps and chocolate. Strangers came and went from the small waiting room. All of them, Airlie noticed, commenced their wait full of concern and uncertainty, but after reassurance from a doctor or nurse, left in high spirits, relieved of worry.

At nearly five o'clock, a weary looking elderly doctor appeared. He eyed Gavin and asked if he was Mr. Swanson. Gavin froze, more color seemed to drain from his already pale face, and he cleared his throat.

"I'm Dr. Marshall." Gavin shook his hand. "Stabilizing her condition after surgery took some time, but your wife is now in ICU and can see only immediate family."

"Is she going to be all right?" Gavin asked.

"Your wife has extensive internal injuries, Mr. Swanson. It's still very early. We simply can't say. I think the most important thing to remember at this time is that she has made it this far. The next few hours, and indeed days, will be a test, but she's in very good hands."

"What about head injuries?" Grace asked.

"Amazingly, Mrs. Swanson doesn't appear to have suffered any major head trauma. Her forehead has a rather large laceration, but scans have shown no obvious damage to the skull, nor is there any bleeding on her brain. I should warn you, she is attached to many machines with various tubes, so please don't be alarmed when you see her. She really is being well looked after."

"So, can we see her now?" asked Gavin.

"I must insist you visit one at a time. Are you all related to Mrs. Swanson?"

Gavin turned to Grace and Airlie. "I'm Olivia's only relative in Ireland. I know she would want Grace and Airlie to see her though." Gavin looked expectantly at Dr. Marshall. "Grace is her closest friend, and well, Airlie," he cocked his head and smiled affectionately, "she's the closest thing she'll ever have to a daughter."

Airlie's eyes twitched, and her stomach lurched lower than she thought possible. Rachel rested a calming, supportive hand in the middle of her back while Grace glanced fleetingly with disdain.

Dr. Marshall smiled briefly. "Very well, come this way."

"I'll wait here, Airlie, okay?" Rachel hooked a finger through Airlie's belt loop, holding her back. "You all right?"

"I think so. I'll be fine." She kissed Rachel's cheek. "Thanks for this. I can't tell you how much I appreciate it."

The impeccable cleanliness, even as they approached the Intensive Care Unit, somehow intensified the seriousness of the situation.

"These people are here to see Mrs. Swanson." Dr. Marshall addressed a young, pleasant looking nurse before he turned to Gavin and advised him they'd speak again in the morning.

"Only one at a time, thank you, Nurse," Dr. Marshall called over his shoulder as he left.

Grace and Airlie were ushered into a small waiting room just outside the ICU as the nurse efficiently swiped her security card and Gavin disappeared through the huge door.

"You'll go in next," Airlie said. It was a statement not a question. "She might not want to see me, and if she doesn't, you can just say she's too tired. I don't want to mess things up, so you go in next, okay?"

Grace nodded. "I'll ask her. If she's not awake, you might as well just go in. You'll feel better for having seen her."

Both Grace and Airlie slouched low in the chairs. Airlie's hangover was a memory, but she was exhausted and emotionally weary. The cream walls of the unimaginative waiting room didn't help. She stared at the small television, situated high in the corner of the room, but she took no notice of it.

Twenty minutes passed before Gavin emerged. Grace and Airlie stood expectantly. "She's okay. So far she's okay. She woke for a little while. They've doped her to the eyeballs on God knows what, but she's alive. Thank God, she's alive." He ran his hands over his hair, and although Airlie couldn't look directly at him, she could tell from his voice that he was holding back tears.

"She mentioned you, Airlie, well, mumbled your name, so I told her you were here, but I really don't know if she heard or not. Do you want to go in next?"

"Grace is next. I think Grace should go." Airlie felt a little frantic.

Grace pressed the buzzer that alerted a nurse to her presence. The nurse ushered her silently through the doors.

On any other day, Airlie would have felt awkward alone in a waiting room with Gavin. She was in love with his wife, and the thought of losing her was incomprehensible, but she was too exhausted to feel awkward. She was even too exhausted to feel happy that Olivia had spoken her name. For all she knew she probably wanted to see her to give her a bollocking for being a bitch on the phone. The silence wasn't anything Airlie felt the need to rectify, and she could tell, out of the corner of her eye, that Gavin had shut his eyes, so obviously, neither did he.

After a short while, Grace emerged. She held the door open for Airlie. "She's awake," Grace said. "She wants to see you, but just take it easy, eh?"

Airlie stepped into the ICU. The room was arranged in a semicircle. The nurses station sat on a raised platform with all the beds facing them, and although the ward was for seriously sick people, the noise and activity came as quite a shock. The nurses outnumbered the patients, and the activity surrounding them was intense—checking machines, administering drugs, recording doses, changing drips, and goodness only knew what else had to be done to keep these people alive. Bland curtains separated the cubicles, and at the far end, being attended to by the sweet looking nurse, was Olivia. She was connected to numerous machines, and her limp body looked helpless.

Airlie's heart sank, weighed down with guilt at the sight before her. Her breathing became short and shallow. Olivia's eyes blinked opened, and their gazes locked.

"Here's the last of your lot then, popular lady that you are." The nurse, whose name was Katie, according to her badge, smiled, checking Olivia's drip one last time before leaving, swinging the curtain partially closed behind her.

Airlie felt fear for Olivia's life and an overwhelming sense of uselessness for the woman she loved. Olivia was pale. The kind of pale you only ever see in the movies because you believe it impossible for an actual human being to be so white. The usual spark in her eyes was gone. They appeared to have lost all color, and for a split second, a wave of panic struck Airlie as she struggled to remember the color of Olivia's eyes.

"Hey, Liv." She cleared her throat with an awkward cough. "It's good to see you." It crossed her mind that that was a stupid thing to say, but anything right now was going to sound ridiculous.

A faint smile of acknowledgment skewed Olivia's dry mouth and she spoke, but Airlie couldn't make out what she'd said. She took Olivia's hand in hers. "Don't try to speak. It's okay."

Olivia spoke again, a little louder this time but still in an inaudible whisper.

"Liv, I really don't think you should speak. Whatever it is, tell me tomorrow when you're stronger."

Olivia frowned and then winced as if frowning hurt. Airlie could see she was struggling, so she moved closer still, her ear near Olivia's lips. "I love you so much."

Airlie froze. Seconds passed before another wave of panic passed through her, and she glanced at the machines to observe any change. Nothing. Olivia had simply drifted to sleep. She watched the rise and fall of her chest and breathed easier. The monotonous measuring devices provided some comfort, although she felt completely uncertain of what to say, if indeed Olivia's words required a response. Of greater concern was the implication of not replying at all. What if she said nothing and Olivia died? Would Olivia die without hearing Airlie say "I love you" one last time? She was annoyed for even imagining such a thing.

A different nurse emerged from behind the curtain and explained to Airlie that it was time for her to leave.

Airlie gently kissed Olivia's forehead. There was no response, not the faint hint of a smile or even a slight squeeze of her hand, and Airlie glanced to the machines again for reassurance. They remained beeping steadily.

"I love you, Liv. See you tomorrow." Airlie's throat constricted with emotion and fear.

"Right, lovey, time to go now. Will you tell Mr. Swanson I'll be out in a moment to discuss arrangements for this evening?"

Airlie heard the nurse, but refused to take her eyes off Olivia until the last second.

"You'll tell Mr. Swanson, love?"

Olivia remained unmoved with steady breathing and peacefully closed eyes. Airlie released her grip, nodding in acknowledgment before leaving.

"Did she speak to you? Did she say anything?" Gavin asked.

Airlie's eyes caught the narrowing of Grace's brow and slight shake of her head. It was enough to reinforce the lie she was about to tell. "No, nothing. She was asleep the whole time. Sorry I was so long."

"There's no need for apologies. I know what you two mean to each other."

Airlie's stomach twisted.

Just as she was about to relay the message from the ICU nurse, another lady in plain clothes arrived and explained the accommodation arrangements to Gavin. There was no question of him leaving the hospital. Grace and Airlie bid him good night with hugs and returned to find Rachel waiting patiently. Airlie agreed to stay at Olivia and Gavin's and Rachel would return to Dublin.

## CHAPTER FORTY

I can stay with you if you want. It's not a bother." Rachel hugged Airlie beside the car.

"Don't be silly. I'll be fine." She was far from fine.

"Why don't you stay with Grace tonight? Save you being alone."

"She knows about me and Olivia. I don't know how long she's known, but she knows."

"Did she say something to you?"

"She didn't have to."

Rachel ruffled Airlie's hair. "She's not rushed you off for an exorcism yet."

Airlie wanted to be alone. She needed space to digest what was happening. The thought of enduring a night with Grace and her obvious disappointment was a situation she wanted to avoid. In any case, Grace hadn't offered.

"Not yet. But this way, you'll be home at a decent hour tonight, I can feel useful by helping out Gav, and in some way," she held back tears, "I know I'll feel close to Liv if I'm at their place."

"You have to find a resolution to this situation, Airlie. The fact that you're here suggests it's not over between you two."

"I know I shouldn't feel the way I do about her."

"See, that's where you're wrong. How you feel about Olivia isn't wrong. They're your feelings, they're valid. It's what you do about them that's become the issue. She chose Gavin, but you're still here."

"She just told me she loves me."

"What? Just now?"

Airlie nodded.

"Shit." Rachel paced. "She's on a lot of medication. Could it be the drugs talking?"

"Could be?"

"But you want to believe it's not?"

"I know it's not. She hasn't stopped loving me."

"You're forgetting Gavin. Or she is."

"How could she? She's still married to him and she's in love with me."

Rachel stood close. "You do realize that Olivia is, for now and ever, a cheater?"

Airlie raised her eyebrows.

Rachel sighed. "Yes. Exactly like me."

"And will you ever do it again?"

"Touché. Please just tell me you'll get this sorted so you can move forward one way or another."

"We all make mistakes, Rach."

Rachel pulled her close. "She's lucky to have you to love her."

"I loved you like that once." Airlie pulled away and grinned.

"You loved me, but never like you love Olivia. I think you learned the hard way that you can't love two people at once. Not successfully anyway."

"I didn't want to love her back then."

"When are you going to realize you don't get to choose?" Rachel cupped her cheek. "Becoming you can take time. It's a process and you're still in it. Give yourself a break."

Airlie ushered her into the car. "Drive safely, Rach, and thanks for everything. Not just today, but everything."

Rachel winked. "Taught you everything you know."

"Okay, you can go now."

"Especially that thing with your little finger."

"Rachel! Bugger off."

"Made you laugh."

"Yeah, you did. You're a good friend."

"And don't you forget it."

As Rachel pulled away, Airlie spotted Grace on the far side of the car park. She was waving to her while talking on her mobile. She had no energy for an argument tonight and hoped to God the drive to Roaring Bay would be over soon.

❖

Ash's snarl at the side gate was a warning, but Airlie ordered his silence, and the ferociousness turned into pathetic cries of excitement. In the strong glow of Grace's headlights, Airlie located the potted plant with the spare key taped to the bottom and unlocked the front door. After a quick wave, Grace disappeared into the darkness. The drive had been uneventful, but Airlie was thankful to be alone on familiar ground.

She busied herself with dinner preparations for Ash, whose head was bobbing in and out of view at the back door. Gavin hadn't washed yesterday's dishes, and Olivia's favorite cup remained dirty in the sink.

She watched as Ash devoured the contents of his generously filled bowl, the thrill of company a forgotten memory now that his tummy was satisfied. The unwashed dishes needled her until she rolled up her sleeves and filled the sink with hot, soapy water.

She washed the dishes, dried them, and neatly put them away, knowing the correct place for everything. The domestic chores provided comfort. Just doing something useful distracted her enough to keep moving. She put on a load of washing and methodically folded the clean clothes, taking special care with Olivia's. She wanted everything to be clean and tidy when she returned home.

She wasn't prepared for the pang of guilt that gripped her when she switched on the light in the main bedroom. It was in a state of disarray. Gav had understandably left in a hurry that morning. She could see Olivia's side of the bed remained unused, and she selfishly thought that a space without Olivia next to him was how it should be.

It was almost midnight by the time Airlie finished. At last, a hint of tiredness crept through her. She poured herself a small glass of port and took a long sip. Airlie opened the door and let Ash charge past and settle on his bed.

There was nothing left to do. The silence threatened to engulf her. She'd worked all night without the company of TV or music. The port had gone straight to her head, via her empty stomach, and the events of the day filled her already congested mind until she felt terribly lost and overwhelmingly saddened.

The tears came as she braced herself against the wall. Her legs gave way and she slumped heavily to the floor, her shoulder brushing firmly against the wall to flick off the light. Her body heaved and jerked as tears dripped into her glass.

She drank the port in one gulp just to be rid of it, but then craved another. Her entire body ached. She remained sobbing and praying to an unknown God to help Olivia. She begged for forgiveness. Forgiveness for loving Olivia in the first place, for making her love her in return, and for the sourness that had turned their love into shame and hurt. Airlie struggled, but positioned herself on her knees. She made promises to that unknown God. She promised to do the right thing if Olivia survived, she promised to do whatever Olivia wanted to make this right. She knew their relationship had ended, and should Olivia never want to see her again, she would say her good-byes and leave without discussion. She begged God for salvation. Salvation for the lying, the cheating, and the lack of self-control she exercised in seducing a married woman. She swore to God she would never fall in love again. Love tainted her, and now Olivia's life was in the balance, and she would do anything to change that if she could.

Airlie curled into a ball and fell asleep. If it weren't for Ash's slobbery kisses, she might have remained on the doorstep all night. She fetched the pajamas from beneath Olivia's pillow. She stared at the side of the bed where Olivia usually slept. While the thought fleetingly crossed her mind, she couldn't bring herself to sleep there, not in the bed she shared with Gavin. Instead, she took Olivia's pillow. She snuggled deeply, hugging the pillow tightly. Within minutes, she drifted off. Her sleep was disjointed and tormented, and the pillow and scent of Olivia remained with her until the phone startled her awake, early the next morning.

The news was positive. Gav reported an overnight improvement, although he'd been warned not to become too excited; there was still a long way to go.

He'd compiled a list of things he needed, and Airlie took notes, thinking how justifiably tired he sounded, yet with a hope in his voice that was absent yesterday. He was refusing to leave the hospital, directly against doctor's orders.

Whatever it was that Olivia and Gavin had, whatever it was that held them together, it was real. It was what made him determined not to leave her in hospital alone. It was what made Olivia stay with him; partners for life. He was everything Airlie wasn't. She had to let it go.

"You still there?" he asked.

"Sorry." Airlie snapped back to the present.

"So, as I was saying, I've called the insurance company, and you're fine to drive my car. I'll see you in a while."

The line disconnected. She read the list: shaving stuff, clothes, toiletries for Olivia and nighties. Airlie had never seen Olivia in a nightie, doubted whether she even owned one, but Gavin had insisted there were nice ones in her bedside drawers. She tossed the list on the table and put the kettle on.

Although she was hungry, breakfast was a chore, and the coffee was terrible. She longed to be the one in the hospital looking after Olivia. *She* wanted to be the one calling someone to collect things, because if that were the case, she and Olivia would be together. She wanted to be the person the doctors sought to discuss Olivia's progress. She wanted to be the one the nurses knew and addressed on a first name basis, saying to Olivia, "Ah, here she is," and smiling as Airlie proudly arrived with a bunch of her favorite flowers. Airlie realized she didn't even know what Olivia's favorite flowers were.

Her head throbbed. She lingered, unshowered and unprepared for the conversation she would have to have with Olivia when she was well enough. She had the entire two-hour drive to Galway to choose the right time to say good-bye.

She shut off the shower and stepped over Ash to retrieve her towel. She studied her reflection in the mirror, hardly recognizing the person staring back. Why did she find her full length, pale reflection so disappointing? What had she expected to see? Her sense of right and wrong was distorted, altered by love, and love was something she was sure she'd never had to contend with before. Airlie had solved the mystery surrounding all the happy people in the world. They were in love. She was in love. So in love, that when the time came, she would leave and never look back.

Airlie's approach to the hospital was, in one way, less morbid than the previous day, but given the conversation she was about to have with Olivia, if she were able, the day was destined to be awful. She'd rehearsed her speech for nearly two hours, but she was nowhere near ready to deliver it.

It was amazing the difference a bit of sunshine made, and in one corner of the ICU ward, sunlight streamed in. If you didn't look closely at the sick faces, you could be forgiven for forgetting the seriousness of the situation.

Gavin sat by her bedside, holding her hand. The gesture, while kind and loving, upset Airlie. She hesitated, but only briefly, and walked over to the bed.

Olivia's eyes were closed.

"She woke earlier, but she's slept since," he said.

Airlie looked at the monitors. "Is she okay, though?"

"So far so good."

Airlie handed Gavin the bag containing the items he'd requested.

"Thank you. You're a life saver. Do you mind sitting with her while I go and freshen up?"

She looked from Gavin to Olivia and back. "Sure. Will you be long?"

"I've not eaten since yesterday morning. I might grab something. Do you want anything?"

There was no way Airlie could eat, not until she had said her piece. She had no way of gauging, until Olivia opened her eyes, if she was capable of comprehending anything Airlie had to say. "I've eaten, thanks. If she wakes while you're away, I'll tell her you won't be long."

"You have my mobile number. She needs all the rest she can get. I think she'll sleep for a while yet."

Airlie sat in the warm seat Gavin had vacated.

"Hold her hand. She won't bite. She needs to know someone's here," he said.

Airlie took Olivia's hand in hers. It seemed smaller than she remembered. It was warm.

Gavin shrugged on his jacket. "Talk to her. You two are never normally lost for words." He smiled and left.

Airlie stared at Olivia. Making small talk to someone who might or might not be listening wasn't on her agenda for the day. Olivia's chest rose and fell. What on earth should she talk about? The weather, current events, never seeing her again. She gulped air as the opening line of her rehearsed conversation played before her eyes.

Olivia's hand squeezed hers. Airlie glanced to her face. Her eyes flickered, then her hand squeezed again. She was waking up.

Airlie freaked out and pressed the buzzer. She jumped up, releasing Olivia's hand just as a nurse arrived.

"Is everything okay?" the nurse asked, then busied herself checking Olivia's monitors.

"She moved."

The nurse stared at Airlie over her glasses.

Olivia's entire body stirred this time.

"See. Just like that," said Airlie.

The nurse raised her eyebrows then smiled. "She's fine. She might be waking up."

Airlie felt her eyes widen.

"That's a good thing. She might speak or she might not. Be patient with her."

Airlie dug her hands deep in her pockets.

"She's on a hefty dose of drugs; it may take a while. I'd sit if I were you."

Airlie was beginning to tire of everyone telling her to sit but she had little alternative. The time for good-byes was looming. She jiggled her legs and perched on the edge of the seat.

"Hey." Olivia's voice was croaky and slurry at the same time. She sounded like a drunk who'd smoked her way through life.

"Hey yourself."

Olivia raised her hand, as if seeking comfort. Airlie took it and rested it between hers.

"Thirsty." Olivia licked her lips.

A jug of ice sat half melted on the bedside. Airlie poured some into a pale green cup that sat beside it. She bent the straw and gently placed it on Olivia's lips. Olivia sucked the tiniest amount but appeared instantly relieved. Her body relaxed.

Airlie patted the back of Olivia's hand. "Are you up for a little chat?" It was a stupid question. There was never going to be a good time for this conversation, but with Olivia off her face on medication, this moment was probably the worst.

Olivia open her eyes, smiled briefly, then nodded.

"I've been thinking," Airlie began.

"Me too," Olivia said. She seemed to be trying to focus on Airlie. "Where's Gavin?" Olivia's hand twitched before her hand and arm went limp.

Airlie leaned forward. "Liv?"

Nothing.

"Olivia?"

Olivia began to gently snore.

Airlie sighed. She was second best now and that would never change. Olivia had wanted Gavin, not her. "He'll be back soon," she said, but she knew Olivia hadn't heard.

Gavin wouldn't be much longer. He'd rush back. He was a good man in that way. Her chance to speak privately to Olivia was lost for the day. She hated the thought of suffering another restless night before she could try again in the morning.

The nurse reappeared. "Must be a relief to see her awake."

Airlie nodded.

"You'll notice a steady improvement now, I imagine. More often than not, it's the way it works."

Airlie smiled and resumed watching Olivia's chest move while the machines kept time.

The following morning, Airlie knew she looked rough. She'd stayed awake until after three watching movies, although she'd struggle to name any of them. If it weren't for Ash snuggled up against her legs on the sofa, the loneliness may have engulfed her again. She'd miss Ash, too.

Although tired, her apprehension of the inevitable conversation hadn't subsided. She hadn't eaten since yesterday lunch.

If the nurse had been correct about Olivia's improvement, she might have her chance to talk to her. It all depended on Gavin.

When she walked into ICU, she was shocked to see Olivia alert and with a dusting of pink on her cheeks.

"Morning." She smiled at Olivia. "You look a darn sight better than you did yesterday."

Olivia smiled. "I feel better, too."

Airlie kissed her cheek.

"Righto, now that the morning shift has arrived. I might fetch the papers so I've got something to read to you later. I'll grab a bacon sandwich while I'm at it." Gavin smiled. He looked exhausted, but his relief at Olivia's improvement was obvious.

Airlie took an extra breath. It was now or never. "Great idea. I wanted a quick chat with the patient anyway." After she said her piece, Olivia would want her to go. The only thing she hadn't been sure of was what excuse they would give Gavin for her leaving. But then, they'd been making up excuses for a long time now. Between them, they would come up with something. It was appalling, but it was what they did.

"Don't go." Olivia's voice was weak.

It broke Airlie's heart to hear her say that to Gavin.

"I'm not leaving, just grabbing some supplies, love. Airlie will keep you company."

"I want to talk to you both," Olivia said.

"It won't be long and he'll be back." Airlie didn't want to drag this out.

"No. Just both of you stay, please. I want to talk to you." Olivia's tone suggested frustration. The twist of her features suggested pain.

Airlie paused by one side of the bed, Gavin the other.

"What happened to me last night was terrifying." She closed her eyes. "I mean the night of the accident."

"You're still weak, my love. Why don't you rest?" said Gavin.

Olivia raised her hand to silence him. Airlie glanced between them. Gavin relented.

"I don't know how I know, but I know I wasn't ready to die. If I'd have died, I would have died a liar, and that lie would have hurt everyone I care about." She turned to Gavin. "I love you, dearly. You're a kind and gentle man and you deserve to be with someone who adores you." She began to cry. "I'm sorry. That isn't me anymore. I'm not in love with you, Gavin."

"You're not well." Gavin's smile had faded. "You've been through a terrible ordeal. You don't know what you're saying. What do you mean you don't love me?" He glanced at Airlie, then back to Olivia. "Why did you want her here? Why is she here for this, Olivia?" He turned to Airlie. "What have you done?"

Airlie couldn't take her eyes off Olivia.

"What the fuck have you done to my wife?"

"Gavin, I'm so sorry," Olivia said. "Please understand this is me. My fault, not Airlie's."

"She made you into a lesbian?"

"No, Gav. We fell in love. It doesn't matter who she is or what label you put on it. And although it's entirely my fault, I couldn't have stopped it. I tried. We tried."

Airlie began to cry. She was watching a man fall apart and have his life ripped from beneath him. That would hurt for a long time. Simultaneously, her life was falling into place. She didn't know what to do.

Gavin's knees gave way and he stumbled into the chair behind him. "I don't understand."

"You deserve the truth. I feel like the truth is all I have. I'm a liar and a cheat, Gavin." Tears left glistening tracks down Olivia's face. "How could I die and have you not know who I really was? I want you to find the person you're meant to be with. Dying in the middle of this lie wouldn't have allowed you to do that."

"I'm losing you anyway." His head dropped into his hands.

"I was already gone. I'm sorry. I'll try my best to explain. I'll answer all the questions you have, but not today. Please, I'm tired."

Gavin's body was heaving with silent sobs. "I'll be back later."

"I've made up my mind."

Gavin stared at Airlie. "You did this. I thought you were family." He left. The timing was terrible. Although, when was the best time to tell someone you were in love with someone else?

"Stop looking at me like that." Olivia held out her hand.

"What the hell just happened?"

"I firmly believe my choice to live or die depended on whether I chose to live a lie. Nothing like a brush with death to give you clarity." She coughed. Airlie could see she was in pain. "All this time I've been an asshole—to you and Gavin. I can't fix what I've done to Gavin, I can only offer him the truth. I've lied and cheated, and nothing can make that disappear. I can fix what I've done to you. If you'll let me."

"Will he ever get over this?" Airlie had to sit. "Should I go after him, make sure he's okay?" She stood.

Olivia shook her head. "Leave him. I might be the worst wife in the world, but I know he'll need to process this alone and in his own time."

Airlie sat again. "I can't believe what's happening."

"Life is fragile. I learned that the hard way. I know I'm all smashed up, but when I woke yesterday, I knew I would be okay." Olivia pressed the self-administering morphine button.

"I feel like this is all a bad dream."

"Bad? I don't know if you noticed, but I just told my husband I'm leaving him for you."

"But you had to nearly die to work that out."

"I'm not the smartest cookie sometimes."

Airlie looked her in the eye. "I came here today to tell you I was going and not coming back."

Tears slipped down Olivia's cheeks.

"I thought I had to set you free." Airlie took her hand and pulled the chair close. "I thought if you loved someone you should set them free. I was going to respect your decision to stay with Gav. To choose him."

"I choose you."

Airlie looked around. Suddenly, she was the person she wanted to be. She was the one Olivia wanted by her side. She was the one who would look after Olivia, who would nurse her back to health, and who would be called Olivia's, and Olivia hers.

"Thank you," Airlie said.

"What for?"

"For acknowledging what we have. For finding the courage to be who you are."

"It took me long enough. Bouncing around in a smashed up car, then waking up with only you on my mind was certainly a hurry along."

Arlie smiled. "Shit. What do we do now?"

Olivia squeezed her hand. "We suffer the fallout of my decision. I imagine it will be a rough time. Then I'll get better, and we work it out from there."

"How about you get better *first*?"

"How about you marry me when I get out of here?"

"How about you get a divorce first."

"That's a given. So, will you?"

"Jesus. You don't waste any time."

"Life's so short; it could have ended for me only two days ago. It's taken so long to finally become me, I don't want to waste a moment longer."

A nurse poked her head through the curtain. "Sorry, ladies." She looked at Airlie. "You'll have to leave now. I think Mrs. Swanson could use some rest."

"She's staying." Olivia smiled. "She's my next of kin. I want her to stay."

The nurse looked confused. "Right. As of just now, is it?"

Olivia nodded.

"Shall I organize some paperwork to reflect that?" asked the nurse.

Olivia nodded. "Airlie's my partner. I want her with me."

The nurse shrugged and smiled. "This place gets stranger every day."

## EPILOGUE

I can't get comfortable," said Airlie. The airplane wasn't full, and she and Olivia shared a row of seats between them. They were only seven hours into the journey from Ireland to Australia.

Olivia rolled her eyes. "I can tell this is going to be a thing with you."

"A thing?"

"Yep. A whining, flying, airplane thing."

"But you still love me, right?"

"I do. Do you think your parents will still love you when you bring your girlfriend home?"

"They know we're coming. They're excited to meet you."

"But you've not mentioned my age."

"What's that got to do with it?"

"I'm halfway between your mum's age and your age."

Airlie eyed her. "Don't you go taking a fancy to my mum."

Before Olivia could reply, a flight attendant appeared. She leaned close, as if what she had to say was a secret. "Sorry to interrupt, ladies, but I have a family with a sick child who could use the benefit of an extra seat."

This was Airlie's worst nightmare—besides the one where Olivia has a car accident and dies—the only time she'd ever had any chance of a decent sleep on the plane and it was about to be snatched from her.

"Would it be okay if we moved you to business class for the remainder of the journey?"

"Us?" Airlie and Olivia said in unison.

The flight attendant leaned closer still. "Business class passengers generally don't take too kindly to screaming children. It's not exactly what they pay for."

Airlie was out of her seat before Olivia even had her belt unclasped.

Her journey had gone full circle. She and Olivia had decided to settle in Australia, close to both their families and somewhere near the sea, where the temperature in winter never reached single figures.

They were going home.

# About the Author

Michelle Grubb (michellegrubb.com) is Tasmanian born and now resides in the UK, just north of London, with her wife. She's a fair-weather golfer, a happy snapper, and a lover of cafés, vinyl records, and bookshops.

Michelle harbors an unnatural love for stray pieces of timber (she promises her wife she'll build her something one day), secondhand furniture shops, and the perfect coffee.

She can play six chords on her guitar, stumble through a song on her drum kit, and if you see her wearing headphones, she's probably listening to Mumford & Sons while dreaming up stories and plot twists.

It goes without saying that writing is Michelle's favorite thing to do.

# Books Available From Bold Strokes Books

**Amounting to Nothing** by Karis Walsh. When mounted police officer Billie Mitchell steps in to save beautiful murder witness Merissa Karr, worlds collide on the rough city streets of Tacoma, Washington. (978-1-62639-728-6)

**Becoming You** by Michelle Grubb. Airlie Porter has a secret. A deep, dark, destructive secret that threatens to engulf her if she can't find the courage to face who she really is and who she really wants to be with. (978-1-62639-811-5)

**Birthright** by Missouri Vaun. When spies bring news that a swordswoman imprisoned in a neighboring kingdom bears the Royal mark, Princess Kathryn sets out to rescue Aiden, true heir to the Belstaff throne. (978-1-62639-485-8)

**Crescent City Confidential** by Aurora Rey. When romance and danger are in the air, writer Sam Torres learns the Big Easy is anything but. (978-1-62639-764-4)

**Love Down Under** by MJ Williamz. Wylie loves Amarina, but if Amarina isn't out, can their relationship last? (978-1-62639-726-2)

**Privacy Glass** by Missouri Vaun. Things heat up when Nash Wiley commandeers a limo and her best friend for a late drive out to the beach: Champagne on ice, seat belts optional, and privacy glass a must. (978-1-62639-705-7)

**The Impasse** by Franci McMahon. A horse-packing excursion into the Montana Wilderness becomes an adventure of terrifying proportions for Miles and ten women on an outfitter-led trip. (978-1-62639-781-1)

**The Right Kind of Wrong** by PJ Trebelhorn. Bartender Quinn Burke is happy with her life as a playgirl until she realizes she can't fight her feelings any longer for her best friend, bookstore owner Grace Everett. (978-1-62639-771-2)

**Wishing on a Dream** by Julie Cannon. Can two women change everything for the chance at love? (978-1-62639-762-0)

**A Quiet Death** by Cari Hunter. When the body of a young Pakistani girl is found out on the moors, the investigation leaves Detective Sanne Jensen facing an ordeal she may not survive. (978-1-62639-815-3)

**Buried Heart** by Laydin Michaels. When Drew Chambliss meets Cicely Jones, her buried past finds its way to the surface. Will they survive its discovery or will their chance at love turn to dust? (978-1-62639-801-6)

**Escape: Exodus Book Three** by Gun Brooke. Aboard the Exodus ship *Pathfinder*, President Thea Tylio still holds Caya Lindemay, a clairvoyant changer, in protective custody, which has devastating consequences endangering their relationship and the entire Exodus mission. (978-1-62639-635-7)

**Genuine Gold** by Ann Aptaker. New York, 1952. Outlaw Cantor Gold is thrown back into her honky-tonk Coney Island past, where crime and passion simmer in a neon glare. (978-1-62639-730-9)

**Into Thin Air** by Jeannie Levig. When her girlfriend disappears, Hannah Lewis discovers her world isn't as orderly as she thought it was. (978-1-62639-722-4)

**Night Voice** by CF Frizzell. When talk show host Sable finally acknowledges her risqué radio relationship with a mysterious caller, she welcomes a *real* relationship with local tradeswoman Riley Burke. (978-1-62639-813-9)

**Raging at the Stars** by Lesley Davis. When the unbelievable theories start revealing themselves as truths, can you trust in the ones who have conspired against you from the start? (978-1-62639-720-0)

**She Wolf** by Sheri Lewis Wohl. When the hunter becomes the hunted, more than love might be lost. (978-1-62639-741-5)

**Smothered and Covered** by Missouri Vaun. The last person Nash Wiley expects to bump into over a two a.m. breakfast at Waffle House is her college crush, decked out in a curve-hugging law enforcement uniform. (978-1-62639-704-0)

**The Butterfly Whisperer** by Lisa Moreau. Reunited after ten years, can Jordan and Sophie heal the past and rediscover love or will differing desires keep them apart? (978-1-62639-791-0)

**The Devil's Due** by Ali Vali. Cain and Emma Casey are awaiting the birth of their third child, but as always in Cain's world, there are new and old enemies to face in Katrina-ravaged New Orleans. (978-1-62639-591-6)

**Widows of the Sun-Moon** by Barbara Ann Wright. With immortality now out of their grasp, the gods of Calamity fight amongst themselves, egged on by the mad goddess they thought they'd left behind. (978-1-62639-777-4)

**Arrested Hearts** by Holly Stratimore. A reckless cop who hates her life and a health nut who is afraid to die might be a perfect combination for love. (978-1-62639-809-2)

**Capturing Jessica** by Jane Hardee. Hyperrealist sculptor Michael tries desperately to conceal the love she holds for best friend, Jess, unaware Jess's feelings for her are changing. (978-1-62639-836-8)

**Counting to Zero** by AJ Quinn. NSA agent Emma Thorpe and computer hacker Paxton James must learn to trust each other as they work to stop a threat clock that's rapidly counting down to zero. (978-1-62639-783-5)

**Courageous Love** by KC Richardson. Two women fight a devastating disease, and their own demons, while trying to fall in love. (978-1-62639-797-2)

**One More Reason to Leave Orlando** by Missouri Vaun. Nash Wiley thought a threesome sounded exotic and exciting, but as it turns out the reality of sleeping with two women at the same time is just really complicated. (978-1-62639-703-3)